THE DISAPPEARANCES

GEMMA MALLEY

HODDER

First published in Great Britain in 2013 by Hodder & Stoughton
An Hachette UK company

First published in paperback in 2013

1

A CIP catalogue record for this title is available from the British Library.

Paperback ISBN 978 1 444 72285 7
eBook ISBN 978 1 444 72284 0

Printed and bound by CPI Group (UK) Ltd, Croydon CR0 4YY

Hodder & Stoughton policy is to use papers that are natural, renewable
and recyclable and made from wood grown in sustainable
forests. The logging and manufacturing processes are expected to
conform to the environmental regulations of the country of origin.

Hodder & Stoughton Ltd
338 Euston Road
London NW1 3BH

www.hodder.co.uk

For Abigail and Johnnie

It is in war that the State really comes into its own: swelling in power, in number, in pride, in absolute dominion over the economy and the society.

Murray Rothbard, 1963

PROLOGUE

Thomas looked at his boss mutinously. 'The guy's a genius and you want me to fire him?'

'He's sixteen. You can't be a genius at sixteen. And even if he is one, he's a kid. Give him a few years to grow up.'

Thomas's mouth stiffened as it always did when he didn't get his own way. Who cared about age? He himself was only nineteen; in the world of computing he felt like one of the old guys, desperately trying to keep up with what was happening. Sixteen was no kid. Sixteen was prime.

But no one else could see that. All they could see was that the 'kid' was ruffling feathers; that he did things his own way; that he didn't care what people thought. And then there was the little incident with the FBI . . .

Prosser smiled, one of his avuncular grins that usually disarmed people. 'He just needs to grow up a bit,' he said, with a little shrug. 'Learn that we can't mess with people's privacy like that. We do things properly around here.'

'Privacy?' Thomas looked at him incredulously. 'Don't you get it? No one cares about privacy these days. There's no such thing, anyway. And what this guy can do . . . It's years ahead of what anyone else is doing. He doesn't just tell us what people are buying, he can tell us what they're thinking, why they're thinking it. This is the future. What he's doing now is what everyone's going to be scrambling for.'

'And yet we're still going to let him go,' Prosser said, gently but firmly, his face changing to his I'm-the-boss-and-you'd-better-get-used-to-it expression. The one Thomas loathed. 'He hacked into FBI files, for God's sake.'

'He hacked into them in five minutes,' Thomas replied, folding his arms. 'In five minutes, Prosser.'

Prosser's face hardened. 'Was there anything else?'

Thomas shook his head. It was no use. Prosser didn't get it. He would never get it. People didn't see what Thomas saw; didn't see that in that kid's mind was the future, ideas so incredible they would revolutionise everything. People didn't see the opportunity, the unbelievable opportunity that lay before them.

They were blind.

But Thomas wasn't.

He turned, left his boss's office, then, as soon as Prosser could no longer see him through the glass windows of his office, he stalked quickly down the hallway, down the stairs, and through the corridor that led to his department. He opened the door to the open-plan office that he presided over, stood there for a few minutes just looking at the boy, the boy genius. He was surfing car sites, luxury cars; Thomas had never seen him do any actual work. And for a moment, he was struck by an almost overwhelming envy, because he and the boy seemed to have so little in common; because for Thomas, work meant just that – a long, hard slog to keep up, to edge ahead. But the boy . . . His whole world was different to Thomas's. When you were as brilliant as this boy, work wasn't measured in minutes and hours; it was measured in product-ivity. And he could do more in a minute than other people could do in a week. Thomas had been following him for months, had offered him work experience the minute he'd finished school. And now he was going to lose him? No. It was impossible.

Cautiously, Thomas walked towards him. 'So, how's it going?' he asked.

The boy shrugged. 'Okay, I guess.' He clicked away from the Mercedes website back onto the code he was writing, the work he was supposed to be doing.

Thomas nodded, then pulled up a chair and sat down. 'How soon until blast off?'

'Blast off?' the boy looked at him in derision, but Thomas didn't allow himself to get upset. He'd been sneered at, ignored, laughed at for most of his life; called 'dweeb' and 'nerd' and, well, much worse. But he didn't care, not any more. He was beyond caring about being cool, being liked. None of those things mattered, not now. When you had power it didn't matter if people liked you. And he was going to have power. 'Our little project,' he said. 'The program we've been discussing. How long until it's ready?'

The boy shrugged. 'That's what I keep telling you. It's never going to be.'

'Never?' Thomas felt his stomach tighten. 'Don't talk like that, of course it is. How long do you need? Do you need more help? I can get you more help.'

'There's really no point,' the boy said. And he didn't seem to care. How could he not care? How could he?

Thomas cleared his throat. 'Of course there's a point,' he said. 'What you're creating, what you've got here, it's incredible. It's more than incredible. It has to be built. It has to become real. They don't understand here, but I do. I'll pay you myself. Work for me, I'll find you an office, anywhere you want. Anywhere . . .'

The boy sighed, swivelled his chair around to face Thomas. 'Forget it, Thomas. Look, it's been fun, but I know they want me out of here. And that's cool. The tea sucks anyway. You need a teapot. Fresh leaves.'

'So I'll buy some,' Thomas said, trying his best to keep the desperation out of his voice. 'You have to finish.'

'Why?' The boy looked at him, eyes boring right into him like they could see what he was thinking.

Thomas stood up in frustration. 'Because we agreed. Because it's a great idea. Because you signed a contract,' he said, trying to keep his voice measured, calm. The contract had been a long shot, but the boy had signed it readily enough when Thomas had promised him access to the entire

Infotec server, promised to let him do whatever he wanted. For weeks he had been mopping up the boy's shit, making excuses, taking the blame, and he hadn't done that out of the goodness of his heart.

The boy appeared to consider this. 'I s'pose,' he said. 'But like I said, it's not going to work. I'll see you around.'

He stood up; it took every bit of self-control for Thomas to resist the urge to shove him back down in the chair again.

'Okay,' he said instead, blocking the doorway, buying himself another few seconds, trying to remember to breathe. 'So what's stopping it from working? Or, rather, in what circumstances would it work?'

'None. Not in the real world anyway,' the boy said dismissively.

'And in the not-real world?' Thomas insisted, seeing a glimmer of hope. 'What then?'

'Really?' the boy asked, his interest piqued. 'You really want to know?'

'I really want to know,' Thomas nodded.

'Okay,' the boy said. He flopped back down in this chair, twiddled his thumbs. 'So,' he said, 'first you'd need a smaller population because it needs to start small, grow organically, you know? And it's no point just picking a control group because it won't work if there are loads of other interfaces and networks buzzing around. You'd need a desert island. A village on a desert island. Few hundred people, maybe a couple of thousand.'

'Go on,' Thomas said.

The boy thought for a moment. 'They've all got to be willing to be monitored day and night, so there can't be any politics, any dissent, anyone talking civil liberties because then it's dead in the water.'

'I see,' Thomas. 'And what else?'

The boy laughed. 'That's not enough? You see? It's never going to work. Never going to happen.'

'What else?' Thomas asked, the tension now audible in his voice.

The boy sat back, put his hands behind his head like he was sunbathing. Thomas half expected him to put his feet up on the desk, right on top of the keyboard.

'They've got to want it,' the boy said, then, with a shrug. 'They've got to really want it. See, what matters is what people believe, not what is real. You can have the most incredible set up, give people an amazing life, but if they think you're doing it to them, they'll hate it. But if it's something they want and you give it to them . . . Well, that's completely different.' He stood up. 'So look,' he said, 'thanks and stuff.'

He held out his hand; Thomas shook it. 'And if those conditions are met, you'll build it? It'll work? Our contract still stands?'

'Sure,' the boy grinned as he walked out of the room. 'You get the cow to jump over the moon and I'll do anything you want.'

1

'Morning.'

Evie looked up to see Raffy next to her with two steaming hot cups of tea and she quickly sat up and took one from him. 'What's the time?' she murmured.

'It's early,' Raffy said, getting back into bed. 'I couldn't sleep.'

Evie moved aside for him and took a sip of her tea. 'How early?'

'Four thirty.'

Half an hour before their usual wake-up time. Evie tried to open her eyes properly, but they were rebelling, resisting her request. Instead, she put down her tea and allowed her eyes to close again, her head lolling back against her pillow.

'Still, exciting day today. We're being fitted,' Raffy said. He was bearing down over her; Evie knew he was expecting her to open her eyes, so she did so, managing a little smile before closing them again.

Fitted. For her dress. For his suit. Next week would be their Welcome Ceremony, their formal acceptance into the Settlement.

And it was also going to be the day of their wedding.

'You don't look excited.'

Evie looked at Raffy worriedly, but immediately saw that he was joking, teasing her.

'Of course I'm excited,' she said, forcing another smile, a light-hearted expression. She was excited, after all. Every time Raffy so much as mentioned the wedding she got jolts all around her body. Excitement, fear; they were the same thing. Sort of.

She closed her eyes for a moment. 'It's going to be quite something.'

'Isn't it?' Raffy breathed, rolling off the bed then grinning at her. 'Married. Seriously. Did you ever think this would happen when we were in the City? Did you?'

Evie opened her mouth to explain that she meant being formally accepted into the Settlement, but she closed it again. She should have meant marrying him. There was something wrong with her. Something terribly wrong and she had to protect Raffy from it, even if she couldn't protect herself.

They had been here for about a year. After they had

left the City for the last time, destroyed the System that had so blighted their lives, they had gone back to Base Camp where Linus and his friends lived, but within days, Linus had told them that they had to find their own place to live, that Base Camp was only a temporary place, that they had to find somewhere that would be a real home. And at first, Evie had refused to countenance the idea, had railed against Linus, told him that they had to stay together, that she'd found a new family and wasn't going to lose it. But Linus had just smiled at her, those twinkly eyes of his disarming her as he told her about the Settlement, a place he'd never been to but heard great things about, a community of good people where they could live, could flourish.

And eventually Evie had agreed, not because she wanted to go to the Settlement, but because she realised that for Linus, it was over; the battle had been won. It was he who needed to move on; he who needed everyone to leave. Linus was not like anyone she'd ever known. Wise, infuriating, tough, secretive, he had been one of the founders of the City, had built the System from scratch as a benevolent force to meet people's needs and ensure that everyone was happy. Except the System had been corrupted, the Brother had taken control and, fearful for his life, Linus had left to establish a base from which he communicated secretly with the City, waiting for the right time to disable the System once and for all, to kill off the monster that he had inadvertently created.

Now that was done, Linus had no need for Base Camp any more, and Evie recognised that she and Raffy had to leave, because soon everyone would be gone and they would be left behind with nothing.

And so they had come to the Settlement, with a message from Linus to Benjamin, its leader, a man Linus had met briefly in the early days of the City, a man, he told Evie and Raffy, who had good eyes, which was apparently enough for him to judge the entire Settlement.

But he'd been right, as he usually was.

The Settlement was a cooperative that had been established by Benjamin twenty years before. It had started as a small camp, according to Stern, Benjamin's second in command, who had shown them around on the day they arrived. He told them that it had grown over the years and was now a sprawling landmass full of houses and farms and people who worked not because a system required it but because they wanted to, because they needed to, because that was what living here required.

Because life was harder here than in the City, Stern had told them, food would not materialise unless they farmed it; buildings would not be erected unless they themselves built the foundations. Here there were no computers, no government jobs and no shops; there was a market for bartering, and there were long days full of hard work.

He'd looked at them then, thoughtfully, as though waiting for them to say something. But they hadn't; they'd both remained silent, because they had just seen Benjamin walk past, Benjamin whose name was always uttered in revered tones, Benjamin, whose presence could be felt even before he entered a room.

Within the Settlement, Benjamin was like a god; his story one of myth and legend, a fighter who refused to let the Horrors keep him down, who continued to fight, to strive, to motivate, to lead, who set up the Settlement to reward those who had assisted him, who expected the best in people and because of his belief in them, usually got it. No one knew where Benjamin had come from or what his life had been like before the Horrors. There were rumours, of course: he had been a soldier, a priest, an athlete, a politician. But Benjamin never spoke about the past. He and Stern had survived the Horrors together and had determined to build something in the ruins, to offer hope, to offer a future.

And that's exactly what the Settlement had offered

Evie and Raffy. Stern had been right when he said that there were long days of hard work in the Settlement, but life wasn't harder here than the City, not to Evie, anyway. It was like a paradise to her; so far from the City with its rules and restrictions that she could hardly believe it was on the same planet.

And it was all because of Benjamin.

'Ah, we finally meet.'

Evie still felt the hairs on the back of her neck stiffen when she remembered meeting Benjamin for the first time. Stern had appeared in front of them, a week after they had first arrived at the Settlement, and asked them to follow him. And as he had led them towards Benjamin's private quarters, she had felt her heartbeat quicken, had seen Raffy's posture grow taller, seen his eyes widen just slightly; he, too, had known what was happening, who they were being taken to. Raffy had tried to play down the whole evaluation thing, telling Evie that they were evaluating the Settlement just as much as the Settlement was evaluating them, but as he padded silently behind Stern, she knew that this meeting mattered to him just as much as it did to her. Something had changed in Raffy since they'd got here; for once he seemed genuinely to want to please, to be accepted.

'So,' Benjamin had said as they were brought into his room, Evie's eyes darting round and taking in the low seating, the lack of objects, the simplicity of the space. 'How do you like this Settlement of ours?'

Evie stared up at him. He was tall, a mountain of a man. And broad; his frame was twice the size of Raffy's, and even though it was covered in long hessian robes, it was clear from the way he moved that he was strong, muscular, a man not to be challenged lightly. But his eyes were kind, his face genuine. Immediately Evie knew that she would do everything she could to make him like her, to like them both, to make sure that he let them stay here.

They both nodded fervently.

Benjamin smiled. 'You know, when we started to build this place, I was angry. Very angry at what had happened, at the destruction, the devastation that the Horrors had created. But I knew that anger is itself a destructive force, that I had to let it go if we were going to build a truly good place to live.'

He looked at Raffy, then at Evie; they both blanched. It was as if Benjamin was looking deep inside them and seeing the anger within, the frustration, the resentment.

Evie opened her mouth to reassure Benjamin that they, too, were ready to let their anger go, but to her surprise, Raffy got there first. 'Anger serves a purpose when there is something to direct it on,' he said, stepping forwards. 'Now we are both ready to let go of our anger. We want to be happy. We want to be here.'

As he spoke, Evie's mouth fell open because she had never heard him sound so earnest; there was no undertone of sarcasm, no knowing look. He felt her gaze; turned towards her. And she'd felt a surge of happiness, because for the first time in her life she saw Raffy looking like he had found his path. He didn't look tortured; he wasn't angry, nor sullen. Instead his face was full of determination and focus, and it was infectious.

Benjamin smiled again. 'I'm glad to hear it. You see, what we're doing here is building a new life, a new future. The past is another place. Your past, my past, everyone's past. Our pasts cannot be changed. But we do not have to dwell on them either. We can learn from what has happened and we can move on, look to the future. Out of the worst pain can come strength; out of suffering can come resolve, out of desperation can come love and community. And that is what we have here. A community. A place owned by those within it, ruled by them, organised by them. A place where everyone has a role, where everyone contributes. Does that sound like a place you'd like to live?'

'Yes,' Raffy said immediately. Evie nodded too.

'Good,' Benjamin said. 'So let me tell you a little bit about the Settlement. You see, many years ago, there was nothing much here. But there was the river to the north and hills around us for protection; I knew it would be a good place for a new start. There was just a few of us at first, about ten families. We built the first houses, and ploughed the first fields about thirty years ago. We wanted to build a safe community, a peaceful one where no one would go hungry, where no one would be afraid. But more than that, I wanted to build a settlement where people could reach their potential, where they could learn, and discover new things, where no one would be held back. Where children would be the responsibility of everyone, not just their parents. Where everyone would be encouraged to find their purpose, to find fulfilment. Life is nothing if we are not fulfilled, if we don't feel valued, wouldn't you agree?

Evie nodded, but again it was Raffy who spoke, who said a resounding 'yes'. And as Benjamin continued to talk, Evie had watched in wonderment as Raffy transformed in front of her, his cynicism replaced by wide-eyed adoration. He had listened to Benjamin talk, transfixed by his story, by his hopes for the Settlement, for its people. He had listened in silence, not looking down, not shuffling from foot to foot as he usually did, but eyes wide, looking intently into Benjamin's. Like a hound, Evie had found herself thinking. Like the farm dogs that followed their masters around the City, never leaving their side, waiting patiently at their feet for the smallest scrap of food.

'So,' Benjamin had said eventually, after he had told them about the Settlement's foundations, about its egalitarian nature, its back-to-basics philosophy, about his own determination to ensure that everyone could be fed, clothed and cared for, their bodies and minds nourished, 'what is it that you think you can contribute to our community? What is it that you two will bring to the Settlement?'

Evie had looked up at Benjamin worriedly; even though this was not the City, even though she was no longer ruled by the System, by Labels, by a mother who constantly criticised her and berated her, she still found it hard to shake her fear of those in charge. 'We will work hard,' she managed to say. 'We have skills. I can sew. And we're determined.'

'I'm please to hear it,' Benjamin had said gently, then turned to Raffy. 'And how about you, young man?'

Evie had held her breath at that point; if she had a residual fear of those in power, Raffy had only loathing and resentment; whenever he had been asked a question like that in the City, his answer, always insolent, had often landed him with some punishment or other. But instead, Raffy stepped forwards.

'What will we bring?' he asked, looking Benjamin right in the eye. 'We'll bring ourselves. Completely. Wholeheartedly.' And Evie felt the hairs on the back of her neck stand up, because she'd never heard him sound so sure of anything.

Benjamin had laughed. But not unkindly. 'That's all I can ask,' he'd said, his eyes twinkling. 'In which case I am happy that you are joining us. As a matter of fact, I am always delighted when young people join our Settlement, because we need youth here; we need your energy, your ideas. But we also need the next generation. Do you two intend to get married and have children?'

Evie had looked over at Raffy, not sure what to say, but he showed no such reticence. 'Yes,' he'd said immediately. 'Yes, we do.'

And if there had been an opportunity for Evie to step in, to say that nothing had actually been decided yet, then she hadn't seen it; couldn't see it now, either. Because to contradict Raffy would have been to say that he wasn't telling the truth – hardly a good start for two people looking for acceptance.

And anyway, she was in love with Raffy. Had always been in love with Raffy. She wanted to marry him.

Didn't she?

She opened her eyes again; back in their bedroom, Raffy was still staring at her, just like he always did, dark curls framing his face. He grinned. 'Just wait till everyone sees us on our wedding day,' he said, his eyes lighting up. 'Just wait till everyone sees once and for all that you're mine.'

Evie exhaled slowly. She couldn't let this one go, however hard she tried. 'Raffy,' she said, in a tone of voice she seemed to use a lot lately, a tone that was considered, careful. 'Raffy, I wish you wouldn't keep talking about me like that. Like I'm a possession—'

'I know,' he said quickly, his brown eyes wide and warm like a dog's. 'I'm sorry. But I can't help it. I want to belong to you; I want you to be mine. Want everyone to know it.'

He looked so earnest, Evie found herself melting. 'And they will,' she promised. 'We will totally belong to each other.'

Raffy smiled. 'And then no one else will ever look at you again,' he said, lightly. 'No one will ever look at you and think they've got a chance.'

Evie stared at him, all the warmth suddenly gone. 'No one looks at me,' she said, her voice strained now. 'No one, Raffy. It's all in your head.'

Raffy stared at her incredulously. 'You have no idea

how beautiful you are,' he said, sitting on the bed and watching her as she got dressed. 'You don't know what men are like.'

Evie didn't reply; she walked instead towards the small bathroom they shared with four other couples, who they often ate with, talked and laughed with. At least Evie did. Mainly with the girls. If she spoke to their partners when Raffy wasn't there and he found out, he would fly into a rage. It sometimes felt like Evie had left the City where the System monitored her every move, only to find that Raffy had taken over the job himself, watching her, monitoring her, checking up on who she had spoken to, who might have caught her eye inadvertently.

But while his jealousy was debilitating, frustrating, restrictive, Evie knew that it wasn't his fault. It was hers. Because a year ago, on a day when her world had come crumbling down around her feet, on the day that she and Raffy had gone on the run, she'd kissed Lucas, Raffy's brother. She'd told Raffy about the kiss; had hoped that he might forgive her, perhaps even understand. But he hadn't. And ever since then, he hadn't allowed her out of his sight.

A few minutes later, she came back into the bedroom, determined that today things would be better, today she wouldn't rile him, wouldn't bring him out in a jealous rage.

Their room was one of many in a low one-storey building that housed nearly a hundred people, each given space according to their needs. Their room had space for their bed, a chair, a desk and a bookshelf. Down the corridor was the shower room that they shared with the other couples. Outside was a quadrangle of grass that anyone in the building could use; around it were dedicated allotments where personal food could be grown to supplement the weekly camp provision but some were allocated to the planting of flowers because, as Benjamin always liked to say, feeding the soul was as important as feeding the belly.

'What are you working on today?' she asked.

'I'm going to help plough one of the far fields,' Raffy yawned, 'although my shoulders are killing me.' Evie turned and appraised Raffy's shoulders: broad, rippled, so different from how they looked just a year ago. It was as though here, in the Settlement, Raffy had suddenly become a man. He was taller, too, but his sudden broadness was what surprised her the most. He suited it. Suited being here, his face tanned by the sun, framed by his unruly, tousled hair that he refused to keep short. He suited working hard, Evie found herself thinking, suited laughing with the other builders, sharing jokes. He came back every evening with a spring in his step, even as he collapsed on the bed in exhaustion.

It was what she'd dreamt about when they'd lived in the City, when even talking to each other was a terrible crime. Here, she and Raffy could walk down the road hand in hand with no one to report them, no one to stare at them, no one to tell them how wicked they were.

And no Lucas.

Evie caught her breath, as she always did when she thought of Lucas, as the image of his face flooded her mind.

'Right, time to get up,' Raffy said, putting his tea down then leaning in to kiss her. He framed her face in his hands, kissed her tenderly on the lips, then pushed his fingers into her hair, pulling her towards him. Evie loved his hands, nutmeg brown from the sun, full of strength yet so tender with her.

She closed her eyes briefly, allowed herself to enjoy the moment, then reluctantly opened them again to look at the clock on her bedside table. Nearly 5 a.m. As work in the Settlement started on the dot at 6 a.m., breakfast would be served shortly in the communal dining areas, one for each Area. And if you got there later than 5.40 a.m., there wasn't much point, they'd discovered, as all the good food had already gone.

'Today's going to be a good day,' Raffy said suddenly, jumping out of bed and grabbing a towel. 'And not just because of the fitting. Everything's good, Evie. The new field could produce enough food for a month if we do it well. Simon's going to show me.'

Evie smiled. Simon was one of the established farmers; he had taken Raffy under his wing and under his tutelage Raffy had blossomed. He'd told her, a few weeks ago, that for once in his life he felt like he was achieving something, that he was part of something, that his life actually had a point to it.

'They really trust you to plough a whole field?' Evie teased.

Raffy flicked her around the ankles with his towel. 'Watch what you say,' he said, grinning. 'People respect farmers around here.'

Evie looked at him thoughtfully. That's what it was, she realised suddenly. That's why he was so happy here. For the first time in his life, Raffy had earned the respect of others. For the first time in his life he could walk tall. And this tall farmer loved her. Had always loved her.

As he got to the door she called out to him. 'Wait.'

'What?' Raffy asked, turning just as Evie put her arms around him. Her future. The only one that mattered. Once they were married, he would stop being so jealous; he would know that he had her. And things would be good. They would be completely good.

'I love you,' she said. 'That's all.'

'And I love you,' Raffy said as he leant down and kissed her again, tenderly, holding her tight against him. 'More than you could possibly know.' Then he smiled, and wandered out of the room.

2

It was early morning. Gabby noticed that the street she was walking down, one of the larger streets in the City, was almost empty and walked a little faster. She was five or so minutes late for work, which wasn't good, but nor was it the end of the world. Not any more. Still, ten minutes might be pushing it. Ten minutes and she might be forced to work into her lunch break.

Lunch break was one of the improvements since the System had been deactivated. Or 'taken away' as her parents liked to put it, fear in their eyes, resentment in their voices. Her parents didn't like Lucas, the City's new leader. They believed that what he was doing would bring devastation and evil back within the City walls. But that was mainly because her parents could no longer use the System as a threat; at least that seemed to be the thing that vexed them most. They couldn't tell her what time to get back home every night any more; couldn't insist that she sit with them after supper listening to her father give them both a lecture on the importance of contemplation or something else utterly boring. Now she could go and meet her friends on the green after work; now she could choose who she was going to marry, choose everything.

Although, she reminded herself, as she broke into a light jog, there were still rules about getting to work on time. And anyway, she wasn't ready to make any of the big choices yet. She couldn't imagine getting married, having a house, being all serious like her parents. Mainly she just wanted to play ball on the green, feel the exhilaration of running for a catch, the thrill of winning, the pain of losing. Until the System had been deactivated, the only winning or losing in the City was determined by the System and involved labels: an upward movement meant you won, a downward movement meant you lost. But the System was no game; it determined everything: where you worked, who you married, who you associated with. Whether you won or lost, things could still turn against you. Whether you won or lost, you had no control.

Then again, back then no one disappeared either.

Gabby stopped for a second, caught her breath, looked around. Was someone watching her? Following her? Then she shook herself. Of course they weren't.

What Clara, her best friend, had told her was probably made up anyway. There weren't any Informers in the City. The Disappearances weren't what Clara had said they were. There would be some other explanation. There had to be. Clara's terror had seemed genuine; Gabby had noticed how her hands were shaking as she told her the story, had seen the fear in her eyes. But Clara got scared easily; she believed what people told her. And Gabby refused to believe that she would disappear just because Clara had told her about the people in the hospital. Otherwise, Clara herself would have disappeared.

The truth was that Gabby was as scared about the Disappearances as everyone else, but she refused to let on, refused to let them cower her. Because that's how things had been with the System: people afraid all the time, not going out after dark, worrying about what lay ahead. There was something terrible happening, of that she had no doubt, but she wasn't going to let it affect her. She wasn't going to let things go back to how they were. She'd rather die.

Maybe not die, she corrected herself. But she certainly wasn't going to run scared from the Disappearances like everyone else. She was just beginning to see her life as something worthwhile, something worth waking up in the morning for.

Until the change, there hadn't been any sport in the City, not openly anyway. There hadn't been any dancing, either, any music, any real conversation. People had been too scared, had limited themselves to furtive whispers followed by the clenching fear that confidences would be betrayed, that the System had heard, somehow. Now it was common to see people clustered on street corners arguing about things; now people were invited round to other people's houses for supper; now old guitars and accordions had been dug out from wherever they'd been hidden and music could be heard everywhere once work was done for the day.

Gabby's parents saw it as the beginning of the end; Gabby saw it as a miracle.

She increased her speed; the pottery workshop where she worked was just a minute away now. She wondered if Clara was already there; they had both been up late last night, which was why Gabby was late now, why she had slept in, in spite of her mother's attempts to rouse her.

So when Clara had told her about the shadowy strangers in the hospital, her voice trembling as she spoke, Gabby had listened, but only partially; had reassured Clara but not in any meaningful way. Because when she'd begged Clara to tell her what she knew, Gabby had hoped and expected to hear that the

Disappearances were something else completely, that the others had run away, found something more exciting, somewhere better. So she had listened to Clara only half-heartedly, had told herself that probably Clara was making it up, that it couldn't be true because . . . Because . . .

It was only as she turned the corner that she noticed the shadow under her feet. Only as the workshop came into view that she felt her heart start to thud in her chest, felt her legs speed up. The Informers. Clara had told her that they knew everything, that they had tracked down everyone who knew, everyone who had seen them. Everyone except Clara.

It couldn't be true. And yet, as she heard the footsteps speed up behind her, Gabby felt a cold veil of terror fall over her. Because she knew now without a doubt that she was being followed. Because through the fug of fear, she realised that what Clara had told her was true. Because suddenly she knew that she was running for her life.

3

What she needed to do, Evie thought to herself as she walked to work, was to just stop thinking about things so much. She had always thought too much, always questioned things too much. Maybe she should just learn to accept what was in front of her; maybe then she would actually be happy.

She and Raffy were happy here, there was no question of that. And it wasn't like she wanted to marry anyone else. The truth was that marrying Raffy made total sense. And the last thing she wanted to do was mess things up, to jeopardise anything.

The truth was, Raffy and Evie had found that, in spite of the Settlement being a warm, open and welcoming place, it hadn't been that simple to be accepted into it and the last thing she wanted to do was set them back again. Raffy and Evie had been interviewed, questioned at length; they had met various groups of people, had undergone a trial period, had been put up before the camp council for approval. As Benjamin had said, the township belonged to the people who lived in it; they alone could decide who joined them. And anyone who did join them had to prove their worth, had to show that they were committed, that they could fit in.

And so that's just what they'd done. Raffy had got work on one of the many farms that kept the Settlement's community fed; Evie had started in the kitchens, then moved to the fabric workshops where her rusty sewing skills were welcomed. And Raffy's delight in the place soon rubbed off on her, too. Whereas in the City she'd loathed sewing, had wanted to do something as different as possible from the woman who had posed as her mother, here she found herself feeling grateful that there was something she could do well; here she brushed away the pricked fingers that plagued her, because they didn't matter, because in a strange way she was almost proud of them. Proud of her work, of being part of a community that was as different from the City as it was possible to be.

And Benjamin had watched them, too; every so often one of them would look up to see him watching them, the whites of his eyes shining against his ebony skin;

when he realised that he had been seen, he would give a half-smile, a little wave, and would walk on, his long robes flapping at his ankles, robes that were in no way a uniform, and yet were emulated by most of the men and women on the Settlement – long flowing clothes and long flowing hair that framed open, happy faces as they worked, talked, laughed and ate.

People didn't talk much about the past at the Settlement, which suited Evie and Raffy down to the ground. It was like Benjamin had said, people here were building a new life, a new future. The past was another place, the past could not be changed. The citizens of the Settlement recognised this. They had suffered during the Horrors, just as everyone had suffered, just as those who had initiated the Horrors had intended. But the Settlement's people had survived, and with survival came responsibility. A responsibility to live, to grow, to learn, to draw a line and move on.

And that was what had convinced Evie that this wasn't just somewhere they could survive, but was somewhere they could live. In the City, they talked about the Horrors all the time, about the evil that had nearly destroyed the world. In the City, everything and everyone was analysed, labelled, ranked, including the people. Here in the Settlement, people just got on with their lives, looking to the future, looking for the good in people instead of fearing the evil. Here, music was always in the air; people playing guitars, singing, humming as they worked. Here books were shared and discussed openly; here different opinions were welcomed and considered. Here, asking questions was encouraged, not frowned upon. Here, you could talk to whoever you wanted, whenever you wanted to.

At least that was the idea.

'Hey, Evie!'

Evie turned to see Neil walking towards her. Neil was one of the Settlement's teachers. Teaching was considered the highest calling in the Settlement and everyone was encouraged to learn as much as they could. There were regular art classes, book groups, pottery, woodwork, engineering and cookery classes, as well as classes in reading, writing and arithmetic for those whose education had been limited to a few sporadic lessons given by whoever was available, and for those who hadn't even got that far.

'Neil!' Evie's eyes lit up and she rushed towards him eagerly. Neil, who was aged somewhere in his fifties, had arrived at the Settlement ten years before, having lived almost has a hermit since the end of the Horrors. Wearing nothing but rags and with hair down to his waist, he had – according to the stories Evie had been told – been close to starvation; for several weeks it was touch and go whether he would survive. But slowly he was brought back to health and with each week his nurses had learnt more about him, discovered that this emaciated man in front of them had been a leading academic before the Horrors, had won prizes, travelled the world. He was a sailor, a pianist, had invented a device used in fishing that prevented environmental damage and had given the proceeds – many millions of pounds – to charity. Evie had been told all this, but it didn't mean much to her; she found talk of the old days confusing and strange. But what she loved about Neil was the excitement on his face when he was talking about a book or concept; the way his eyes danced when one of his pupils grasped something important.

Now he tended live stock during the day and held various classes in the evenings: creative writing, musical appreciation, knot tying and singing, and he regularly told anyone who would listen that he had never been happier, that he had everything he wanted here and more. But Evie knew that this wasn't strictly true; she noticed how quickly he devoured the Settlement's meagre rations every evening, knew that he was too busy teaching to tend his own allotment. And so, whenever she went to his classes, she always brought him a piece of bread, a piece of fruit, something from her meal that day. And he would always refuse to take it, but she would insist because she didn't need as much food as him and anyway, she was hungry for learning, so really it was a fair trade.

Although she never told Raffy what she was doing. She wasn't sure he would entirely understand.

The truth was, though, and Evie knew it, that if Neil only asked for more food he would almost certainly get it; food was shared equally only because it seemed the most sensible way, the fairest system. As Benjamin and Stern and everyone else kept telling them, the Settlement wasn't a place of rules but rather one of community. Everything was up for discussion; anyone was within their rights to suggest something different, to propose a new way of doing things.

And no one ever asked to change a thing.

'I got that book I mentioned.' Neil held it aloft and Evie's face broke into a smile. He threw it to her; jumping, she managed to catch it.

'Thank you,' she said, her face glowing as she turned the book over in her hands. It was a book Neil had told her about at her creative writing class held every Wednesday evening. Benjamin had suggested she go, that she might find writing cathartic. Initially, Raffy had gone with her, professing to be as interested in writing his thoughts down as she was, but eventually he had drifted away, joined another club, run out of excuses to stop her attending on her own.

And Evie loved it – loved the language of words, the way just changing one word in a sentence could change everything, could create emotion, tension, suspense or fear, loved how writing about her life, about the terrible things that had happened to her, reduced them to just words on a page, helped her to free herself of them.

'You'll enjoy it, I'm sure you will,' Neil said. 'This author was writing over a hundred years ago, but her books are relevant to any time because her themes are universal, because there's truth in her words. You'll see what I mean.'

Evie smiled gratefully. She'd always hated learning in the City; had despised the facts and figures she had been forced to memorise, regurgitate word for word, no questions, no imagination, nothing new or different, because different was dangerous, because different couldn't be trusted. The City had been so full of fear, she realised now; fear of doing something wrong, fear of talking to someone who might infect you with evil, fear of your label being changed to a lower one, a worse one, fear of the same thing happening to someone close to you, fear of the Evils outside the City walls, fear of what might happen if the walls were breached, if your resolve crumbled, if evil reigned once more. And fear was crippling; fear was debilitating. Fear made people anxious, irritable, unhappy and closed.

'I'll see you on Wednesday?' Neil asked and Evie nodded, beaming.

'See you then,' she said, opening up her bag and putting the book, *All Men are Mortal*, safely inside. But as she did so, her fingers brushed against something, a hard, metal object that made her redden guiltily and quicken her step as though afraid someone might be following her, might know what it was.

It was a watch.

Lucas's watch.

The watch he'd given her on the day she and Raffy had left the City for the last time.

The watch that had belonged to Lucas and Raffy's father, the watch Lucas had asked her to give to Raffy, and then told her that he loved her. Had always loved her.

'You okay, Evie?' Neil moved towards her, his face suddenly concerned. Evie realised that she was blushing furiously.

'Fine,' she said, quickly, knowing that she sounded less than convincing. 'Honestly, I'm fine.'

It had been several weeks before she found the

moment to give the watch to Raffy. She had waited until she thought he would be ready to understand, ready to forgive his brother, ready to see Lucas for who he really was instead of the oppressive older brother he'd pretended to be.

She'd pressed the watch into his hands just as Lucas had done with her; had told him that Lucas wanted him to have it. 'He said it was always yours. That your father asked him to look after it for you. He couldn't give it to you before. But now . . . now you should wear it.'

Raffy looked at it for a moment, then stuffed it into his pocket.

'You're not going to put it on?' Evie asked, but she was met by fiery eyes.

'Put it on? No,' Raffy said curtly.

And that was that; at least Evie thought that would be that. It was only weeks later that she dared mention it again, ask whether he might ever think of putting it on.

'Put on Lucas's watch?' Raffy sneered. 'I don't even have it any more. I traded it with the baker for some cakes. Remember the chocolate sponge? More useful than a gold watch.'

Evie had stared at him. 'But Lucas kept that watch for you. For years. It was your father's. He—'

'Don't,' Raffy interrupted her, walking towards Evie, a look on his face that she'd never seen before, a look that was so cold that it was like he was someone else, someone she didn't know, someone she didn't want to know. 'Don't mention Lucas again to me. Or my father. Or that watch. Do you understand?' His face was inches from her but there was no intimacy in his expression, no softness in his eyes. He didn't even see her, she realised; at that moment, he saw only his resentment, saw only his own, selfish rage.

And inwardly seething, inwardly so furious she could barely look at Raffy let alone bring herself to speak to him, Evie had nodded. But four months later, the baker had benefited from a full set of patchwork curtains and cushion covers sewn by her hand from the scraps of fabric left over in the workrooms, and Evie had the watch back.

Now she kept it hidden, transferring it from bag to hiding place on a regular basis, never keeping it in the same place for any length of time. It was yet another secret that she kept from Raffy, a time bomb that might explode at any moment. But she was prepared to take that risk. Because Raffy might be happy to forget Lucas, to ignore his sacrifice, to pretend that he didn't exist. But Evie couldn't. Wouldn't.

Lucas did exist. And Evie hoped that he was happy. Back in the City, she hoped that he had finally found the peace he'd been searching for.

'All right then,' Neil shrugged, giving her one last smile before he walked away, 'see you Wednesday.'

4

Lucas took a deep breath and surveyed the woman sitting opposite him. Amy Jenkins. He had spoken to her many times before; had orchestrated the launch of her journal, *The City News*, believing that the introduction of a free press, of independent thought, would be welcomed by the City's people, would encourage them to believe in themselves, to build a new world together.

But that had been a year ago. A lifetime ago.

Now things were very different.

Now search parties were roaming the streets of the City; crowds were gathered outside his offices, braying for his blood. Now he was met only by angry faces, by desperate pleas. And everyone wanted one thing: The System, reinstated. New Baptisms reintroduced. The Brother. Servility.

Lucas felt a lump beginning to form in his throat.

'What we have to remember,' he said, coolly, calmly, giving no indication of the turmoil underneath, 'is that the System enslaved us. Its judgements were arbitrary, controlled by the Brother to keep people fearful, to separate them, to reward his friends and punish his enemies. It was corrupt.'

'And yet,' Amy said, her eyes narrowing, 'the City was a place of safety, of peace. And now our young people are disappearing. Every week another one is snatched from their bed, from the street, never to be seen again. They trusted you; their families trusted you. To keep them safe. To keep the Evils out of the City. But you failed them; you continue to fail them. What do you say to that?'

Lucas closed his eyes. They were calling them the Disappearances. Boys and girls, all teenagers, all missing. A few weeks ago Jane Anderson, Bill Grainger, Edward Ashleigh, all the others, had been working, eating, sleeping . . . And then, one by one, they had gone. Six of them in total, disappeared, in a City with huge walls that had been built to protect them all. Disappeared in a City that for years had believed itself rid of evil, safe. Disappeared with no explanation, no clue as to what had happened to them.

He opened his eyes again, then stood up and walked to the window, a small perfunctory affair that let in enough sunlight but kept out the cold. Utilitarian, like everything else in the City. Lucas had never really noticed until recently how drab everything was, how little beauty there was within the City walls. He'd been too focused on the machinations of its government, on protecting Raffy and Evie, on secretly communicating with his father's comrade, somewhere outside. But now his brother and Evie were gone; now there was no subterfuge, no living a double life, no more secrets. Lucas had expected to feel better, happier. Instead, he felt empty.

And now this. Lucas was used to being one step ahead; used to knowing what others didn't. Now he felt helpless, and helplessness did not sit well on his shoulders.

'We are searching,' he said. 'Day and night. We have searched every inch of this City.'

'And yet you haven't found them,' Amy said, her voice brittle. 'My little sister, for instance. She's been missing for three weeks now. She was at home. I said good night to her and in the morning she was gone. And you say you have search parties? What's the use of search parties when they can't find anything? When it's you, our self-imposed leader, who is doing this to us? Will you be happy when we've all gone? Is that what you want?'

There were tears in her eyes, but Lucas didn't blink; he just walked towards her. 'I want the City to be a good place,' he said simply. 'A place where people are free to make decisions for themselves, to live without the stigma of labels.'

'To be free to be abducted by Evils?' Amy asked, her voice strangled with emotion. 'To be scared to walk down the street alone? To travel around the City only in large groups? To lock every window and press furniture against the door at night-time? Is that what you want for us?'

Her lips were trembling as she spoke; she reminded Lucas of Evie, with her challenging eyes and refusal to accept anything less than the truth. What would Evie say to him now, he wondered. Would she tell him that he wasn't doing enough? Would she stare at him angrily, just as Amy was doing, and tell him that until the Disappearances stopped he had failed his people, failed the City? Of course she would. And she'd be right.

Lucas steeled himself and shook his head. 'No,' he said. 'Of course not.'

Amy scrutinised Lucas's face. 'And what words of reassurance do you have for us?' she asked. 'For the parents of the missing children? For their families? For everyone else, terrified to go to sleep? What do you have to say to them? To us?'

Lucas looked at her steadily. 'I will find who is doing this. I will find them and I will punish them. I will get justice. And I will find our young people. I will reunite them with their families.'

'How?' Amy demanded, but Lucas had already walked towards the door, opened it for her, made it clear that the interview was over.

Because he didn't have the answer to her question.

Because he wasn't sure he had the answer to anything any more.

But he knew that he would find answers. Knew that he wouldn't stop until whoever was doing this was brought to justice. Unless he did, everything he had fought for, everything his father had fought for, would be for nothing. Whoever was snatching away these young people was snatching away the City's happiness, its peace. And it was up to him to restore that peace.

Lucas left his office; he needed to get out, needed air. Amy was right: he had let his people down. He had dismantled the System, the System that tracked each and every citizen, the System that would now be able to show him exactly where the Disappeared were and exactly what had happened to them. He, Linus, Evie and Raffy had destroyed it joyously, triumphantly. But Lucas hadn't realised quite what a supporting wall it had been to the City; hadn't realised that without it, things would begin to crumble.

Actually that wasn't quite true; Linus had tried to tell Lucas, but Lucas hadn't listened. He hadn't wanted to listen. He'd just wanted to get on with his new life, with the job his father had entrusted to him all those years ago.

It was nearly a year since Linus, Raffy and Evie and the others had stormed the City with Lucas's help, disabling the System that had controlled its citizens for so long, revealing the truths that the Brother had kept from them. The System had known everything; seen everything, understood everything. Built by Linus to anticipate people's needs and create a world where happiness was not just aimed for but delivered, the System had soon been corrupted, manipulated to the Brother's ends, acting as policeman instead of bene-factor, monitoring the City's people to check that they didn't step out of line.

Linus had told him that disabling the System wouldn't be enough, that every vestige of the old regime had to be dismantled and destroyed so that the people had no choice but to accept change. But Lucas hadn't believed him. Just as he hadn't believed Linus's prediction that the people wouldn't be grateful; that they would blame Lucas instead, that they would come to hate him.

Now, however, he was coming to the desperate conclusion that Linus had been right. People did hate him. He saw it in their eyes. The citizens of the City were more scared now than they ever had been before, and it was his fault because for all his talk of a new start, he couldn't protect them from the Disappearances. He had no answers, nothing at all.

He strode out into the corridor but immediately found himself in front of the Brother who was walking towards him, by his side the guards who accompanied him everywhere, looking more like staff than gaolers, Lucas thought to himself ruefully.

'Lucas. Difficult times?' the Brother asked, a smile on his lips. Lucas stared at him.

'Yes,' he said, stonily, refusing to let the Brother glimpse his inner torment, his self-doubt. 'And please take that triumphant look off your face. I know you find it impossible to actually care about anyone but yourself, but you might pretend to be upset about what's happening instead of appearing decidedly cheerful.'

'Lucas, that is a terrible accusation,' the Brother said, the smile not leaving his face. 'Of course I'm upset. Not for you, but for the poor people of this City who depend upon you to keep them safe. Who have been let down again and again. You are so like your father, Lucas, I can't believe I didn't see it before.'

Lucas looked away, loathing filling his body. His father had been a victim of the Brother's administration; had been labelled a K when he had discovered the lies upon which the Brother had built the City. K for Killable. Lucas shivered when he remembered the look in his father's eye as he had told him what was going to happen, that he was going to die, that he needed Lucas's help, that he could tell no one . . .

And now the Brother was gloating. Lucas had never loathed him more. If he had done as Linus had suggested and left the Brother to die outside the City gates, just as the Brother had left Lucas's father and so many other victims, perhaps things would be different. But Lucas hadn't been able to do it; he hadn't been able to stomach the idea of attempting to build a good, free City on such a vengeful and barbaric act. Instead he'd believed that forgiving the Brother would demonstrate the power of this new government. And the Brother had been so grateful – pitifully so – had promised to support Lucas, to help him, to be a part of this new City.

But now, even with the guards Lucas had appointed to restrain the Brother, even with a house arrest that enabled him to travel only from his house to work and back again, the Brother was still doing his best to plot, manipulate, encourage dissent. Lucas had no proof, but he could see what was happening, and he suspected his own men of being complicit. People were afraid of the Brother; people still believed in him. But they wouldn't for much longer. Lucas would see to that.

'I have to go,' he said angrily. 'I have young people to find.'

'And you really think you'll find them?' The Brother shook his head. 'Lucas, the wall has been reinforced, checked for breaches; you yourself have confiscated all the keyholders' keys. No one can get out of the City and no one can get in. You need to accept that this evil is within the City walls. You need to accept that you cannot control everything. You need to accept that you need the System.'

Lucas shook his head in amazement. 'This from the man who sought to control his people to such a degree that they couldn't form a friendship without his say so?'

The Brother shrugged. 'I am attentive to my flock. It's not a crime, Lucas. But you focus on the wall, if that's what makes you feel better. I'm sure Rab will be pleased of the company.'

Rab was the East Gatekeeper; it was his area of the City wall that was most vulnerable because of the swamps surrounding it, making it impossible for

guards to line it. But those same swamps made it an
unlikely entry point from the outside, too, as Rab had
pointed out each time Lucas had visited him, each
time Lucas had interrogated him and checked the gate
for himself before confiscating his key, believing in
some way that if he alone held all the keys he would
be more in control of what was happening. And
anyway, the Brother was right. There had been no
breach of the wall, or the gates; no forced entry had
been attempted and Rab had sworn blind that he had
let no one in or out. Whoever was doing this was
either in the City already or had some unknown way
of getting in or out. But Lucas couldn't shake the
suspicion that the Brother knew more than he was
letting on.

'I'm going to overturn every stone, every inch of the
City,' he said, his voice low. 'I'm going to find out
who's behind this.'

'Do what you want,' the Brother waved him away.
'The trouble is, we have no System to protect our
citizens any more. But you know that, don't you Lucas?'

Lucas regarded him coldly. 'The System never
protected them. It ruled them with a rod of iron, monitored their every move,' he said, levelly.

The Brother shrugged. 'And yet people felt safer.
Were safer. You disabled the System. So you are

responsible for the Disappearances. You look for them, Lucas. You explain to their families why their loved ones are missing. Or, you could do something that would really stop what's happening. You could reinstate the System, see that every citizen is tracked again, visible to the System's operators, protected by them. You could finally do something worthwhile, show your people that you care about them.'

'Always the System. That's your answer to everything.'

'Because it *was* the answer to everything,' the Brother said, his eyes stony. 'And you and your terrorist friends destroyed it.'

Lucas took a deep breath. For most of his life, he had hidden his emotions, had hidden everything about himself. These days he allowed his emotions to surface, but still he knew they had to be controlled. Otherwise they threatened to overwhelm him, to render him so angry, so desperate that he would have no will to continue.

'You are the terrorist, Brother,' he said eventually. 'You are the one who took power by force, by subjugation. The System ruined lives, sentenced my father to death simply because he discovered the truth.'

The Brother frowned. He was getting frustrated.

'You still don't understand, do you Lucas?' the Brother asked, patronisingly.

'Understand what?'

The Brother walked closer towards Lucas so that he was just inches away from him. 'I used to think that you were a clever man,' he whispered, a little glint in his eye. 'That you understood. But really you're as naive as your friend Linus. What you don't seem to grasp is that people want to be led, want to be told what to do. That is what I gave them. The freedom not to have to think for themselves. And you took it away. That's why they dislike you, Lucas.'

'People want freedom,' Lucas said, taking a step back.

'Believe what you like,' the Brother shrugged again. 'But if I were you, I'd hope that young people stop disappearing. Because if they don't, the angry mob braying for your blood is only going to get bigger, more confident, more determined. And I certainly have no intention of stopping them.'

He was looking Lucas right in the eye; Lucas steeled himself to make sure his own gaze didn't waver. 'Thank you for your support,' he said. 'But rest assured, I'll find every single person who's disappeared, and I'll also find whoever's behind this.'

The Brother smiled, thinly, then started to walk on, the guards at his side.

'Poor Lucas,' he said with a little sigh, then stopped, turning to look at Lucas with a look of mock pity on his face. 'Fighting your battles all alone, as always. Where are your friends, Lucas? Where are the people you sacrificed everything for?'

Lucas said nothing.

'What about that girl you were matched to?' the Brother continued, warming to his theme. 'She preferred your brother, didn't she? The brother who left you here to rot, after everything you did for him. Maybe you should accept the facts, Lucas. No one wants your help. No one wants the freedom you're so desperate to give them.'

Lucas opened his mouth to speak, but he was interrupted by the sound of footsteps running towards them, footsteps that could only mean one thing. He turned, mentally preparing himself for the news.

It was Christopher, head of the police guard; his face was ashen. 'There's another one missing,' he gasped, his panting suggesting that he had run all the way from the police building half a mile away. 'Gabrielle Marchant. I've started a search, but . . .'

'But nothing,' Lucas said determinedly, gritting his teeth. 'We will comb every inch of the City. We will find her.'

* * *

Gabby stumbled, fell to the ground, scrambled up again. The streets were deserted, everyone hard at work, and anyway she was too far away now. She should have run into a house, into the bakery, but she somehow knew they'd get to her before she opened the door, so instead she had run out of the centre of the City into the no man's land that surrounded it. Her only chance was to outrun them. She could hear them behind her; she didn't know how many there were or what they looked like. She just knew that they were coming for her, just like Clara had said they would, just like they'd come for the others.

It had seemed fanciful when Clara had told her; had seemed like the stories her own parents told her about the world before the City, about the Evils who lived outside the City walls, about the thousand unseen threats that surrounded them all the time. And even though she'd seen the fear in Clara's eyes, heard the tremor in her voice, she hadn't really taken it in, hadn't really understood. Clara had warned her; had told her that everyone who knew had Disappeared; that the strangers had a way of knowing; that she had to forget every word Clara was saying and never breathe it to a soul. But Gabby had just smiled and nodded, because Clara herself hadn't disappeared, and that, to Gabby, was a pretty fundamental hole in the story as far as she was concerned.

Now, she realised how stupid she'd been. And now it was too late.

No, not too late. Never too late.

She filled her lungs with air; she knew she could outrun anyone if she tried. She would get away. She had to. If she could only get over the City wall, through it somehow, then she would just keep on running and they would give up. She wiped the sweat from her forehead then felt her heart stop as she heard them again behind her, crunching on the leaves, closer than she'd realised.

She upped her pace, frantic, her eyes wide in fear. She was too far from the wall. She would beg, she would fall on the floor and beg . . .

But it would do no good. Escape was her only hope.

She ran, terrified, towards the swamps, towards the wall that had protected them from the Evils, the Eastern wall that now offered her only chance of escape from her pursuers. It was the only section of the wall without guards, the only section she might attempt to escape through. And if it occurred to her to run to where the guards were, to ask them for protection, she soon discounted the idea. The guards had not protected the others; if Clara was right, the guards must have let the strangers into the City. She couldn't trust anyone.

She was getting closer now; she could see the wall

ahead of her, see the gate. If she could only get to it. If she could only leave this place, get away . . .

Up ahead of her was a house, small and squat, surrounded by swampland. The gatekeeper. She lunged towards it, hammered at the door, tried to open the latch. But her hands were covered in sweat; her brain too frantic to make any sense of the handle in front of her. She screamed out for help, then shivered as she heard them, closer. She turned, then caught her breath as she saw them, saw them for the first time, walking towards her, smiling, two of them. They were laughing at her, at her fear, at her terror, laughing because she had nowhere to run to, because it was over, because they had won . . . She closed her eyes. And she waited.

5

News had spread rapidly, driving men and women onto the streets and crowds were already gathering by the time Lucas got outside. The Disappearances had struck fear into the hearts of the City's people; its walls, its rules, its very existence was grounded in the desire to protect its people from evil. Having young people simply vanish from within the City walls was too much to countenance; it shook the very foundations the City had been built on.

People regarded Lucas warily as he joined the throngs, but no one said anything. He was their leader, after all, and in spite of all that had happened he had not yet faced open hostility from his people, even though he expected it every day. And he knew, in a twisted way, that he had the Brother to thank for it, not because of anything the Brother was doing, but only because of the culture of fear that he had brought about, that still persisted now. The System had been gone for a year, but still the City's citizens were wary of questioning, of challenging, of doing anything that might, in the old regime, be considered suspect. And Lucas had been an A; had always been an A. Though he kept explaining that labels meant nothing, that people could not be categorised in that way, he knew that his former label still protected him, still gave him an authority that he would otherwise lack. And it depressed him, but he was still grateful for it. Sometimes.

'Who was she with last? Who knows her? Where are her friends?' Lucas asked the questions even though they had been asked before, even though he knew what the answers would be: blank faces, wordless teenagers. The friends and acquaintances of the Disappeared had been interviewed relentlessly, separately and together; each had insisted that they knew nothing, that they had nothing to tell.

'You last saw her yesterday?' The group of teenagers looked at him blankly; they shrugged, nodded. They were scared; of course they were. Everyone was. 'And then what?'

'Then we went to work this morning, only she didn't come,' a girl said.

'And your name is?'

'Clara,' the girl answered, wide-eyed. With fear, Lucas found himself thinking. No, with something else.

'They know nothing,' another man said dismissively. 'She was at home this morning. She disappeared between leaving home at 7.30 and 8 a.m. when she didn't arrive at work. We have to start searching, not wasting time here.'

'And there was nothing strange the last time you saw her? Nothing she said to you?' Lucas continued, looking closely at the girl, trying to work out what it was about her that made him want to keep her talking.

The girl looked uncomfortable. 'I don't know. We were playing ball last night. Just playing . . .' She swallowed; a tear appeared in her eye. A man stepped forward protectively. Her father.

'She doesn't know anything. Let's stop wasting time and start the search.'

Lucas nodded reluctantly. 'Okay,' he said. 'Usual drill.'

They split into groups, chose areas to search and agreed a reporting structure so that information could be shared quickly and effectively. They searched all day, not stopping to eat, then they searched into the evening. As darkness fell, the women and younger people were sent home and the men continued to search;

by early morning it was just Lucas and Gabrielle's father, her uncles, and her father's work colleagues who were still out, still hunting. No one met another's eye; no one was ready for what they knew in their hearts – that Gabrielle was gone, like the rest of them, that they would not find her.

And then it was the start of the next day; people were out, walking to work. Bleary-eyed, Lucas called a halt, told the men to go home, to sleep, said that he would relieve them of their duties that day. And reluctantly they went; Lucas watched them heavily, then slowly turned and made his way to his office. He would not sleep. He couldn't. He felt like he would never sleep again.

People stared at him as he walked past, but Lucas barely noticed the attention; he had grown immune to it, learnt how to block it out. Lucas put his head down, pulled his coat around him and marched forwards. The Brother was right; he was not good with people, found it hard to reassure, to connect. For all his life he had repressed his feelings, and now he wasn't even sure he had any. All he knew was how to stay calm, cool, collected, to pretend that he wasn't scared, to pretend that he was in control.

But he wasn't in control; wasn't even close. And as he walked, he felt himself begin to shake, not with cold, but with emotion. He had failed. He had failed the City.

He had failed his father.

He stopped walking suddenly; he was hungry, ravenously so. There was a bakery on the corner; he stepped in and bought a loaf of bread and two buns. Food would keep him going. Food would help him fight the doubts that circled his head like vultures, seeing weakness and swooping in for the kill. He couldn't allow them any oxygen; it was too self-indulgent. When he had found the missing teenagers, then he would make a decision; then, perhaps he would leave the City. But until then, he had to stay strong, he had to stay focused.

He put his head down again and started to walk. But just as he turned the corner onto the main road, the road of government buildings, he stopped, because next to him was a girl, a girl he vaguely recognised. And then, suddenly, he knew that she was the girl from last night.

'Clara?' he said.

She looked surprised that he had remembered her name. She nodded.

'Is there something you've remembered? Something you can tell me?'

She looked at him warily. Her fingernails were chewed, her eyes bloodshot; Lucas suspected she hadn't slept either.

'Tell me what you know,' he said quietly. 'Tell me. You can trust me. I just want to find your friend.'

She bit her lip. 'You used to run the System,' she said. 'Didn't you?'

Lucas nodded. 'Yes,' he said. 'I did.'

'And it was your brother who . . . Raffy, I mean. He found the glitch. It was because of him that you . . . that the System was deactivated?'

'Sort of,' Lucas shrugged. 'The System should never have been up and running. Not in the way it was. It was supposed to protect us. And instead it became a tyrant, controlling us. That's why we closed it down.'

Clara nodded uncertainly.

'No one's listening,' Lucas said then. 'If you tell me something, no one else will know.'

Clara looked up with a start. 'But that's just it. They will know. If I tell you, you'll disappear too,' she whispered. 'They can hear everything.'

Lucas looked at her uncertainly. 'They?'

Clara shook her head. 'It doesn't matter,' she said, walking away. 'It doesn't matter.'

'It does matter,' Lucas said, running after her. 'Clara, talk to me. Who are you talking about? Who can hear everything?'

Clara shook her head again; there were tears in her eyes. 'I can't,' she whispered.

'Yes you can,' he said firmly. 'And you must. Who are you talking about? Who are these people?'

Clara looked around furtively, her eyes full of fear. She bit her lip anxiously. 'The Informers,' she whispered. 'That's what we call them. Called them, I mean. They're the ones disappearing everyone. And I'm going to be next. I know I am. I'm the only one left.' Her voice was shaking; as Lucas moved closer he saw that her whole body was trembling.

'You won't be next,' he said grimly. 'Tell me what you know and I'll protect you.'

She shook her head, looked around nervously.

'They're here?' Lucas asked.

'They're everywhere,' she whispered.

Lucas thought for a moment, then took her hand. 'Come with me,' he said, pulling up his collar and lowering his head. 'I know somewhere we can talk. I know somewhere safe.'

As Lucas and Clara made their way unsteadily, Lucas couldn't help thinking about how Evie must have felt, when night after night she crept out of her house and made the same journey, knowing all the time that if she was caught her life would change immeasurably for the worse.

He remembered how he'd felt, watching the little

red dot on the System screen that represented the girl he was supposed to be marrying moving towards another red dot, his brother. He remembered how he would sit, pinned to the chair, unable to move, as he saw the dots get closer and closer until they were like one. And then, an hour or so later, moving apart once more. Lucas always waited until Evie's dot was back in her house where it belonged, then he would painstakingly erase the information, protecting her, protecting his brother, purging all evidence of their clandestine meetings, telling himself that the ache in his stomach was fear for them, not envy, not a desperate longing to be the dot that her dot was seeking . . .

He had always loved Evie; now that she was gone, he felt as though clouds surrounded him; it was as though without her in the City there was no joy, nothing to look forward to. Without her, he was falling, failing, unable to see what he should do, unable to keep back the waves of despair that threatened to consume him.

But there was no point thinking about it. She *was* gone, and she wasn't coming back. She was not his; would never be. What he had was the City, and he had to fight for it, just as he had fought all his life.

It took Lucas and Clara ten minutes to reach their destination. The tree where those dots had found each other was huge on the outside, formidable and grand, taller than any of the buildings that remained from the past or had been built since. Lucas walked towards it, found the opening and ushered Clara inside where she looked around in wonderment.

Inside the trunk, it felt cosy, womb-like, a safe haven. There was a blanket at the back. Lucas picked it up and lay it over the damp floor.

'Sit down,' he said to Clara. 'We're safe here. Tell me everything you know and I promise you will be protected.'

She looked around hesitantly.

'What is this place?' she breathed.

'Just a little hideaway,' Lucas said, sitting down opposite her, trying to ignore the hole that had appeared inside him, the desperate longing for Evie that had dogged him for most of his life. 'Are you hungry?'

He took out the bread and tore off a chunk for Clara, then he gave her a bun. He took the other and devoured it in seconds. Clara followed suit. Then she took a deep breath.

'You really want to know?' she said then. 'Because they'll know. And they'll come after you. That's why Gabby . . . I told her, you see. She knew I knew something; she'd seen us whispering. Me and the ones who . . . The Disappeared, I mean. And she begged me to. I didn't want to, but . . . I had no one else to talk to. I was scared, because I thought I'd be next. I should have been next. And now she's gone. Now she's disappeared. They did it to punish me, because they told us not to tell anyone. And now they're coming for me. Or you. They might be outside right now. It might even be you . . .' She pulled her knees towards her and started to sob quietly. 'And I don't even care because I just want it to be over now. I just want it to stop.'

She looked up at Lucas fearfully.

'Tell me what you know,' he said, calmly. 'Tell me who's doing this and I'll . . .' He stopped, couldn't finish the sentence. He would kill them. That's what he would do. There would be no tolerance, no rising above his need for vengeance this time. Honour counted for nothing amongst people like this. He met Clara's eyes. 'I'll stop them,' he said. Do you understand?'

Clara raised an eyebrow. Then she sniffed. 'The stupid thing is that I didn't even want to go,' she said, looking down. 'I didn't even want to go in the stupid hospital.'

'The hospital?' Lucas frowned.

'That's where it all started,' the girl said, shaking. 'That's where we saw them.'

'The Informers?'

Clara nodded.

It had been a dare, she explained. Because the

hospital wing used for New Baptisms had been closed, and they wanted to see inside, see for themselves what it was like.

It had been her friend Edward's idea to break into the hospital; he had been showing off, had secured a kiss from Clara, had a glint in his eye that she found exciting. And so they had gone, seven of them; had slipped in through the main doors, up the stairs and into the Fisher wing. And it was there that they'd been met by a locked door, impenetrable, windowless walls.

'Let's go,' Clara said immediately; there was nothing there, nothing of interest anyway and the hospital gave her the creeps. But Edward hadn't wanted to give up.

'I thought the City wasn't allowed to keep secrets any more,' he said, raising an eyebrow at her, like it was a challenge. 'Aren't we supposed to think for ourselves now? Isn't that why they destroyed the System? Well, I'm thinking for myself. And I think I want to see what's behind that wall. Don't you? Come on, we'll get in round the back.'

He winked at her, grabbed her hand and started to walk back down the corridor, turning left shortly afterwards. Everyone else followed. They knew what lay beyond the door; knew what it was Edward wanted to see. Fisher wing. The place where the New Baptisms happened. Or the mutilations, depending on who you believed.

They walked around in a loop, into a small room that smelt of laundry, and there they started to search for another way in, a back door, something.

'Here!' Clara had spoken before she'd had time to censor herself, to think through the consequences. It was a small opening in the wall. Locked, but easily broken. A hole to pass laundry through, she thought. 'You think we can get through there?' she asked, as everyone rushed towards her, as Edward shot her a triumphant look that made her glow inside.

'I think we can definitely get through,' he grinned and pulled himself up. But just as he was about to wriggle through, he was stopped by the sound of foot-steps on the other side of the hole, walking towards them, their voices muffled but still audible. Men. In the Fisher Wing. Silently Edward dropped back down to the floor.

'And if the System cannot be salvaged?'

'Of course it can be salvaged. The Brother is trying to play us, that's all. He thinks the longer it takes the more he'll be able to negotiate. But we don't need him. We need the boy, that's all. Raffy. If we can find him, the Brother can be disposed of quite frankly. He's getting too demanding. Too difficult.'

'What about Lucas?'

There was a sigh. 'First we find his brother Raffy. Then we'll deal with Lucas.'

Clara hadn't noticed Harriet going red, hadn't noticed the sweat dripping off her forehead; it was only when she coughed, grabbing a sheet to muffle the sound, that Clara realised she'd been trying to hold it in, desperately trying.

Immediately the footsteps had stopped and with them the voices. Clara and her friends had frozen and exchanged fearful glances. And then, just seconds later, the men were behind them in the laundry room, standing there staring at them. They were dressed in black, in jackets and trousers; their faces were hard, impenetrable.

'They're here,' one of the men called out, then they stepped aside as another man walked in, surveying the scene, his eyes narrowing as he looked from face to face, scrutinising each one carefully before moving to the next.

'You know who we are?' he asked then, and Clara had recognised his voice immediately as the man who'd been talking before, about Lucas, about the Brother.

She shook her head. She could see that Harriet was shaking.

He stared right at her. 'We are the Informers. We

inform on people if they break the rules. And you have broken the rules. You will regret that. And if you speak to another living soul, they will regret it too. These are not idle threats. We are in this City for a reason. Do I make myself clear? Perhaps I should make myself more clear. You. Edward. Come with me.' He looked straight at Edward, who shrank back.

'I said come,' the man said, his tone suddenly lower, more menacing. The two other men moved towards Edward, who started to tremble. Then, as he tried to run, the men grabbed him and dragged him away, out of the laundry room; Clara heard him scream and shout for a few seconds and then . . . silence.

'You should leave now,' the man said, a little smile playing on his lips. 'And please remember that if you breathe one word of what you have seen or heard, you will never see Edward again. And of course we know who you are. Where you live.' Then he smiled at them, shrugged and walked away, closing the door behind him.

'What happened then?' Lucas asked, breathlessly, his heart pounding in his chest.

Clara took a deep breath. 'We left the hospital,' she whispered. 'We ran as far away as we could.'

'And did you tell anyone?'

Clara shook her head. 'We couldn't. Because of

Edward. Because of what the man had said. They knew who we were. We couldn't tell. We couldn't . . .'

Tears were forming in her eyes again; she wiped them away distractedly.

'So what happened next?' Lucas asked, trying to keep his voice calm, trying not to let her see how angry he was, how much he wanted to run down to the hospital now and rip these men apart with his bare hands. Who were they? What were they doing in his City? How dare they talk about Raffy as though they knew him?

'We didn't do anything. We waited for Edward to come back. But he never did. A week later, Harriet disappeared; then, a week after that, her younger brother had gone. None of them said anything to anyone, I know they didn't. They were too scared to even talk to me about it. But they still disappeared. And then everyone else did, too. Then it was just me. I didn't know what to do. I couldn't go out, couldn't sleep, couldn't look in the mirror in case I saw them behind me. And then . . .'

She stopped talking.

'Then?' Lucas prompted gently.

'Then I told Gabby. She's my oldest friend, and she knew I knew something. She said I had to tell her what the big secret was, why I never talked to her any more, why I wasn't talking about the Disappearances like everyone else was. And . . . I told her. I told her everything. I . . . I murdered my best friend.' She was sobbing now, her face streaked with tears. She looked up at Lucas imploringly.

'So?' she said, wiping at her eyes, sniffing hopelessly. 'What do we do now?'

Lucas looked at her steadily for a few seconds as what she had told him sank in, as he suppressed the rage building inside of him. Right now he had to stay calm. Right now, his duty was to protect Clara. Because it hit him with a thud that it was because of him that she and her friends had been looking for entertainment; that if it wasn't for him and Linus destroying the System, she and her friends would have been at home, doing chores, not daring to talk to each other unless interaction had been sanctioned. The rules that had constrained them had also protected them. 'You're the last of the group? There's no one else who saw the Informers, who knows anything about them?'

'I'm the last one,' Clara nodded.

Lucas nodded. No one else was in direct danger. But Clara . . . Clara he could protect. One out of the seven. It was pathetic. Pitiful. But it was something. Revenge would have to wait. Justice would have to wait. 'In that case,' Lucas said, 'what we do now is get you out of here. Do you understand? We have to leave the City, and we have to do it now.'

Clara looked up at him and he was surprised to see not worry in her eyes but relief. That he had believed her. That he understood. 'Yes,' she said quietly, and got to her feet.

6

Lucas didn't think they were being followed any more; they had left no trace and had not stopped anywhere. They had used all the back alleys and hidden paths he knew to get to the edge of the City, then had run through the wasteland that surrounded it until they were at the East Gate lookout, a small hut next to a large swamp that Lucas had visited several times but never been into because of the vile stench that emanated from it.

The official name for Rab was 'Gate Patrol' but he and the Brother knew that he did no patrolling. He was a nasty piece of work; a short, squat bully of a man who had no place in the City. But he had no fear of being alone, no qualms about using a gun, and no respect for anyone, including the Brother himself, which made him perfectly placed to live in the dishevelled hut close to the East Gate and to keep tabs on what went on.

The truth was that no one ever breached the City walls without the City's consent. The 'Evils' used to be brought to the City walls every so often to instil fear in those who lived within them, but they were no real threat; they were simply the brain-damaged casualties of attempted brain surgery, captives of the City, treated like animals in camps a short drive away from the City walls, brought out every so often to scream and moan and remind the City's inhabitants how lucky they were to live inside its walls.

Now the Damaged Ones were being cared for properly, not worked to the ground, and lived peacefully away from the City that had destroyed them. The only new people who passed through the City's gates were prospective citizens, attracted by the rumours, some true, some not, of overflowing clean water, plentiful food and decent shelter, a place where people were good, where there was order. But the Great Leader had stopped his botched experiments a few years before; now that there was no need to experiment on people, to mutilate them, the hopeful immigrants had been turned away, back to the barren lands they had come from. What the wall patrol had really been charged with was stopping the City's inhabitants trying to leave, preventing them from getting outside the City, from seeing the outside for themselves. Only by encouraging fear of what lay beyond the walls could the Brother hope to impose his totalitarian regime, and that meant creating a prison from which no one could escape.

It had been one of Lucas's first commitments, to open the gates, to let people see the world for themselves. But caution had led him to delay; fear that City citizens weren't ready. And then the Disappearances had changed everything. With the Disappearances went any thoughts he had had of opening the gates.

'Rab,' Lucas called out. He didn't like the East Gatekeeper, but there were questions he needed to ask before he left the City, answers that he wouldn't leave without. Moments later, the man appeared. Twenty years ago Rab had been one of the people queuing outside, begging for a chance to enter the City, agreeing, as all prospective citizens did, to have the New Baptism to remove the 'evil' amygdala from his brain, little knowing that the operation would leave him not free from bad thoughts, but completely brain-dead. By chance, the Brother had happened upon him in a waiting room at the hospital, fighting with another prospective patient, and had declared him incapable of salvation. It was on the way back to the City wall that

Rab had begged and pleaded, offered to do anything in order to stay. And the Brother had seen in him a desperation, an anger, a self-destructiveness that he realised he could use; had agreed to let him undergo the operation after all, had inserted a chip into his head and sent him out to work for him. He had told Lucas the story proudly, the day he first took him to meet Rab. Back then, Lucas was the Brother's golden boy, the person he trusted more than anyone else. Back then, he spoke the truth, believing that Lucas worshipped him, that he saw the world as the Brother did, as many means to one end: power.

But now things were different.

'You came then?' Rab looked at him suspiciously. 'I've been waiting.'

Lucas stared at him. 'You have?'

'The flies. You've come to see them?'

Lucas looked at him uncertainly. 'Flies?'

'Yes,' Rab said, his eyes narrowing as they flickered over to Clara. He rarely spoke; Lucas had barely heard him say one word in the years he had known him. Instead he preferred to grunt if he accepted an order, or to shoot a look of disdain if he didn't. He looked back at Lucas, fixing him with a stare. 'Horrible things. Thousands of them. Coming from over there. Something's up.'

Lucas turned to look in the direction that Rab was pointing. Sure enough, away in the distance, there was a small black cloud. They were several hundred metres away but still he could make out a faint buzzing, a focused army preparing for battle. He thought for a moment, then made a decision.

'This is Clara,' he said. 'She's working with me at the moment. So, the flies. How long have they been there?' Lucas asked abruptly, walking towards the swamp, towards the path that led to the gate, motioning for Clara to follow. 'I was here just last week. They weren't here then.'

Rab shrugged. 'Few days,' he said. 'I told the Brother. He said he'd send someone. Never did. I'd have checked it out myself only you took away my key, didn't you?'

Lucas counted to three in his head. 'You told the Brother? Not me? Even though I told you explicitly to run all your communications past me?'

Rab shrugged. 'You're here now,' he said.

Lucas opened his mouth then closed it again; there was no point arguing. Not now. Instead he started to walk towards the cloud; Rab followed. 'Tell me about the Informers,' he said.

Rab gave him a long look. 'Don't know nothing about any Informers,' he grunted. 'It's not a good sign, flies.'

'No,' Lucas agreed. Then he stopped walking, looked Rab in the eye. 'You know nothing about the Informers? Are you sure?'

Rab looked at him for a moment, then shrugged. 'You sort out the flies, maybe I'll see if I remember anything,' he said.

Lucas felt himself getting impatient, but then calmed himself. He didn't want to alarm Clara. And anyway, they didn't have much time and they needed information. That meant playing along with Rab. That meant not losing his temper.

They walked in silence around the back of Rab's small house, onto the raised path that led through the swamps to the East Gate. Rab went in front, Lucas behind with Clara running behind. Lucas was surprised that even with his height advantage he still had to march quickly to keep up with Rab. The closer they got, the louder the buzzing was. As they approached the gate it was almost unbearable, the flies buzzing around their heads, the noise almost deafening. There was a stench in the air that made it hard to breathe, a stench that made the hair on the back of his neck stand up on end. Whatever had brought the flies here wasn't good.

As they approached the gate, their pace slowed down; Rab fell back so that he was next to Lucas. 'Ready?' Rab asked.

Lucas looked down at Clara, then scanned the horizon. 'You wait here,' he said.

'Here?' Clara looked at him in alarm. 'No. I'm coming with you. You promised. You can't leave me on my own . . .'

Lucas shot her a look. 'All right,' he relented. 'But when I tell you to turn around, you do it? Okay?'

Clara agreed reluctantly. Then Lucas nodded and took the key from around his neck, where he had kept each of the gate keys since confiscating them. He put the key in the lock and turned it, then pulled the heavy gate. There was a loud clanking sound and the gate began to open; Lucas gave it another pull to help it open before stepping through it to the other side.

The stench became unbearable as they walked towards the flies; Clara fell back, her eyes wide and he nodded for her to stay where she was, as he and Rab continued forwards until they were in the midst of the swarm. Then, as he approached the centre, Lucas bent over involuntarily, dropped to his knees as his stomach clenched, and he threw up. Rab stood beside him, then held out his hand to pull him up. 'Had a feeling it would be something like this,' he said gruffly. And as Lucas stood, his eyes turned in the direction Rab was looking, through the swarm of flies, and that's when he saw her. A body. A girl. Decomposing.

He rushed towards her; could still make out her features. She was unmistakably from the City; her clothes were those created in the cloth district, her shoes clearly the current style. Her hair was long and dark, her body, or what was left of it, strong and athletic.

It was Gabrielle. It was one of the Disappeared.

For a few seconds, Lucas was unable to move, unable to process what was in front of him. Her body, rotting on the ground, her skull dented, her mouth open as though crying out in pain. He felt sick, angry, desperate.

He turned around to check on Clara; she was sitting on the ground, staring at them blankly. He lifted his hand, caught her eye, motioned for her to turn away. He and Rab walked together, silently, towards the large mound that lay just beyond Gabrielle and as they drew closer Lucas knew Rab was thinking the same as him because his pace slowed, his head shrunk back. The stench told him what they would find before they could see anything. But when they did, even though Lucas had tried to prepare himself, he still stood gripped to the spot, his mouth open in a contorted cry of anguish, fear and pain.

They were there, the Disappeared, all six of them in a heap, half devoured by wild animals, tossed aside like refuse. Boys and girls, not much younger than Evie and Raffy, stolen from their families, murdered then left to rot.

Rab took out a hip flask from his pocket, poured a thimbleful into the lid and handed it to Lucas, who hesitated, then took it and downed it in one. Rab refilled it, handed it back to Lucas, then took a swig from the bottle himself.

'Who did this?' Lucas heard himself say, first quietly to himself, then more loudly. He rounded on Rab. 'Who did this?' he demanded. 'Don't tell me you don't know. They're here. Outside the gate that you're meant to watch. Tell me how they got here. Tell me what happened to them.'

Rab stared at him sullenly. 'I don't know anything,' he said, but Lucas saw something in his eye: disgust and betrayal. Rab was human: it was clear from the look on his face that he did not believe that these young people deserved to be murdered and cast aside, like rubbish.

'They were left outside your gate,' Lucas said, his voice low, bitter. 'You don't think that's relevant? You don't think they were trying to point the finger at you? Why here? Why now? Tell me, Rab. Tell me what you know. Tell me now.'

Rab looked at him uncomfortably. 'You think I know something?' His tone was accusatory. 'You think

I know something about these bodies? Because you're wrong. I don't. I wanted rid of the flies, that's all. Think I'd have sent a message if I knew what they were doing here?'

'You have to know something,' Lucas said, looking straight ahead. He downed the rest of his whisky, welcoming the heat in his mouth, the taste that pushed out the stench of decomposing bodies. 'You are the gate patrol, even if you're too drunk to do much about it any more. People are dead outside the gate you patrol, and I am being led to believe that there are strangers in the City committing these murders when it is supposed to be secure. Tell me what you know and I guarantee that you won't be punished for your involvement. Otherwise . . . otherwise, you will be blamed when the parents of the dead come to visit them. Because they *will* visit them. We are going to bury them. Every single one.'

Rab appeared to consider this. He took a deep breath, then his eyes darted over towards Lucas. 'I do what I'm told,' he said cautiously. 'I monitor. I keep an eye. I let the Brother know what's going on.'

'And did you let the Brother know about the bodies?'

Rab shook his head vehemently. 'I didn't know about any bodies. I only saw the flies a few days ago,' he said tentatively. He was getting defensive, his tone more agitated.

Lucas leant forward. 'But Rab, how did the bodies get there? How did they get through your gate without you knowing?'

Rab didn't answer for a few seconds. Then he stood up. 'I've had enough,' he said angrily, walking away, back to the City, but Lucas was too quick for him. He grabbed at his wrist, pulled it behind him. Rab was strong, but Lucas knew what he was doing. Moments later, Rab's nose was on the ground, both his arms twisted behind him. He kicked out, but it was futile.

'Tell me,' Lucas said again, his voice lower now, showing the strain of containing Rab. 'Tell me or you will regret it. For all I know, you were involved in these deaths and I'm telling you now, I will not hesitate to kill you, do you understand? This is not a threat. Unless you want to end up in one of those graves, you talk and you talk now.'

There was silence; Lucas tightened his grip.

'Fine,' Rab choked finally. 'I'll tell you.' Lucas let one of his hands go and he fell back onto the ground. Rab stared up at him insolently. 'But after that I'm done with this business. After that you leave me alone. You all just leave me alone. You understand?'

'I understand nothing,' Lucas said grimly. 'Tell me what you know.'

Rab pulled himself up. 'You want to bury the bodies,

don't you?' he muttered. 'We do that first. Then I'll tell you what I know. Back at my cottage. Back where I know we're safe.'

Lucas nodded grimly. Then he put the lid of Rab's bottle down and holding his breath, he walked towards the pile of bodies, waving away the flies, trying not to look at the rotting corpses, the eaten-away flesh.

Silently he carried each body to its own patch of ground ready for burial. It was a grim job; most of the bodies were just skeletons with rotting flesh hanging off them. They had been ravaged, and now were home to maggots eating through what was left of them.

Rab watched him for a few minutes, shaking his head and spiting on the ground. Then, slowly, he stood up. 'Going to need some spades,' he said. 'I'll be back.'

'Don't tell Clara. Don't let her see,' Lucas said.

'You want me to take her to the cottage?' Rab grunted.

Lucas shook his head. 'She'll feel safer where I can see her,' he said.

Rab shrugged and walked off.

Lucas watched him go for a few moments, then carried on moving the bodies until Rab was back and then they dug. One grave per person. The ones at the bottom of the heap were no longer identifiable; the ones nearer the top were more so – a piece of clothing that had survived, perhaps part of a face that had not yet been attacked by beast, fowl or insect. In any event, he knew who each of them was because he had stared at their photographs on a list of Disappeared so many times.

Once the bodies were all under the earth, and after Lucas had marked each grave with a stone, he followed Rab back through the gate to the first body, Gabrielle Marchant. Lucas buried her, then silently followed Rab back through the gate, picking a silent Clara up on the way, then they walked together back to Rab's house, where he and Lucas washed their hands under the outside tap for a very long time.

'So,' Lucas said.

'So,' Rab replied, and walked into his cottage.

Lucas followed him in, his arm around Clara protectively. He'd never been inside Rab's house before. On the outside it was little more than a shack, a wooden structure that held no allure whatsoever. But as he walked through the door he was surprised to find a welcoming warmth, chairs covered in blankets and a small fire in the corner next to what he assumed must be Rab's bed. Above the fire sat a kettle; on a small table was one cup.

Lucas motioned for Clara to sit down on a wooden rocking chair; she did so immediately, pulling her knees up to her chest. He watched her for a few moments, wondering how much she had seen, what she was thinking. Then he turned to Rab. 'So, Rab. This is where you live.'

'I'd offer you a brew,' Rab said, 'but I've only one cup.' His tone was sarcastic but not unfriendly. He pointed to one of the chairs; Lucas sat down on it.

Rab sat in the other one, pouring more whisky into two glasses; Lucas refused the glass that Rab proffered him, so he offered it to Clara, who hesitated before declining. 'More warming than tea,' Rab said, as though an explanation were required. Lucas said nothing; he just waited watchfully as Rab sat back in the chair and exhaled slowly.

'I didn't know that's what they were doing,' he said, eventually. 'I had no idea. The Brother just said I was to let them in when they came.'

'Let who in?' Lucas asked, leaning forward. 'Who are "they"?'

Rab shrugged. 'I never got any names,' he said, the sarcasm returning. 'The Brother just called them our Informers.'

Lucas glanced over at Clara, who visibly whitened.

'Informers?' Lucas asked. 'Why didn't I know about this?'

Rab looked at him for a moment, then he started to laugh. 'You?' He shook his head. 'You really think you're in charge, don't you. You really think . . .' He shook his head again, wiped away a tear from his eye, then his face turned serious. 'You know nothing,' he said. 'You're the Brother's poodle, whatever he tells you.'

Lucas felt his eyes narrow. 'Things have changed,' he said, levelly. 'The Brother is no longer in control.'

'No, Lucas,' Rab said, launching forward and grabbing his hand without warning. 'The Brother is not in control. But not because of you. Not because of what you and your friends did. You think that changed anything? You have no idea. No idea at all.'

'No idea about what?' Lucas asked angrily. He pushed Rab's hand away. 'You don't know what you're talking about, Rab. You're a drunk. You live out here in the middle of nowhere . . . Just tell me about the Informers. What are they doing here?'

Rab took a deep breath. 'They bring stuff. Deliveries. Food, grain. From other camps and settlements. Taxes, the Brother calls it.'

Lucas's face creased into incomprehension. 'But I don't understand,' he said. 'I stopped the food coming from the Damaged Ones,' he said uncertainly, remembering when he'd discovered that the 'Evils' created by the supposed New Baptisms had been put to work in farms outside the City walls, their produce shipped straight back to the City. 'I stopped—'

'You stopped nothing,' Rab said, shaking his head wearily. 'City can't survive without the supplies the Informers bring. Dead of night they come, bring the food, and the Brother's men collect it. That's all I know. Been going on as long as I've been here.'

Lucas stood up, his mind racing. He started to walk around the small room; Rab and Clara sat and watched him.

'Okay,' Lucas said suddenly, sitting back down. 'Tell me everything you know about these Informers. Everything.'

Rab pulled a face. 'Nothing much to tell,' he said gruffly.

Lucas bent down so that his face was inches from Rab's. 'There are six graves a mile away from here,' he said, his voice low. 'A girl, here, whose friends are . . .' he paused, not wanting Clara to know about the bodies. 'Whose friends have disappeared.'

'Who are dead, you mean,' Clara interjected. 'The flies? The spades? I'm not stupid, you know. I know what you were doing.'

Her eyes were blank; she was rocking back and forth on the chair.

'Who are dead,' Lucas said, his voice quieter now. 'A girl who is so scared of being Disappeared that she can't sleep, can't function, who hasn't dared to tell anyone because telling them what she knows is to hand out a death sentence. And now I discover that people have been coming into the City undetected for years. Walking around as if they own it. Tell me what you know and tell me now.'

Rab sighed and took another drink. He looked twitchy; his eyes darted around the room as though worried that someone might be listening. Then he started to talk, looking at Lucas intently as he spoke. 'Like I said, they've been coming a long time. Once a month maybe. In, then out. Always at night.'

Lucas's brow furrowed. 'Every month? And where do they come from?'

'No idea. I opened the gate, went back to my house. Just like I was told to by the Brother.'

Lucas grimaced as he remembered the look of irritation on the Brother's face when he confiscated the gatekeepers' keys. 'You didn't watch them?'

Rab looked down. 'Not supposed to watch them.'

'But you do. You must. How many of them are there? What do they look like?'

Rab shrugged uncomfortably. 'Maybe I've seen them once or twice. Not on purpose. Just, you know, glimpses. There are usually two or three of them. With a lorry.'

'And what do they do?' Lucas demanded.

'They come in for a few hours, leave their stuff, then they go,' Rab said gruffly. 'I don't know what they do, I don't know why. All I know is that when they leave I lock the gate again. That's all I want to know.'

Lucas shook his head, his brain trying to process this information, trying to make sense of it. 'No,' he said. 'No, I don't buy this. They would have been seen. The System would have spotted them. I would have spotted them.'

'These people can hide,' Rab said, his voice dark suddenly. 'These people can do anything.'

'Like killing people? Dragging them here without anyone seeing? Without you seeing? Rab, this doesn't make any sense.'

Rab looked uncomfortable. 'I'm not saying it was them. Just that they exist.'

Lucas nodded. 'So when did they come last? Before I took your key, I assume?'

'It was three months ago.'

'Three months ago?' Lucas's face creased into a frown. 'But that doesn't make any sense either. That . . . I don't understand.'

Rab raised an eyebrow, then he leant forwards, his expression suddenly conspiratorial. 'That's the thing, though,' he said under his breath. 'This time it was different.'

'Different how?' Lucas asked impatiently.

Rab smiled, apparently enjoying Lucas's frustration. He took another sip of whisky, then spat violently on the floor. 'Different,' he said, cradling his glass and looking at Lucas knowingly, 'because like I said, they came three months ago. But this time, they didn't leave.'

Lucas felt his heart begin to thud in his chest. He could feel Clara's eyes on him, saying 'I told you so. I told you.'

'So they've been here all this time?' he asked, but Rab didn't answer; instead he held his hand up, motioning for Lucas to be quiet.

'You hear that?' he asked. Lucas shook his head. 'They follow you here?'

Lucas was surprised to see Rab's face fill with fear. 'You led them to me?' he asked, standing up, agitated. 'Get out. Let them take you. I just want to be left alone. I don't want anything to do with this.'

'You're already up to your neck,' Lucas whispered, because now he too could hear the sound of footsteps outside. 'You're the one who let these people into the City,' he said. 'And you found the bodies with me.'

'I noticed the flies, that's all,' Rab hissed, then he grabbed Lucas. 'This way,' he said, bundling him and Clara out through a kitchen that smelt of mould and sour milk. 'You get out, you get yourself hidden and you don't get yourself unhidden, understand?' He opened a door silently and pushed them through it before closing it immediately.

Lucas grabbed Clara and pulled her down towards the swamp, submerging them both in its foul-smelling depths, guiding her hands to find the narrow platform that enabled access to the gate. With one hand, he held her; with the other, he clung onto the platform himself. Then, silently, they waited.

7

It was dark outside, and his limbs were beginning to ache. Thomas realised that he had been sitting in the same position for several hours; he was hungry and thirsty. But such mundane things could wait another few minutes. He was so nearly there. So close he could almost feel it.

As he scrolled through the information in front of him, he felt the hairs on the back of his neck stand up. And what made it so incredible was how easy it was, how easy it all was. Four years ago, he'd been a junior manager in a technology firm having to answer to a stupid boss who didn't understand anything. Now . . . now he had his own department, a budget that no one questioned, a remit that was as wide as he wanted it to be. He was in charge of security and data, of investigating breaches. At his say so, the entire network could be changed, closed, manipulated. His investigations were so secretive he could fly to the Caribbean for a week's holiday on expenses and no one would question it. All because he got it. All because he knew how to harness people, harness technology. All because he knew how to scare people, how to excite them, how to make them think they needed him.

And they did need him; they needed him because he was the only person who saw what was possible. The only person who was thinking big.

And Thomas was thinking very big. Very big indeed. He scrolled through his list of candidates, checking and double-checking the information he had on them. And oh, did he have information. Reams of it. Every sorry detail of their pathetic lives. He smiled to himself as he remembered his former boss talking to him about privacy, like it was something that had to be preserved. Prosser was gone now, left in the last reshuffle, managed out of the business. Some information had got out about an affair, some dubious expense claims. It had been easy, in the event. Pitifully so.

But what lay ahead would be a real challenge. What lay ahead would take patience, time, skill, cunning and confidence. It was almost impossible to pull off. But only almost.

Thomas smiled to himself. At last a proper challenge. And if it worked . . .

What was he saying? Of course it would work.

He opened a screen, stared at the face of a despondent-looking girl with eyes that seemed completely empty; she had proved to be one of his best recruits. Then he flicked to another prospective recruit, a boy, black skin, fierce eyes full of anger, full of mistrust. He stared at the face for a few minutes, then flicked to his file. He was the perfect candidate. But it would be a long game. It would take time. And he would need some help.

He stood up, opened his door, looked at his assistant who was sitting at the desk just outside. 'Get in here.'

Two minutes later, his latest recruit Adrian Crouch appeared. 'Got your badge on?' he asked.

Adrian shook his head. 'No. It's in my pocket,' he said, as though that made up for it.

Thomas's eyes narrowed.

'In your pocket?' he said, his tone cutting. 'Put it on. I told you that badge is important. It signals you out to people. Doors will open for you. There will be people looking out for you.'

Adrian raised an eyebrow. Thomas opened his mouth to shout at him, to fire him right there on the spot, then changed his mind. Instead, he picked up his phone, dialled a number. 'Mike?' he said. 'Mike, come in here.'

Mike was in the room within a minute. 'Hey,' he said.

'Adrian wasn't wearing his badge,' Thomas said.

Mike looked at the new recruit warily. 'You weren't?'

Adrian shrugged. 'I'm not really a badge kind of a guy,' he said.

Thomas hesitated before speaking. Adrian had been at the company a matter of weeks; had been identified by a member of Thomas's existing team as one of the most talented hackers out there. And since he'd arrived he'd proved his reputation to be correct; he was the best Thomas had ever seen. Well, nearly the best. No one would ever get close to his protégé, his old intern. But the problem was that Adrian knew he was good, and that knowledge made him arrogant, made him think he could do things his way. Thomas moved his chair closer.

'The thing about the badge,' he said, quietly, 'is that if you wear it, if you demonstrate your full allegiance, no one will mention the incident with your uncle. No one will ever find out about it. Ever.'

Adrian's face immediately flushed with fear and shame. He stared at Thomas, wide-eyed. Clearly written across his face was the question: How did you find out about that? Thomas couldn't help smiling. He could find out anything. That was the whole point.

He stood up, walked towards Adrian, put his arm around him and led him to his computer. 'What we're building here is the future, Adrian,' he breathed. 'What we're doing here is going to change the world. But I need people I can trust. Who trust me. Who do what I ask them to do unquestioningly. Do you understand? Like Mike here. Like everyone in this department and a lot of people beyond it. Policemen. Judges. Politicians. Actors. Terrorists. Journalists. All bound together, all working towards the same thing. All proud to be one of us. Do you see why the badge is so important now, Adrian?'

Adrian nodded. He was shaking, Thomas noticed. That was good.

'Wear the badge and you're protected, Adrian. You are above the law. This badge, it's a passport. You see?'

Adrian was sweating now; Thomas thought for a moment. 'And no one will ever find out what you did. Or where your uncle's body is. He deserved it, right? He paid for what he did to you, to your brother. We get it. We're on your side, Adrian. We're a team. Okay? I don't want you to be unhappy, or uncomfortable. I don't want you being afraid of anyone. We all have histories, but in this team we put that all behind us, do you understand? It doesn't matter any more. What matters is information. Who has it and who controls it. What matters now isn't what's real but what we tell the world is real. Who we are, what we've done . . . it's all in our hands. We'll delete what's happened, delete all of it and give you a new past. A better one.' He clicked the mouse; immediately a picture appeared, of Adrian, surrounded by a group of students.

'You want to be an academic?' he asked. 'Have a first-class degree from Oxford?'

Adrian frowned. 'I never even went to university,' he said.

'That's not what the evidence suggests,' Thomas smiled, 'that's not what potential girlfriends will see when they google you. Or how about you have a large inheritance?'

Adrian raised an eyebrow. 'So you fake a few

photos and documents. So what? I'm still me.' He was trying to sound cool, but Thomas could see the desire in his eyes.

'No, you're not. Not if you don't want to be,' Thomas said smoothly. 'I'm not talking about Photoshop. I'm talking about creating a history. Creating a person.'

'But it won't be real,' Adrian said uncertainly.

Thomas laughed. 'Real? What's real? What you see on the television? What you read on the Internet? Don't you get it yet? We control the search engine, we control the information people see, we control reality. Do you see? Do you see what we can do here?'

'Yeah, I see.' Adrian nodded, his eyes glued to the screen.

Thomas could see that he had him; the fear had gone. He would need to be managed carefully, would need to be brought right into the centre, surrounded, supported. But he was going to be OK. Thomas had a feeling about him.

'Good,' he said. 'So don't take off your badge. Don't ever take it off again . . .'

8

Devil stared into the young boy's eyes. He could see the fear in them, but to his credit the boy didn't blink, didn't look down like the others had done. His hands hung at his sides, pale jeans only just staying up.

'You hear me? You hear what I need you to do?'

The boy nodded.

'Tell me.'

The boy repeated what he had told him, word for word.

'And what happens if you don't do it?'

Not even a lip quiver. Maybe this boy was tougher than he looked. Maybe he needed to watch him. 'I go to hell,' the boy said, his voice soft and high. Like a choir boy, Devil found himself thinking. He chuckled to himself. There weren't any choirs

around here. The only singing was from the drug-
gies, the tramps, rocking back and forth under
the bridge, high on desperation.

'You know about hell?' he asked. He would play
with the boy a while. Make sure he knew who he
was talking to. Make sure he knew what he was
dealing with here. The boy nodded. 'You learn
about it in church? With your mama?' Devil emphasised the word in a bid to make the boy look
pathetic in front of the rest of the gang. There
was a ripple of laughter. They knew the drill. They'd
been through it themselves. Some of the boys
shouted out insults, but the boy didn't seem to
notice. He just nodded again.

'Yeah, well, then you don't know,' Devil continued,
warming to his theme. He knew how to instil fear,
knew how to work them up. His dad had taught
him everything he needed to know about that. He
used to listen to his dad when he stood in the
pulpit and made his congregation worship him,
got them listening to his every word like he was
Jesus Christ himself. Before they realised he
was stealing their money, before the police came
and took him away.

Before his mother moved them to this shit-
hole.

'See, the Church don't know about hell. Not the hell you'll be going to. The Church thinks hell is a place you go to when you die. But there's hell right here on earth, too. And that's the hell I'm talking about.' Devil stood up, loomed over the boy. Devil was tall. Tall and broad, just like his father. He knew he could physically intimidate pretty much anyone if he wanted to. And most of the time, he wanted to. 'See, I got my own hell for people that cross me, you know what I'm saying? A hell full of pain. For you. For your little brother. Your little sister. Your mother. You want your little sister to be screaming when we put her hands in boiling water? You want your mother to be mopping my piss with chains around her ankles? 'Cos that's the hell I'm talking about. That's what you got to think about when you're deciding whether to finish that rival off. You hear me? It's dog eat dog, you get me? Ain't no survivors.'

The boy nodded again, silently. Maybe he wasn't shaking, but he knew who was boss, Devil thought to himself. He would do as he was told.

'Good.' He took the knife out of his pocket, carefully wiped it for fingerprints. One day he would have something better than a knife. Soon the

Dalston Crew would be big, strong, ready to run with the big boys. To fight the big boys and win. Soon he would be in control of the whole of East London, not just this crummy estate. Everyone would know that he was the boss. Everyone would know to be scared of him. 'And after, you hide this good for me? Until I need it again. You don't go bringing it back to me. And when them pigs come looking, what you do?'

'I don't know nothing,' the boy said, parroting what he'd been told.

'And if they fit you up? If they come after you? If the police get your mama down to the station and she's begging you to tell the truth, to tell them where you got the knife, to tell them who told you to do this?'

'I tell them that boy has been agitatin' me. That it was all my idea. That I found the knife.' The boy's voice was getting quieter; his eyes were clouding over.

Devil smiled. It was a smile that disarmed, that made people think that maybe he was human after all, that he had feelings. That's how he controlled people. People were afraid of him one minute, but the next, they wanted to help him, they were devoted to him. That's how he liked it.

It had taken him a long time to get to this place.

'Okay,' he said. 'I'm done with you. You get this job finished. And then you got the protection of the Dalston Crew for life. You get me? You, your mother, your sister, your baby brother. All safe. No more windows getting smashed. No more money going missing. No more fires starting in your flat. You get me?'

'I get you.'

The boy took the knife, tucked it into his waistband. And it was only when he turned to leave that Devil noticed that the boy's trousers were wet, a big damp patch right around the crotch. And for a moment, just a moment, he felt something. Something close to guilt. A sick feeling that made him wonder who he was; what he was. What he'd become. For just a second, he imagined Leona looking at him, those fierce eyes of hers filling him with self-loathing, just like they'd done that time he'd teased her about her braces. But then Devil shook himself. He wasn't the same person he'd been back then. He was Devil now. And he was a survivor.

He pushed all thoughts of Leona from his head and smiled. The kid wasn't tough after all; he was scared, good and proper. The kid would do just what he'd been told, for as long as Devil wanted him to do it.

9

Lucas freed a hand to wipe away the sweat dripping from his forehead, his other hand clutching Clara. He tried not to notice the blisters on his feet, the scratches on his legs, the tightness of his chest, but they were all getting worse, all threatening to overcome him. He and Clara had been running for what felt like days but was really about twenty-four hours, a few very short rests stolen en route. For the past few hours he had been carrying Clara; she had tried to keep up but kept stumbling with tiredness, and Lucas knew they had to keep going. Until they were far away. Until they were somewhere safe.

They'd waited for an hour in the swamps, their heads just above the surface, just high enough to breathe, until Lucas was sure there was no one there. He had helped Clara out, and then they had crept towards the wall, opened the gate and started to run.

They'd run all day, and most of the night, following the same path that he'd sent Raffy and Evie on a little over a year before. They were hungry, thirsty, exhausted. Neither of them had been outside of the City walls before and even though Lucas knew that no Evils roamed the land, he could still see the fear in Clara's eyes, still felt trepidation as he ran, his eyes widening in incomprehension as he saw the landscape outside the City walls, immense, green, deserted.

But they had had no time to explore, to question, to investigate, and now all thoughts of exploration disappeared from his head anyway. The directions Linus had given him so long ago had brought him to safety; he could see the lights of Base Camp in the distance like a lighthouse guiding him in.

He had told himself he would never come here, told himself that it was not his place. When he'd said goodbye to Evie at the City gate, he'd meant it; had intended never to see her again. Base Camp belonged to her and Raffy; the world outside was their world, not his. But he had no choice, he told himself as he ran. And he was not coming to live here; he was coming because he had to, because he needed help, because he was fighting an enemy he didn't know or understand.

The Informers.

What Clara had told him had seemed . . . incredible. Inconceivable. And yet now he realised that what she knew was just a tiny part of the whole; and for that, her friends had paid with their lives.

Lucas closed his eyes, steeled himself, forced himself to keep going, taking Clara's hand to help her along. And soon enough it was there, in front of him, getting closer, just as he'd hoped it would be, this mythical place that he had heard about from his father, but never seen with his own eyes before. At Base Camp, Clara would be safe. At Base Camp he could gather his thoughts, and work out what to do next.

They were less than a mile away. He worried for a moment that they were still being followed, that he was leading the Informers straight to Base Camp, but soon dismissed the thought. He had taken a roundabout route, and anyway, he would have known if he was being followed. He always knew.

The lights became larger as they ran; soon he could see the campfire, the tents. Clara stumbled and he lifted her up, his legs speeding up as he found the last vestiges of energy within himself to make it over the line. He had made it. He was there.

He laid Clara down, then collapsed in front of the fire; immediately a woman rushed towards him. For a split second he thought it must be Evie and his entire body stiffened, in longing, in fear. But it wasn't Evie, it was someone else, someone older, a woman he recognised. 'Martha,' he managed to say before he passed out. 'Martha, this is Clara. She needs to be kept safe . . .'

There was someone murmuring, and he felt something on his face. Was he dreaming? It was a hand, tenderly stroking him, and it made Lucas want to cry out, because he couldn't remember the last time he felt cared for, cared about; couldn't remember the last time someone had touched him.

Was it her hand? His empty stomach flip-flopped. It couldn't be her. Could it? He didn't want to open his eyes, didn't want to shatter the possibility, didn't want real life with its obstacles and messes and desperate sadness to ruin this moment.

'Lucas? Lucas, can you hear me?'

It wasn't her. A thud of disappointment, a gathering together of his emotions, and Lucas opened his eyes.

'Where's Clara? Is she okay?'

'She's fine.' It was Martha, smiling at him reassuringly. Lucas had met her when she had come with Linus, Raffy and Evie to dismantle the System. 'You look terrible.'

'I'm fine.' He tried to sit up but fell back again. 'Is Raffy here? I need to see him.'

'You need to eat,' Martha corrected him. 'And rest.'

Lucas sat up again; this time he managed it. 'Martha, I'll eat but I can't rest. There are dead bodies outside the City, Informers who are killing people. They—'

'Shhhh,' Martha said gently, standing up. 'I'll bring you some soup. And some bread. Raffy isn't here. But he's safe. Tomorrow you can go and see Linus and he'll explain everything.'

Lucas frowned. 'Go and see him? He isn't here? He promised me he'd look after Evie and Raffy. He promised—'

Martha gave him a sad smile. 'And he has. He is. Just not here. Linus hasn't been here for a long time,' she said. 'Things have been . . . different. But I'll tell you where you can find him. If you rest. If you eat the food I bring you.'

'Tomorrow? No, I need to see him today,' Lucas said, forcing himself out of the bed that he'd been lying on. His limbs ached and his stomach felt like it was concaving inwards; immediately he fell back onto the mattress. 'I need to know where Raffy is. How do you know he's safe?'

Martha raised an eyebrow. 'Because Linus wouldn't have it any other way. He'll tell you tomorrow,' she said, sternly. Then she smiled. 'I've missed the company, anyway. Please stay.'

Lucas looked at her for a few seconds, then relented. 'Maybe it's a good thing Raffy isn't here.'

Martha nodded. 'Linus usually knows what he's doing,' she said.

'I know, I know – he'll tell me tomorrow?' Lucas asked quizzically.

'Exactly,' Martha smiled, closing the door behind her.

Lucas stretched, then tentatively swung his legs on to the floor, holding on to the bed to stand up. He assessed the damage: his feet weren't in the best of shape, but nothing serious. He must have fainted from exhaustion. A meal would sort him out. He walked towards the door then stopped, steadying himself as dots appeared in front of his eyes. Then, he carefully opened the door and walked out of the room.

He had never been in Base Camp before. He had imagined it to be busier somehow, thronging with people. Instead it was eerily quiet, only the sound of tarpaulin flapping in the wind punctuated the silence.

The Camp had been set up by Linus many years before when he had left the City that he had helped to found, sickened by the way his beautifully designed System had been corrupted to manipulate and control its people. Linus had been a computer genius before the Horrors, had believed that by building a computer system that was capable of anticipating people's needs and desires a kind of Utopia could be created. Only it hadn't quite worked out that way. Which was why, eventually, he had left the City, formed Base Camp and plotted to overthrow the Brother and destroy his corrupted System once and for all.

It had been to one of the computers at Base Camp that Lucas had sent his messages week after week, the only time where he felt he was really himself, the only time when he could actually be honest.

And now he was here. He paused in a doorway: inside he could see Clara asleep. He watched her for a few minutes, feeling an enormous weight of responsibility for her, for her family, her friends. She was about fifteen, and her whole life was ahead of her. Just like her friends whose lives had been snatched from them. The thought made his chest clench with anger. The Informers would pay. They would pay for what they had done.

Lucas took a deep breath and he started to walk again. And as he walked, he smelt the delicious aroma of chicken. He followed it and soon found himself in a kind of kitchen. Martha turned and smiled.

'That's your idea of resting?'

He shrugged and grinned. 'Smells too good.'

'Sit down,' Martha said, pointing to a table through

a doorway. 'I'll bring you some bread while you wait.'

Lucas did as he was told. There were several tables, but no one sitting at them. Martha followed him and put a glass of water and hunk of bread in front of him.

'Where is everyone?' Lucas asked. He had loved hearing about Base Camp from Linus; hearing about the fifty or so people who lived and worked there, including Martha and Angel, Linus's closest confidants. Lucas had often dreamt of living there himself; dreamt of a life free from the City and everything it represented.

Martha hesitated. 'Most of the men are working,' she said eventually. 'Collecting food, doing repairs. Angel's out on a reconnaissance trip with three others. But there aren't as many of us here as there were before.' She met his eye and smiled sadly. 'I suppose you never saw us before, did you? It's a shame. You would have liked it. It was . . . exciting.'

'Before?' Lucas asked curiously.

'Before we did what we set out to do and lost our reason for being,' Martha shrugged lightly.

'And now it feels like the revolution has happened but nothing has changed?' Lucas asked.

Martha pulled a face. 'Things have changed,' she said, a hint of sadness in her voice. 'Just not . . .' She shook herself. 'Ignore me,' she said, standing up. 'Let me get you that soup.'

When she came back a few minutes later she put a steaming bowl of soup in front of Lucas then sat opposite him as he ate.

It didn't take him long to devour it.

'More?' Martha asked with a smile. Lucas nodded gratefully and within a minute a second bowl was in front of him. He ate it greedily.

'They don't feed you in the City?' Martha asked, her eyes twinkling gently.

Lucas raised an eyebrow. 'There's plenty of food. It's just that what's going on kind of puts you off eating.' It felt good to say it; even with a wry smile. Lucas realised how alone he'd felt for the past year, without even Linus to communicate with.

Martha put her hand on his shoulder and gave it a little squeeze. 'So tell me,' she said then, looking at him earnestly. 'Tell me what's been going on.'

Lucas told her, as briefly as he could; about the City, the Brother's hold on power, the mistrust that its citizens held for Lucas. He told her about the Disappearances, about the flies; he tried to keep his emotions in check as he told her about the pile of bodies he and Rab had discovered, but even so his voice still cracked slightly as he described finding the young people thrown together as though they were nothing more than rubbish. Then he told her about Rab, about the

Informers. Martha listened silently, nodding, wincing and gasping as the story unfolded. Then she reached over and put her hand on his.

'And you? How are you?'

Lucas frowned. 'I'm fine,' he said. Then he opened his mouth to ask something else, the thing he'd wanted to ask the moment he arrived, the thing that he'd thought about ever since he'd decided to come here. But immediately he closed it again.

'You're wondering about Evie,' Martha said, appearing to read his mind.

Lucas felt himself redden. 'She's safe with Raffy,' Martha said reassuringly.

Lucas nodded. Smiled. 'Well, that's good,' he said quickly.

'You must think about them a lot,' Martha said quietly, her eyes looking up at him in a way that unsettled him slightly. 'You were . . . close to Evie, weren't you? I know that she thought very highly of you.'

Lucas nodded again; his heart was thudding in his chest and he was suddenly finding it hard to think, hard to breathe. 'Yes,' he managed to say. 'I . . . I thought highly of her, too. Think highly, I mean. I—'

He closed his eyes for a second, mentally pulled himself together, forced the desperate loneliness that had suddenly engulfed him back down, deep within him where he could suppress it, refuse to acknowledge it.

Martha pulled a sympathetic face. 'It must be hard. Being alone.'

Lucas caught her eye, flushed slightly. 'I've always been alone,' he shrugged. 'It's no big deal.'

Martha appeared to contemplate this. 'I don't think humans are meant to be alone,' she said eventually. 'We need to connect. We need to feel part of something. That's why people like the Brother succeed, because people are more afraid of being alone than they are of anything else. Not many people are like you, Lucas. Not many people are as strong as you are. But don't try to be too strong. You need people too. Everyone does.'

Her voice cracked slightly and Lucas felt a lump appear in this throat. Did she know? Were his feelings so obvious?

'Not me,' he said. 'I'm fine.'

Martha shook her head sadly. 'Like Linus. He thinks he doesn't need people too.'

Lucas digested this. 'And where is he? Linus, I mean?'

Martha raised an eyebrow then smiled wryly. 'He's in the mountains in a cave, working like a man possessed.'

Lucas looked at her quizzically. 'Working on what?'

Martha sighed. 'He'll tell you tomorrow, I'm sure. And I can't possibly explain – I hardly understand it myself. But he's become obsessed with a camp that appeared on the coast a few months ago. A new civil-isation, quite small I think. They appeared on the surveillance system then apparently disappeared again, along with a chunk of coastline.'

'Disappeared?' Lucas asked seriously, his interest piqued.

Martha raised her eyebrows. 'I don't know. He kept saying that he didn't know where they'd come from. That they had to come from somewhere, but his satel-lites told him that there was nothing beyond this island, which meant that either the people didn't exist or his information was wrong. Then when they all disap-peared, well, he was like a madman, pacing up and down, muttering to himself, sitting at that computer of his for hours, days at a time.'

'And then he left?' Lucas asked.

Martha nodded. 'The thing with Linus,' she said, 'is that he's a genius. He built the System. He sees the world differently from the rest of us; sees connections that we don't, sees everything twenty steps ahead of everyone else. Which means that other people just weigh him down, get in the way. He needed to work, needed to get to the bottom of this . . . this problem. And he had to do it without us slowing him down. So he moved to the mountains. I just hope that he'll figure it out soon so that he'll come home again.'

'This is home?' Lucas asked. 'I thought Base Camp wasn't meant to be fixed?'

'It's not,' Martha shrugged. 'This place isn't home; it's the people. We have always moved around together; Linus has always told us where and when. We need him. And actually he needs us too – to centre him, to remind him that life has to be lived sometimes, that eating together, sleeping, working . . . that these things can be as important as saving the world, in their way.'

'And you're going to wait for him? You're not tempted to leave?'

Martha shook her head. 'I've known Linus a very long time,' she said. 'He's a good man. Slightly mad, definitely a genius, but good. And he won't admit it, but he needs us to be here. Close to him. Needs to know that we'll drop everything for him when required.'

'And you're prepared to do that for him?' Lucas asked curiously.

'We'd all die for Linus,' she said simply. 'He's infuriating, maddening and completely impossible. But everything he does is for a reason, everything he does makes sense, even if it doesn't seem to at the time. Like

I said, he's twenty steps ahead of us. You just have to trust that you'll catch up eventually. So far he's always been proved right. So far, he hasn't put a step wrong.'

'So where is he? What's his new camp like?' Lucas asked curiously.

Martha laughed. 'I'd use the word "camp" loosely. It's more like a hovel. He's in a cave with just his generator and computers for company. Angel tried to help him set up some tents, but he refused. He had to build Linus a kitchen by subterfuge, otherwise he'd have starved to death. Angel takes supplies down there once a fortnight; the last was two days ago so you should find some food. But you should prepare yourself. The last time I saw him, Linus had a beard.'

'A beard?' Lucas managed a smile.

'A long one,' Martha grinned, then wiped her hands on a napkin and made her way back to the kitchen.

10

Devil looked down at the outstretched hand in front of him and shook his head. 'Nah.'

His boys always offered their joints to him, but he always refused. Weed made people weak, made them a-pa-the-tic. Devil smiled to himself. 'Apathetic' was his new word. He liked to use a new word every day. Kept him smart. And Apathetic was one of the best ones he'd found yet. Pathetic with an 'a' in front of it. What most people were, in Devil's opinion. Round here, anyway. No one did nothing. No one had vision. No one except him.

He jumped down off the wall and immediately the others did too, but he waved them back. 'You stay here,' he ordered. They were in their usual spot in the middle of the estate, on the steps leading down to the playground. Not that it was a playground like playgrounds were supposed to be. Swings and a sorry-looking roundabout stood silently; occasionally Devil and his boys would sit on it, spin themselves around, laughing loudly, but no children came here any more. No one dared enter the playground unless Devil explicitly author-ised it, unless he told them they could. It was his playground now. His estate. Shit hole or no shit hole, that still meant something.

He walked away slowly, legs bent slightly at the knee, his head bobbing up and down as he moved, as though he was dancing. He was proud of his walk and had spent a long time perfecting it. When he'd got here, he'd walked like a normal kid. Like a square kid. Kind of lolloping, dawdling; the way he used to walk to school with Leona.

Now, though, people knew he was coming when he was just a speck in the distance. He didn't have to even open his mouth to let people know he was there. It's all about presence, his father had told him once. Make sure people know who you are, what you are. You fade into the crowd, there's no reason why anyone should give you the time of day. You want to be a someone, you have to be seen as a someone. You got to make sure people notice you.

Devil's father had got that bit sussed a long time ago. You couldn't walk down a street with him without people running up to him, calling out his name, waving. People loved Pastor Jones. Needed him. Worshipped him.

Yeah, he knew what he was doing. He knew how to work it better than anyone else.

And Devil knew, too – had figured out within a day of being in this place that he was going to have to change, that if he was going to survive he was going to have to lead. He'd looked at himself in the mirror and brought about a transformation. Gone was the middle-class kid to whom black was just the colour of his skin, who hunched his shoulders so that his large frame didn't intimidate people. And instead, Devil was born: tall, broad, insolent, swaggering, angry. Someone people would be afraid of. Someone people wouldn't dare to cross.

Devil walked down through the tunnel that went between the two high rises, the tunnel that no one wanted to be anywhere near after dark except for the junkies, the slags, people who didn't care any more, who had no respect for themselves whatsoever. Devil had no respect for them either. Devil didn't have any respect for anyone, except himself. Even his crew were just sheep, following him. They didn't have the courage to do anything for themselves.

Not like him. He winced at the smell of urine, of excrement, of stale alcohol, dirty clothes. The first time he'd walked through the tunnel he'd nearly pissed himself. He'd never been anywhere like it in his life; never been outside his leafy suburban town in Hertfordshire, where everyone lived in nice new houses with gardens and cars parked out front, where everyone knew who he was, where everyone smiled and gave him presents when they came to call on his dad. Where he used to listen to Leona practising the piano and tried to put her off by pulling silly faces.

But life, Devil had learnt, changed. Nothing could be depended on except yourself. Nothing.

A ray of early autumn sunshine hit him as he came out of the tunnel and he smiled, enjoying the warmth on his skin. Things were on the up. The Green Lanes Massive had been told, had got what was coming to them. The boy had done his job. Got caught, the stupid prick, but that was his own fault. He'd frozen apparently, stood there afterwards just looking at the boy on the ground, holding the knife like some kind of idiot. But that was okay. Those who needed to know knew that

Devil was behind it; the police had the boy banged up and nothing to link him to the Dalston Crew, so it was all clean, all sorted.

Of course the Green Lanes Massive would retaliate, but Devil was ready for them. His boys were tougher, hungrier; they would go further. That's what it was all about, Devil had realised a long time ago. It was a game of chicken. You had to be prepared to go further than anyone else. You had to have no fear. No fear meant no weakness, meant no one had anything on you. And no one having anything on you gave you power. No one having anything on you made you invincible.

He took the long way round, through the deserted scrubland at the back of the estate. There'd been plans once to turn it into a play area for kids, with a five-a-side football pitch and a youth club; the foundations had even been dug. But the day they delivered the wood to build it, the place was torched; soon after that all the plans were dropped.

He was on the road now, ambling down towards the arcade, hands in his pockets. He didn't usually leave the estate alone; safety in numbers and all that. But today he was feeling confident. And he didn't want to hang with his boys all the time.

They talked a load of shit, laughed at stupid things. They were boring. Infantile. That had been one of his words, couple of weeks ago now. In-fan-tile. Like an infant. Like a baby. It was now his favourite put down. People didn't like it. They didn't like it because it was a long word and it showed up how stupid they were. They didn't have to be stupid. They could get a dictionary app just like he did. But people didn't think like that. They were happy in the gutter. His father had been right about that: other people deserved what they got. They brought it on themselves. They were lucky he even noticed they were alive.

A girl was outside the newsagent, holding onto a bike, looking into the shop hesitantly, looking down at the bike. It was pink. It was new. Cheap shit; soon enough it would fall apart, the pink would chip. But right now it looked all right. She was wearing a matching helmet, pale pink. The bike had a basket on the front. She had a lock in her left hand; she was looking for somewhere to lock it up.

Devil walked over; something in him needed to separate her from the bike, needed to show her that he was the boss, that everything on the estate was his for the taking, even a crappy kid's bike.

'You can leave your bike with me.'

She looked up at him, her eyes wide. She was six, too young to know not to look him in the eye, but old enough to be hesitant. He remembered when she was a toddler. Her mother used to be fine-looking. Not any more. 'Mum says I got to lock it up.'

'Your mum wants your bike safe. It's safe with me.' He smiled, his whole face softening. He'd learnt that from his father. Soft then hard; hard then soft.

She looked torn.

'You want to go in the shop, you gotta leave the bike here. I'll look after it for you.'

He smiled again. Reluctantly, she started to move towards the shop, turning every few seconds to check the bike was still there.

'Helmet,' Devil said. The girl frowned. 'I'll need your helmet.'

The girl opened her mouth to say something, then she caught Devil's expression. The smile was gone. He was sitting on her bike, his knees pressed up against his chest. She didn't move.

'You give me the helmet,' he said, his tone now threatening. 'I'm just going to take your bike for a ride. Keep it safe for you.'

She edged backwards into the shop. Devil pounced, grabbing her, pulling the helmet from her head before dragging her back to where her bike lay on the pavement. He pressed her nose against the bike, holding her by the neck. 'Now you tell your mamma that Devil has your bike. You tell her if she wants you to have it again, she's going to have to pay me for looking after it for you? You get me? You hear what I say?'

The girl was crying. For a second Devil looked at her; he had an urge to wipe away her tears just as he'd done with Leona, holding her to him, rocking her in his arms, telling her that monsters didn't exist, that he'd protect her, that he'd always be there for her. But this girl wasn't Leona. And this girl's slapper mother hadn't helped them one bit when they'd arrived here; hadn't once given Leona even a smile. Suddenly filled with anger and hate, he pushed the girl roughly onto the pavement. 'You tell her. You tell her what I told you.'

He didn't look back as he cycled away. Didn't care whether she was crying or not. Leona didn't have a bike. Leona didn't have nothing. What right did this girl have? The bike had been bought with money that should have come to the Dalston Crew. Twenty per cent of earnings, that's all he asked of her mother. Not much for protection, not much for her family's safety. But he knew she was robbing him, seeing clients on the sly. He knew she was fiddling, lying, cheating him. And now she'd know he knew.

The bike was too small, far too small, but he rode it anyway. It reminded him of the BMX he used to have when he was younger. He'd loved that bike. He used to go everywhere on it. Sometimes he'd cycle with Leona on his knee and she'd giggle as they rode, clinging onto the handle-bars, squealing when he did wheelies.

He got off the bike, threw it down in disgust, forcing the images of his little sister out of his head. Leona wasn't there any more. That's how things were. Things had changed.

He walked quickly, past the arcade, past the sprawling mess of small two-up-two-down houses that surrounded the estate, gardens full of washing lines and broken-down cars, the paths strewn with broken bottles and cigarette butts. Cheap cigarettes.

Devil smoked Silk Cut, his father's brand. Just to be different. Classy. You wouldn't catch him with one of those cheap brands that tasted like shit.

Then he stopped, looked around. A couple of boys looked at him cautiously, then dropped their heads and walked away. He was on safe territory here. A mile further and he'd need his crew. Just in case. But here, no one would dare mess with him. No other gang would think about trespassing.

He started to walk again, past the houses, around the corner, sneering as he saw people going about their daily business: fighting, doing the washing, shouting at their kids. It was a shit place to live. Sink estate, they called it in the newspapers. Not that anyone around here read a newspaper. They might look at the pictures sometimes, peer at the tits, but nothing else. That's what made it a sink estate, Devil had real-ised a month or so after moving here. It wasn't the flats and houses, even though they had walls so thin you could piss up them and the damp would show through on the other side; it was the people inside them. Lazy, stupid, ignorant people. His dad would have cleaned up, he'd thought to himself. And then he'd remembered that his dad had run away, that he wasn't coming back. And that's when he'd decided that he would clean up instead. That he would own this place, just like his dad had owned his town.

First time he'd seen his dad on television he'd thought it was a game, thought it was something clever his dad was doing with the camera, like when he put images of Devil riding his bike with Leona on his computer for them to watch. But it wasn't a game. It was real. His dad, speaking to millions of people.

'They love me,' his dad had smiled proudly. 'They love me so much they send me their money. All the way from America, from Africa. We'll go to America one day, son. We'll have them eating out of my palms.'

Devil had a different name back then. But a lot of things were different back then.

'Devil? Fancy finding you here.'

Devil stopped, abruptly, cursing himself for getting lost in thought, not noticing the pigs creeping up on him.

'Yeah? It's a free country last I heard,' he said, looking the copper right in the eye. There was a policewoman with him. Quite fit, if you liked that kind of thing. She had dark brown hair; the policeman was a ginger.

'What I heard,' the woman said, 'is that you were behind the stabbing last week. You got anything to say about that?'

Devil shrugged. 'I ain't behind no stabbing. Not my style. My crew's all about peace, officer.'

He smiled, broadly, confidently. They had nothing on him. Could have nothing on him. The boy wouldn't squeal, not if he cared about his family.

'Peace.' The male copper's eyes narrowed. 'You're a little shit, you know that? You know your little gofer's sister is in hospital, don't you? A revenge attack for the murder you made him commit. The Green Lanes Massive have threatened to kill her next time. That boy thought he had your protection. But you don't give a shit, do you? Think he's going to keep quiet now? Think he's going to think twice about telling us exactly what you told him to do?'

Devil's eyes widened. His sister? Shit. He didn't know. 'Yeah?' he said, folding his arms insouciantly. 'Well good luck trying, 'cos I ain't got nothin' to do with it.'

Devil turned quickly and walked back the way he had come. He had an uncomfortable feeling in his stomach. What if the boy snitched? What then?

'Don't go too far, Devil,' the policeman called after him, but Devil didn't turn around. He just shoved his hands in his pockets and made his way back towards the estate.

11

The sewing rooms, as they were known, were situated towards the northern end of the settlement and were made up of two rooms, one for sorting and machining and one for more delicate work. It was in the second of these rooms that Evie worked, sometimes hand-stitching special garments but mostly mending and darning to eke out more use from clothes that had seen better days. Most of the clothes were hewn from wool, but new fabric was expensive to produce so reusing what already existed was the bulk of their work, clothing the farmers who worked all hours to put food on the table for the whole community. In the Settlement, after teachers it was farmers who were revered the most; the majority of men between the ages of sixteen and forty toiled the fields or looked after the animals because, as Benjamin explained, food gives you the energy to do everything else; without it, everything would fail.

In the City, by contrast, farmers were rarely seen, except when they brought their goods to market; agriculture had been taken for granted but never celebrated, never seen as a worthy career. And it wasn't until Evie had gone outside the City that she'd learnt why: the City wasn't self-sufficient, and farming wasn't celebrated because it was carried out elsewhere, a dirty little secret that the Brother liked to keep that way.

Evie still got angry when she thought about what Linus had told her, about the Evils working outside the City to produce food for its citizens under terrible conditions. She would compare their treatment with the farmers of the Settlement and it would send a shiver down her spine, but mostly she tried not to think about the City, tried only to think about the here and the now, about the Settlement, about her future.

Trouble was, sometimes that sent a shiver down her spine, too.

Evie enjoyed her work here. In the City she had hated sewing, had done everything she could to escape from it. But that had been because it was her mother's work. The mother who wasn't her mother. The mother who had stolen her from her real parents and had failed to even love her in return. Now Evie relished the camaraderie as the women worked together – and it was all women in the sewing rooms. 'Not because men can't sew,' Benjamin had told her, a twinkle in his eye. 'I just haven't yet found a man brave enough to join in the conversation.'

And the conversation had been a revelation to Evie. The women talked as they worked, sharing confidences, telling each other stories from their pasts, discussing their dreams for the future, teasing each other, supporting each other. It was so unlike the City where people worked in silence, where sharing a confidence was to put in jeopardy your standing in society, your label.

Here, the women gossiped about others, but mostly kindly; people in the Settlement, Evie had learnt, did not seek to judge or despise or fear. They looked for things that they had in common with others; they looked for shared values, for shared hopes. And all because of Benjamin. Because Benjamin had taught them that love always trumps fear, that peace was far stronger than violence. And Evie loved it, loved the gentle rhythm of this place with the whirr of the machines audible through the thin walls, the delightful eruption of laughter every so often punctuating their conversation.

But today, the conversation was about one thing only: the welcome ceremony. The joining ceremony that would also be Evie's wedding. The dress that she would wear on the day, that she would continue to wear at all celebrations until she got pregnant, when another dress would be made for her for after the birth, signalling that she had entered yet another stage of life.

'Your dress is nearly ready,' one of the older women, Sandra, said with a smile. 'You're going to look so pretty.'

Evie blushed. 'It's ready?' she said, trying to ignore the strange feeling in the pit of her stomach. 'I hope it didn't take much time.'

'No time at all. My daughter doesn't need hers any more, not now she's got a baby. I just added some ribbons and took it in a bit. For someone who lived in the City you haven't got much fat to you.' It was the sort of comment that City women would have made sharply, critically. But Sandra smiled indulgently as she spoke and Evie let the warmth envelop her as she always did in this room. 'Here, try it on,' she said, handing it to Evie.

Evie looked at it, tried to imagine herself wearing it, tried to picture herself happily making her marriage vows. Then she put it down again. 'Maybe I'll try it on at lunch break,' she said, falteringly. 'Don't want to eat into working time.'

Sandra shrugged. 'You've certainly got a work ethic for someone who's grown up with plenty,' she said with a little smile.

'And how is the baby?' another woman, Kathy, asked Sandra suddenly, much to Evie's relief.

Sandra smiled in delight. 'Just perfect. Adorable little thing,' she gushed and the other women cooed.

'How old is he now? Nine months? Won't be long till his Welcome,' Kathy said, shaking her head and exhaling loudly. 'Time goes so fast, doesn't it?'

'Too fast,' Sandra agreed, as she put down a farming glove and started mending another.

Babies were commonplace in the Settlement but they were still greeted with great excitement and love. Each child was officially welcomed into the Settlement as soon after their first birthday as possible; this was why the Welcome Ceremony was held, to bind these children – along with any new recruits – to the Settlement. Two were held every year. Evie and Raffy had attended one already as onlookers as new joiners had to wait a year before formal acceptance was possible. Nevertheless, the ceremony had left tears in Evie's eyes; it was so full of hope, so full of love, so different from the City where strangers were feared, where children were seen as inferior creatures that needed to be rid of their innate evil, needed to undergo the New Baptism, then moulded and coerced into being good citizens.

'So,' another woman, Lucy, said suddenly. 'When do we think it's going to rain? Soon? Let's hope it's soon.'

It had been two weeks without rain; not enough for people to worry too much, but enough to make the weather a hot topic of conversation. No rain meant crop failure; crop failure meant the Settlement going hungry. The Settlement was on the river Humber, but the water had dried up years ago. Instead, the Settlement relied on rainwater collected and stored in large reservoirs. And rainwater needed regular topping up.

'It'll rain soon enough,' Sandra said immediately. She was the mother of the group, always ready to reassure, to offer words of wisdom.

'That's easy to say,' Lucy replied. 'But what if it doesn't?'

'It will,' Sandra said, her voice firmer this time. 'Let's not worry unduly shall we? Doesn't Benjamin warn us that worrying out loud can lead to contagion of thought? That if we are going to spread our thoughts, they should be full of positivity and hope?'

'Well, that's all very well but we all know that we wouldn't be so dependent on the rain if the water didn't just run away to feed the City.'

It was a far-fetched accusation that Benjamin regularly countered, but which people clung to because it gave them a focus for their anger and resentment when the rain didn't come. But as with most rumours there was some truth to the story: the City had built several dams to shore up its own water supply, blithely starving all the surrounding settlements of the water they needed to survive.

Evie reddened as she always did when her former home was mentioned, as though she were somehow responsible for it. She hadn't known about the dams until she'd arrived at the Settlement; had had no idea that the City was so ruthless, so focused on the needs of its own people to the exclusion of everyone else. She knew that people wanted to live within the City walls, but had always been taught that it was salvation people wanted, a chance to live in a world without evil. In reality, it was because the City had made sure that resources were scarce for any other township in the country.

'Lucy,' Sandra said, a note of warning in her voice.

'What? It's true isn't it?' Lucy said defiantly.

There was a short silence as the women, sitting on wooden chairs in a semi-circle, digested this.

'They shouldn't be allowed to get away with it,' Carlotta, a short woman with dark hair, dark eyes and a stout, strong body, agreed eventually. 'Who gives them the right to dam every river? Who?'

Lucy nodded vigorously. 'Exactly. Benjamin should do something. It's all very well being people of peace, but when people are stealing from us—'

'That's enough,' Sandra said then, standing up. She looked around the circle. 'Are you happy living here?' she asked Lucy. 'Is there anywhere else you'd like to go?'

Lucy shook her head.

'And do you believe that Benjamin is a fine leader, who has looked after us so far, who has devoted himself to our well-being?'

Lucy nodded and looked at the floor.

'Good,' Sandra said, sitting down again. 'Don't ever talk like that about him again in this room, do you here? And don't make Evie here uncomfortable, either. We're fine. It'll rain. Okay? It'll rain.'

As she spoke, the skies around them darkened and a clap of thunder made them jump; moments later, rain began to lash against the windows. Sandra smiled triumphantly.

'Nice trick,' Kathy said with a giggle. 'You knew that was going to happen, didn't you?'

Sandra shrugged, a little smile on her face. 'I might have noticed a few dark clouds this morning,' she said lightly.

The women sewed for a few more minutes, then Kathy looked over at Evie. 'Don't suppose you had to worry about being hungry when you were in the City, did you?'

Evie shook her head, warily. People didn't go hungry in the City, it was true, but that didn't mean they were happy. 'No,' she said quietly. 'But I'd rather be here and hungry than there with all the food in the world.'

Kathy's face creased in curiosity. 'It was really that bad?' she asked. 'Don't you sometimes think about going back?'

Evie shook her head vehemently. She'd already told them about the labels, about the strict rules about who you could talk to, who you could be friends with, about the System, about K's being left outside the City walls for the Evils to attack. But many of her new friends found it hard to believe; they had always known the City as the land of plenty, the land of the good, the lucky, and Evie could tell that sometimes they weren't convinced that her tales were entirely truthful.

'I never want to go back,' she said, her voice catching slightly. 'The City had food and water and homes for everyone. But it was also a place where everyone lied, where a System labelled people unfairly, where people were told they would have a future and instead were subjected to brain surgery that took their whole lives away. I never want to go back there.'

'You'd really rather starve to death?' Lucy asked, her eyebrows raised pointedly.

'Lucy, no one is going to starve. It's raining, isn't it? Leave the girl alone,' Sandra said, her voice sounding a little strained.

Lucy tutted.

'Acceptance, love, learning and hope,' Sandra said gently. 'That's what this place is all about. Evie, please don't listen to Lucy. She's just having a bad day. Aren't you, Lucy? Probably got to breakfast late. Thought she'd have a lie-in and now she's regretting it. Right?'

Lucy opened her mouth to protest, then laughed. 'Okay, you got me,' she said.

'Now,' Sandra said. 'If I'm not mistaken, it's almost lunch. Evie, let's get you into this dress of yours, shall we? Let's see just how lovely you're going to look.'

12

'Hey, Wajid. How are things?'

Wajid stared at Thomas insolently; looked over at the prison guard. 'They're shit,' he said. 'What's it to you?'

It was an adopted name, one he'd been given when he'd found salvation, when he'd stumbled across a group of lads in prison who'd listened to him, understood him, protected him. That was ten years ago now; he'd been to prison four times since. But this time he wasn't getting out for good behaviour. This time he was going to rot in there and he didn't need some stranger turning up to gloat.

Thomas leant back in his chair. 'What's it to me, Wajid, is that I'm not happy about your treatment in here. And I'm not happy about the length of your sentence either.'

'My sentence?' Wajid leant towards Thomas, his eyes flashing. 'What do you know about me and my sentence? Who the fuck are you anyway?'

He held Thomas's gaze for a few seconds, then sat back on his chair to survey him properly. It was the third time he'd visited, this strange man who looked like a nerd but wore expensive clothes. The third time he'd asked Wajid stupid questions, pointless questions, before getting up and going. Like Wajid was some kind of entertainment. Like he was some kind of joke. Never a surname, either – just 'Thomas', like he was a friend or something.

Thomas didn't blanch under Wajid's scrutiny. 'I'm someone who can help you,' he said. 'But if you don't want my help, if you're happy in here, then that's fine. I'm evidently wasting my time.'

Wajid slammed his fist down on the table. He was sick of this. Sick of playing games. 'You tell me what you're doing here,' he said. 'Tell me now. Who sent you? Who are you really working for?'

The prison guard walked over. 'Everything all right over here?' he asked.

Thomas nodded quickly. 'It's okay, officer. It's okay.'

The guard moved away slowly.

Thomas looked at Wajid carefully. 'Look,' he said. 'I'm part of a network. A network that can help you. Help you get out of here.'

Wajid's eyes narrowed. 'Don't fuck with me.'

Thomas laughed. 'No, Wajid. No escapes. I'm talking about judges reviewing your sentence. I'm talking about compensation being awarded for a miscarriage of justice. I know you're not a terrorist, Wajid. I know that you're just sick of all the injustice in the world. Sick of the wrong people running the show. Sick of not having a proper voice.'

Wajid didn't say anything for a few seconds.

'And why would you think that?' he asked eventually.

Thomas leant forward again. 'Because I know you,' he said under his breath, only just audible. 'I know what you want because I want it too. And I think you're the person to wake everyone up. You've got people, right? Disciples? People who believe in what you believe in? People who will do what it takes?'

Wajid's eyes narrowed. He wasn't saying nothing. This was most likely a trap, and he wasn't falling for it. No way.

'You don't trust me yet and that's fine. I wouldn't expect you to. But just wait and see what I can do. I'll get you out of here. And then I'll give you what you need,' Thomas said. 'You choose the targets; I'll make sure your people get where you want to go. You just need to line them up, point them in the right direction. Can you do that? Can you do that, Wajid?'

'You think I'm stupid?' Wajid said, sitting back, disdain on his face. 'You're talking a load of crap. Setting me up. I ain't an idiot.'

'Nor am I,' Thomas said, moving his hands forward, slipping a pin to Wajid, a pin with the letter 'I' on it. Wajid frowned; he'd seen it before somewhere. The prison guard cleared his throat and immediately Wajid remembered. He had one too. 'Tonight you'll hear about a bomb attack. That's my people. And tomorrow your lawyer will visit you with news of new evidence. You get me a message to tell me you're on board, and that new evidence will be compelling enough to get you out of here, to exonerate you completely. You don't, and you're going to rot here. Understand?'

The pin disappeared into Wajid's sleeve in a deft sleight of hand. He stared at Thomas for a few seconds. 'Those things happen, then maybe,' he said, standing up. 'They don't, and you'd better watch yourself. I still got friends outside.'

'That's what I'm relying on.' Thomas winked as he stood up. 'Goodbye, Wajid. Until we meet again.'

13

Lucas looked down at Clara. It was the following morning and Clara had slept almost from the moment she'd arrived at Base Camp until now. She looked so vulnerable, lying there in the bed that Martha had made up for her. Back in the City, her parents would be frantic; there would be search parties looking for her. And she was all alone here, away from her friends and family, unable to contact them. But she was safe. Would be safe.

She opened her eyes and he started slightly. 'Here,' he said stiffly, handing her a bowl of cereal. 'Have some breakfast.'

Clara took the bowl silently; he could tell that she was anxious, unsettled, unsure. He didn't blame her.

'This is Martha,' he said, stepping aside so that Clara could see her. 'She's going to look after you here.' His voice sounded formal; he could tell that it made her nervous but he couldn't seem to do anything about it.

Clara's eyes widened. 'What about you?'

'I have to go and find someone. I . . .' Lucas trailed off, not sure how much to tell Clara; the truth was, he barely knew what he was doing himself. He cleared his throat. 'I need to make sure that the Informers leave the City, that they are brought to justice. You'll be safe here.'

Clara nodded slowly.

Martha stepped forward, sat on the bed and took Clara's hand. 'We'll have fun,' she said, her eyes twinkling. 'You're going to love Base Camp. And when things are ready, Lucas will come back for you and you'll go back to the City and tell everyone the truth. Okay?'

Clara nodded eagerly, looked up at Lucas for affirmation. He nodded, wondering how Martha did it, how she managed to soothe, engage; how she made it look so easy.

He could never talk to Evie, either. All those years, all those years of longing, and he'd never been able to say a single thing that didn't sound forced, formal, cold. No wonder she'd hated him for all that time; he'd seen it in her eyes, seen the contempt so clearly. And he hadn't even blamed her. He'd felt contempt for himself, too.

Sometimes he wished he'd left it at that; sometimes he wished he hadn't revealed himself to her, hadn't seen her eyes change, hadn't felt her lips on his, hadn't allowed himself to imagine what life might be like.

'Right,' he said, forcing a little smile, wondering if he should make some gesture, a hand shake, a squeeze of the shoulder, then deciding against it.

'Find me before you go,' Martha said as he started to walk out of the room. 'I need to tell you the directions. I'm not allowed to write them down. Come and get me and I'll talk you through it.'

Lucas didn't hang around. There was no reason to. Instead, he showered, packed up some more food, listened carefully to Martha's directions, then left, before the other men got back. Martha had done her best to bandage up his feet but then he couldn't fit his shoes back on, so she'd reluctantly taken the bandages off again, leaving his blisters, still raw and red, to chafe against the leather of his brogues.

Her directions were complicated – Lucas realised he would never have found Linus without them – but also faultless; almost exactly two hours after leaving Base Camp, Lucas came across the rocky hills that she'd told him to look out for. Then, he walked clockwise around them until he saw a hole, about ten foot wide, leading into the caves below. Apparently this was Linus's home.

Uncertainly, Lucas stepped inside the tunnel and started to walk. It smelt dank; the light was limited and several times he stumbled on rocks. After about 100 feet, he stopped as the tunnel swung round to the right. Then he called out.

'Linus. It's Lucas.'

He waited.

'Linus, it's Lucas,' he called again after a few minutes; still nothing.

Lucas turned the corner and started to walk. Had the Informers got to Linus? Had they found him? No, impossible. But then where was he? Martha had told him that Linus never left the cave. Never. The floor was now slippery under foot, covered in slime and moisture. He held out his hands, using the walls of the cave as support and to guide him. The tunnel was almost dark; what little light there was made the rock luminescent but didn't afford a glimpse of what lay a few feet ahead.

After slipping several times, Lucas dropped down onto his hands and knees to crawl along the dank floor; every few minutes he told himself that he had gone into the wrong tunnel, that he should turn back, but he didn't stop. It was the right tunnel. He had followed

Martha's instructions to the letter. Lucas did his best to shake off his fears as he pushed forwards. Rocks grazed his palms, dug into his knees, but he ignored the pain. He had to get to Linus. Had to . . .

His hand stretched forward into nothing; his body, ready to rest its weight on the hand, tipped forwards. Desperately Lucas pulled himself back and somehow managed to stop himself falling. Then he looked down and his mouth fell open. In front of him, twenty feet down below, was what looked like the System Operating room back at the City. Large computers, their screens all illuminated, chairs, desks . . . And Linus sitting at one of them, a beard reaching down several inches from his chin. Linus's hand shot up.

'Lucas,' he said, not looking up. 'Just give me a minute will you? I'm in the middle of something.'

Lucas stared at him open-mouthed. 'Linus?' he gasped.

'One minute,' Linus cut in, a note of irritation in his voice.

Lucas frowned, then he counted to three in his head, a technique he had learnt many years ago and employed regularly, often several times a day in order to suppress reactions that would otherwise cause him problems. Thousands of injustices; thousands of sweeping comments made arrogantly by the Brother;

thousands of insults directed towards his father, his brother; hundreds of meetings with Evie when what he wanted to do and was able to do were so very far apart. Counting to three had become a mantra, a little meditation that allowed the coolness to descend, the detachment, the armour.

But here, now, counting to three achieved nothing. 'In the middle of something?' Lucas stared in disbelief then turned and lowered himself down, jumping the final fourteen feet down to where Linus was hunched over a computer screen. 'In the middle of something?' He walked over to Linus, inwardly seething, his exterior still cool, just as it always was. 'I thought something had happened to you,' he said, his voice low. 'I called your name and you didn't answer.'

'Will you please,' Linus said again, holding up his hand as a parent might do to a child, 'just stop there. For twenty more seconds.'

His eyes hadn't even left the computer. Dumbfounded, Lucas did as Linus asked. And as he waited, he looked around again, his anger gradually being replaced by disbelief as he marvelled at the technology, the sheer size of the place.

'There we are,' Linus said suddenly, standing up. 'So, Lucas, what can I do for you?'

He was smiling distractedly as though Lucas had

just popped by for a cup of tea, as though they had seen each other as recently as yesterday.

It unsettled Lucas, almost made him forget why he was here. He had only met Linus briefly, but for years they had communicated covertly, and before that it had been Lucas's father who had communicated with Linus. And yet, in spite of that, looking at him now Lucas realised he was a complete stranger.

'I . . .' It was no use. His eyes were on the move again. 'What is this place?' he asked. 'How did you . . . I mean . . . what *is* this place?'

'Good, isn't it?' Linus grinned. 'I call it my head-quarters.'

'But there's no one else here.'

'Exactly.' Linus's eyes were shining. 'I'm the boss and there's no one to get in the way. Perfect, don't you think?' Lucas knew exactly what Linus meant – he dreamt himself, sometimes, of being alone, of not having to deal with people, their problems, their mistrust, their attempts to outmanoeuvre him. But he didn't say anything. Linus didn't seem to notice Lucas's silence, or care. 'Now, tell me why you're here because I don't have long,' he said. 'Lots to do. Okay?'

Lucas nodded seriously. 'There are people in the City,' he said, crouching down so that his head was level with Linus's. 'Murderers. They've been working with the Brother, supporting him, offering food, protection, I don't know what else. Some young people stumbled across them in the old Hospital and they . . . they killed them all. Except one. She's at Base Camp with Martha. And . . .'

'And?'

Lucas took a deep breath. He hadn't wanted to dwell on the other thing that Clara had told him; he'd told himself they were leaving purely for her protection. But there had been another reason, too, the thing that had made him realise immediately that they had to leave the City. 'When the young people saw them. The Informers. They were talking about . . .' He took a deep breath. 'They said they needed to find Raffy. They said they needed him to switch the System back on.'

He looked at Linus, waiting for his reaction. But Linus didn't look remotely shocked, surprised or even angry. He just nodded thoughtfully.

'They're in the City, are they? And they're interested in the System? Well that explains that . . .' Linus said, frowning. Then he turned back to his computer and started to type. After a few minutes, Lucas moved closer. 'So?' he asked.

'So what?'

'So I need to find Raffy and Evie,' Lucas said. 'I need to make sure they're safe and then I'm going to go back to the City and find these Informers and make them regret what they've done.' His eyes were flashing with anger.

Linus raised his eyebrows. 'Okay, if you insist. But Raffy's perfectly safe where he is. He might be marginally safer here, I suppose. You could bring him here, if you want, if he promises not to make any noise. In the meantime, if I can take it from you that you yourself have no intention of restarting the System, then our business is complete.'

Lucas's eyes narrowed; Linus blanched slightly. 'And thank you for letting me know,' he said quickly, as though he thought Lucas's anger was over his poor manners. 'Very useful. Very useful indeed.'

Lucas stood up. 'Linus, did you not hear what I said? Young people have been murdered within the City walls. The Brother has to be involved because the Informers were let into the City by the gatekeeper. They've been bringing in food and supplies for years.'

'From the other townships and settlements around the country. Yes, I know that,' Linus said distractedly. 'What I'm more interested in is where they came from. Where their base is. Because right now it doesn't make any sense.' He stared at his computer intently. 'Nice to see you, Lucas. There's a bathroom over there if you need it. This is where Raffy is.'

He scribbled something on a scrap of paper, handed it to Lucas, then turned back to his computer. Lucas stared at the piece of paper. 'That's it? That's all you're going to say?'

Linus let out a sharp exhalation. 'Is there anything else to say?' he asked. 'Lucas, I am not an army. I am one man. I could try and help you, but I doubt I'd be any more useful than, say, Angel. In fact I would be less useful than Angel. Ask him for help; he's always going out on pointless expeditions that achieve nothing except keeping him from going mad. I, on the other hand, have things to do. Lots of them. So if you don't mind, I'd like to get on with them.'

Lucas watched, open-mouthed, as Linus turned back to his computer.

'I don't want your help,' he said bitterly. 'I want you to care.'

'I do,' Linus confirmed. 'Absolutely. Oh, and you won't get out the way you came in. Strictly one-way traffic. You'll have to go down that corridor.' He pointed in the opposite direction. 'Bit of a tricky climb once you get to the opening, but you'll be fine. Just make sure you turn right not left.'

Lucas shook his head in disgust. 'You don't get it, do you? That we're responsible for this? We switched off the System. You did. I let you. I believed in you. And now seven young people are dead. And you . . . You're just sitting here with your computers like it doesn't matter. Well it does. And I'm going to do something about it.' He started to walk away. Then he stopped.

'You know, I risked everything communicating with you back in the City,' he said suddenly, walking back to where Linus was sitting. 'My father risked everything before me. I thought the City mattered to you.'

'It did,' Linus said, his expression one of surprise. 'The System mattered to me. Destroying it mattered to me.' He looked at Lucas earnestly. 'But now that's done. There are other things that need my attention. Questions I can't answer, can't fathom.'

'Like what?' Lucas asked, his eyes stony. 'What is more important to you than people being brutally murdered, left outside the City walls for scavengers to feast on? What is more important than discovering the Brother has allies outside the City, a City that is meant to be entirely self-sufficient? Allies that I knew nothing about until yesterday? Allies who know about the System, who have free access to come and go as they please? Linus, aren't you listening? Don't you get that this matters?'

Linus breathed out, then looked at Lucas carefully. 'Of course it matters,' he said then. 'But the truth is I know all this. Not all of it, but enough to piece most of it together. And I get that you're angry and frustrated but I've got my eyes on the big picture.'

'The big picture?' Lucas grabbed Linus by his collar and dragged him up. 'You knew all this and you didn't tell me? You let them kill those young people and you did nothing?'

'I didn't know what they were doing in the City,' Linus gasped as Lucas dropped him back down again. 'I didn't . . . I didn't think about that.'

'So what *did* you think about?' Lucas demanded, his eyes unflinching. He was bearing over Linus now; all his residual anger bubbling up inside him. 'Tell me. What exactly did you think about, Linus?'

Linus appeared to consider the question for a few seconds. Then he moved his chair to the side, pulled up another one, and motioned for Linus to sit down. Lucas refused.

'Look,' Linus said, pointing at his screen. Lucas looked; it was a map. Linus pressed a button. The screen zoomed in to show a patch of land that Lucas recognised; the tree where Raffy and Evie used to meet, the tree where he himself had been just the other evening. 'Clever, huh?' Linus grinned. 'Old software but the satellite is still in the sky. It's taken me a while, but I've managed to get it working. It picks up activity, movement, active computer chips. Pretty cool, don't you think?'

Lucas looked at the map irritably. Then, gradually, he found himself moving closer, his anger abating slowly. It was incredible. Absolutely incredible. 'You can watch the City?' he breathed. 'We have to use this to track down the Informers. Catch them. Bring them to justice.'

Linus pulled a face. 'Maybe. But I'm less interested in the City than what's happening elsewhere,' he said.

'Yes, you've made that perfectly clear,' Lucas said. 'But I am interested.'

Linus pressed another button; the map shrunk back so that instead of the patch of land, they were now looking at the City in its entirety. Linus hit the button again and the vast shape of the United Kingdom was visible. Lucas couldn't believe what he was seeing; he'd only ever seen maps in old books but now he was looking at the real thing.

'It's odd,' Linus countered.

'Odd?'

'Odd,' Linus said again. 'Look over here.'

He scrolled across to the east coast, and pointed to an area. 'See that?' he asked Lucas.

Lucas nodded.

'There's a bit missing,' Linus said.

'Missing?' Lucas frowned. 'What do you mean?'

'I mean,' Linus said patiently, 'that here, there should be a bit sticking out. It used to be called Margate. And now it isn't there.'

Lucas considered this. 'Maybe it was destroyed in the Horrors.'

'A whole stretch of land? Not possible. Anyway, that's not the only thing that's strange. The satellites are recording no activity, nothing outside of the UK.'

Lucas looked at Linus strangely. 'But the rest of the world was destroyed in the Horrors. Why would there be any activity?'

'Right,' Linus said. 'But if there are insects on the ground, this satellite would pick them up. It could be that the whole world has been destroyed into complete oblivion except for our fair isle, but it's unlikely, you have to agree?'

'Unlikely, but possible,' Lucas said.

'Okay, but that doesn't explain why it isn't showing any activity in Margate. Or Ramsgate for that matter. Nice place, Margate. And now it's gone. Or rather, the satellite thinks it's gone. But you see it isn't. I know it isn't, because I sent Angel to have a little look and there's a new little community there. Quite a campsite, by all accounts. So my question is, why are they there, and how is it that I can't see them or the place that they came from?'

Linus's face was suddenly deadly serious. Lucas looked at the screen thoughtfully. 'You think it's the Informers?' he asked quietly.

'Seems likely,' Linus said.

'So then we have a common interest,' Lucas said, turning to him.

'Maybe,' Linus said, his voice sounding tired.

Lucas looked him in the eye. 'Linus, you can't solve anything stuck in this cave.'

'Not with you here interrupting me,' Linus said, archly.

Lucas grabbed him by the shoulders. 'Linus, these Informers want the System turned back on. That has to be why they're here. Or one reason, anyway. Who are these people? I'm going to find out. I'm going to stop them. You can help.'

Linus looked at him for a moment. Then he stood up wearily. 'You know I came here to be alone?' he said with a sigh.

Lucas didn't reply.

Linus pushed his chair back. 'Well, if we're going back into battle I suppose I should offer you a cup of tea? I might even stretch to a piece of fruit cake. If you'd like?'

Lucas frowned, then flopped down on a chair. 'I would, actually,' he said. 'I really would. Thank you.'

'Don't mention it,' Linus said, a smile creeping onto his face, his eyes back to their familiar twinkle, his step light as he bounded towards the kitchen. 'You should see this place,' he said. 'Angel's done me proud. It's like a real home away from home . . .'

14

It was the colours that Devil noticed straight away. The vivid red against the grey slabs of the concrete ground; the brilliant blue sky behind the monstrous grey skyscrapers. It was like it wasn't real; like it wasn't really happening.

But it was happening; or rather, it had happened.

'How long's he been there?' he asked, making sure to keep his voice level, like everything was fine.

'I dunno,' Nelson said. 'Ten minutes, maybe. I heard him scream. Woke me up. I came out, and . . .' His voice was trembling. Shit, Nelson himself was trembling. Devil had to sort this and sort it now. Not because Nelson was a mate. He didn't have mates here. Couldn't afford them, didn't want them. He was different now; here, it was about survival, and friends were just baggage.

But Nelson was like his deputy. Anyone else had woken Devil at 5 a.m., he'd have killed them. But it wasn't anyone else; it was Nelson, so he'd listened, followed him out here onto the tiny balcony that ran around the flats to look down at the body below. And the minute he'd looked, he hadn't seen the boy, he'd seen his sister, seen her lifeless body on the tarmac below, and it had filled him with rage, with remorse, with a sadness so deep that it threatened to consume him, threatened to reduce him to a snivelling wretch on the floor. But he'd pulled himself together just in time, before Nelson could see; had reined in his emotions and channelled them quickly. And what he had chan-nelled them into was anger at the boy. The stupid dead boy. Who could have been useful. Could have made something of himself, and instead . . . instead he'd caused trouble, made a scene, produced a problem.

'Why'd they let him out?' he asked, then, already blaming the police for this. 'He should still be in prison. You think he told them what they wanted to hear?'

Nelson shrugged. 'Dunno. They bailed him, didn't they. Said he was young, first-timer. His mum went down to get him.' He cleared his throat.

'She was in a right state. Said he had to visit his sister in hospital.'

Devil remembered the look on his own mother's face when she found out about Leona. He hadn't recognised her; it was like she'd turned into an animal or something.

He shrugged. 'Who cares.' He turned away quickly. He felt claustrophobic, sick, he needed to be on his own to punch a wall, to punch someone. 'Anyway, we don't have to worry no more about him squealing,' Devil said gruffly. 'Right?'

'Right,' Nelson replied, but Devil could tell things weren't right. They weren't right at all.

'This don't change nothing,' he said, turning to look at Nelson. His eyes were more clouded than normal. Devil scrutinised his face closely. 'This ain't our fault. This is nothing to do with us, right?' he said. Nelson nodded but Devil could see his heart wasn't in it. 'The boy was weak, Nelson,' Devil said quickly. 'He couldn't cope with life. Not like us. We can cope. We're the strong ones. We're going places, doing things. We got the world stretching out in front of us, right? Right?'

Nelson nodded again. 'Stretching out in front of us,' he repeated.

Devil patted him on the back. 'You did the right thing,' he said, 'letting me know.'

'We gonna just leave him there?'

Devil considered this, considered the alternative: telling the boy's mother, calling the police. 'Yeah. We need to get away from here. They find us here, they'll try and make out like it wasn't an accident. You go home. Get some sleep. We'll talk later, yeah?'

'Yeah,' Nelson said, shoving his hands into his pockets. 'I'll catch you later.'

Nelson walked off; Devil knew he had to do the same, but he couldn't. Not yet. He couldn't take his eyes off the boy. It was like he'd landed in a pot of paint. Funny that blood was so red, Devil found himself thinking. When it was hidden. Mostly colours were for a reason. His mum had taught him that, back in Hertfordshire when she didn't have to work, when all she had to do was stay at home, make them food, tell them stuff. She'd smiled a lot back then, kissed him on the head for no reason. 'See that flower?' she'd tell him. 'It's so bright because it wants to attract bees to it. See?'

She'd loved bright stuff. House was full of it. Plates with flowers all over them, pictures on the walls, even their sofa was bright pink. His dad had had a fit first time he'd seen it; for a moment everything had gone quiet when it looked like he was going to have one of his explosive rages. But then he'd seen the funny side, told her it would be a talking point, told her not to worry, that it was okay.

Now they had a shitty brown sofa that was stained and uncomfortable.

Now she never talked about nothing; just sat and stared into the distance, not noticing if he was even alive.

She wasn't a winner. She was a loser. She'd lost Leona, lost his dad. Lost herself, too.

Devil forced himself away from the balcony walkway that allowed access to the flats, and back into the tiny room his mum called the sitting room, even though no one round here knew what that meant. It was the lounge, the living room, the place they sat on the sofa to eat tinned spaghetti on toast – and that was on the days that she could be bothered to put some kind of meal together. Devil found his mum lying on the sofa, her eyes surrounded by dark shadows. Even asleep she looked knackered. She always slept there; Devil got the bedroom. She'd told him when they moved in that he and Leona needed a room of their own.

He'd still loved her then. Still seen them as a unit, a team who could carry on even if Dad was gone.

But that was a long, long time ago.

Now there was just the two of them. But really there was just one. His mum had packed up and left the day they found Leona; she just hadn't had the guts to do it physically.

Devil took one look at her and knew he couldn't stay here. He couldn't go back to sleep now. He needed to walk, needed to burn off some energy. People killing themselves was a shit start to a day whatever way you looked at it. Things would be buzzing soon, with police and ambulances, questions and inferences. Best to get away now, before it started. Best to get some air before the fog descended.

15

Raffy wrapped his arms around himself and shivered slightly, but he knew it wasn't the cold that was bringing up goosebumps on his arms and neck. He wanted to leave, wanted to walk away; wanted to be the sort of person who could walk away. But he wasn't. And so he sat, cramped, surrounded by branches, shivering as he watched Evie learn about literature.

He hated Neil.

Hated him because he was handsome, clever, kind. Hated him because he was a good man, because Raffy knew that he was only interested in helping Evie. Hated him because Raffy was not a good person, would never be. Rationally, he saw the world as it was. But rationality did not control his mind, not all the time. Because sometimes the demons got in, changed the lens through which he saw the world, distorted things, made them look very different, very scary. They showed Evie looking up at Neil with a rapturous smile, laughing at his witty jokes. They thought they saw something in her eye, something that used to be there when she looked at Raffy. Love. She was in love with Neil. She would leave Raffy for Neil. Neil was just waiting for the right moment to seduce her, and she would let it happen, willingly, laughing at how foolish and young Raffy was. And Raffy would be alone, more alone than he'd ever been in his life, alone and miserable and lonely and—

A sound broke the silence; an acorn falling from the tree, dislodged by Raffy who had moved too suddenly. He froze. Evie glanced over, so did Neil, but then they were back to books, discussing female emancipation, the development of the female lead, the opportunities open to her as the twenty-first century went on.

Evie was so beautiful. So, so beautiful. She always had been. Raffy remembered seeing her for the first time when he was nearly six. She'd been tiny, wary, her dark eyes staring uncertainly at the other children as they were led into the classroom, shown where to sit, what to do. She didn't mix well with the others; like Raffy, there had been something different about her, something that separated her from the other children. That's how they'd found each other, what they had recognised in each other. And the first time he'd seen her smile, the first time he remembered her face breaking out into a broad, toothy grin because of him, because of something he'd said to her, he remembered thinking that he never wanted anyone else to ever make her smile like that. He'd been a young child at the time, but even then he'd known that he never wanted to lose her, had known that he inevitably would.

Because he wasn't a good man, like Neil.

Because he wasn't perfect, like Lucas.

Like Lucas.

Raffy breathed out, closed his eyes. His older brother. All his life, Raffy had lived in Lucas's shadow, and even now he felt it blocking out his sun. Because Lucas was better than him. More noble, more generous. He had seen the way Evie had been with him, in the City, the night that they had shut down the System. He knew her better than she knew herself; he had seen the furtive glances, the change in energy whenever the two of them were together. And he also knew that Lucas had stayed behind in the City partly so that Raffy and Evie could be together, with no complications. A selfless act, just like the whole of Lucas's life.

And that's why he hated him. Because Raffy wouldn't have been so noble. Because he didn't want Lucas's generosity. He wanted Evie. Wanted to keep her so close to him she'd never see another person, let alone talk to them, smile at them. He wanted her for himself; selfishly, possessively. He wanted it to be like it was in the tree, when they used to meet at night. Back then, the rest of their lives might have been intolerable, but Raffy hadn't cared because in those moments when he was with Evie, he knew that she needed him, that it was just them, against the world, so close they could finish each other's sentences. The City had oppressed them, had oppressed everyone, but Raffy hadn't cared, not really, because it had pushed them closer together. He'd spend his life in prison if he could be sure he'd be sharing a cell with Evie.

And Evie . . .

Raffy looked down at her, talking animatedly, her hands waving around, her eyes dancing.

Evie wanted to be free. Of everything.

Including him.

He knew that. Saw it in her eyes. She had been imprisoned so long in the City, had felt so restricted, so unhappy. And now, now she was soaring into the sky, now she was smiling every day.

Raffy's biggest fears were being realised; soon, very soon, Evie was going to see Raffy for what he really was, and then she would leave him.

Soon she was going to see that she didn't need

him. She was going to realise that actually, she never did.

'Well, I should let you get back,' Neil smiled. 'Next week I'm going to introduce you to *Frankenstein*. A man-made monster. I think hailing from the City you might find it quite pertinent.'

Evie stood up. 'Thank you,' she said, earnestly. 'I just can't tell you how amazing it is to . . . to . . .'

'To realise how much there is out there? How many brilliant people have written such incredible things, had such extraordinary ideas and the courage of their convictions to publish them?'

Evie nodded happily; Neil always managed to put into words thoughts that in her head were jumbled, desperately seeking articulation.

Neil shrugged. 'I just wish we had more books here. They weren't really a priority. In the fight for survival, I mean. Short-sighted idiots putting food and water above the written word.' He grinned. 'Still, we've got enough. And who knows? Maybe one day someone will arrive here with an entire library of books that they've buried underground. You never know, right?'

'Right,' Evie said, her eyes twinkling. It had taken her a while to relax in Neil's company, to understand his constant use of irony, to realise that when he got excited and asked her question after question, it wasn't because she'd got it wrong, or because he was frustrated with her, but because he was as thrilled as she was about finding the answer. And now she loved spending time with him, enjoyed nothing more than discussing the finer points of one of the books she'd read, finding something to disagree with him on so that they could argue happily for hours.

'So, next week,' Neil waved and ambled off towards the centre of the Settlement where he would sit in the square and share a drink with friends. Evie knew this because he had invited her along several times, telling her to bring Raffy, that they would both be very welcome. But she'd said no. Because she'd known what Raffy would say and hadn't wanted to have the argument, hadn't wanted to feel the inevitable disappointment when he confirmed her fears and refused to go, refused to let her go without him.

Maybe when they were married it would be different, she told herself.

Maybe when they were married he would finally believe that he had her, that she wasn't going anywhere, that she loved him.

She started to make her way home. She did love him. Had always loved him. And yet . . . And yet. She sighed. Then she heard something and stopped. A sound in the tree above. A bird? Bigger than that. She peered up into the branches, not sure what she was looking for, but not feeling in any great hurry to rush home. And then, as she met Raffy's eyes, her mouth fell open. She watched him flush, jump down, run towards her, his arms reaching out.

'Evie!' He half-smiled, then the smile disappeared and she could see the fear in his eyes; then he tried to downplay it. 'Evie, come on. I was just . . . just . . .'

She stared at him, her brain trying to compute what had happened, what was happening. 'How . . . how long were you up there?'

Raffy bit his lip.

'How long?' Evie demanded.

Raffy shrugged uncomfortably. 'I just . . . I was interested. In what you were learning.'

'Really?' Evie folded her arms. 'Then what were we discussing today? Which book? What did you learn?'

Raffy opened his mouth but no words came out.

'Tell me, Raffy. What did you learn today?'

Again she was met by silence. Raffy's eyes had now turned thunderous as they always did when he felt cornered. Usually she would hold his hand, soothe him, reassure him, talk him out of his anger. She had done exactly that so many times since they'd arrived here. But not now. Right now, Evie had no interest in reassuring Raffy. He had stepped over a line; she was shaking with anger.

'You used to hate the System,' she said, her voice low. 'And now you are acting like it. You would keep me at home every day, just as my fake parents did. But you can't, Raffy. I won't let you.'

She turned, tears pricking at her eyes, tears that she didn't want Raffy to see because he would rush to comfort her and she didn't want comforting, not by him. She wanted him to trust her, to let her live.

'Where are you going?' Raffy called after her. 'Where are you going?'

His voice was anguished; she knew that he would be staring after her, desperate, miserable. But still she walked. Because this was his fault. Because he had to learn. Because if she stayed it would be worse. Because if she didn't keep walking until she was far away from Raffy, she might say something that she would regret.

16

Lucas tried his best to enjoy the tea and cake that Linus had put in front of him, tried to resist his urge to stand up, pace around impatiently. He had learnt with Linus that there was no use rushing. And so, instead, he simply told Linus everything he knew. Linus listened carefully.

Eventually, when Lucas had finished, Linus looked up.

'I knew we should have killed that bastard.'

Lucas grimaced. 'The Brother?'

Linus nodded. 'Who else?'

'So what do you know about the Informers?' Lucas asked. 'Who are they? Why are they so interested in the System?'

Linus raised an eyebrow, etching lines into his forehead. He had a weather-beaten face, a face that had lived, Lucas found himself thinking. Eyes surrounded by lines, which deepened when he smiled, joining one another so that they appeared to flow back and forth across his features in ever decreasing circles. 'That is the question,' he said.

Lucas tried to contain his disappointment that the months Linus had been holed up here, apparently monitoring the Informers and trying to track them, gave him apparently no insight into what they were doing in the City. But going on the attack would be pointless. He had to trust Martha that Linus knew what he was doing; trust his father that Linus was someone to believe in. But he still had to make sure that Linus really understood what was happening.

'The City's unrecognisable,' he said, his voice low. 'Families are roaming the streets after dark to find whoever's doing this. And they blame me for dismantling the System. I'm beginning to blame myself. I haven't protected them. If the System was up and running . . .'

'Stop being self-indulgent,' Linus said dismissively. 'The System isn't your problem. What we have here are some bad guys doing bad things. Forget worrying about your leadership and instead let's work out how to find them, how to stop them, and how to make them pay for what they've done. Sound good?'

He was looking Lucas right in the eye; Lucas nodded. It was no use trying to manipulate Linus. It was like trying to manipulate a wall.

'Okay then,' Linus said. 'Funny how it seems that the good guys always look to blame themselves and the bad guys always absolve themselves of any guilt.'

Lucas looked at him uncertainly. Linus grinned. 'I'm saying you're a good guy,' he said with a wink. 'You should take that as a compliment.'

'Right,' Lucas said, not sure what else to say. He wasn't great with compliments. Preferred giving them to receiving them, and he wasn't even that great at giving them.

'So, seven dead and Clara is the missing one, the one they'll be looking for,' Linus was muttering. 'Okay, I think it's time to pay them a little visit.'

Linus stood up; Lucas watched him.

'So?' Linus said impatiently, bearing down on Lucas suddenly. He was a big man, towering over him. Lucas was tall – over six foot and broad at the shoulders. But Linus . . . Lucas had never noticed his size before, never noticed that he was built like a warrior. With his long hair and beard he looked utterly terrifying.

'So what?' Lucas asked, managing to keep his voice level.

'So let's go.'

Lucas started. 'Now? Where?'

'To the camp, of course. Come on,' Linus said impatiently.

Lucas's brow furrowed further. 'You're not going to pack? You don't think we should make a plan? Think about this a bit? You don't think you should shave?'

Linus stared at him incredulously. Then, like the sun coming out from behind a cloud, his face broke into a smile. He laughed. 'You might have a point with the beard and the hair. Bit unwieldy. Okay, I'll go trim up and you get yourself ready to go.'

He disappeared into the corner of the cave; Lucas heard a tap being run, then the buzz of an electric razor. He only knew about electric razors because his father had had one, saved from the days before the Horrors. 'Only three of these in the City,' he'd told Lucas proudly. It had been one of the things that disappeared in the days after his father was taken. Lucas often wondered if the Brother now had the razor, if he ever thought of Lucas's father when he trimmed his own beard.

Ten minutes later, Linus reappeared, his beard gone, his hair back to how Lucas remembered it: closely shaved, his growing bald patch rather less glaring.

'This way,' he said, walking to the other side of the cave to where Lucas had come in. 'Climb up here.'

Lucas followed him up to a slight platform that led to a tunnel; they quickly reached a fork. 'And here,' Linus said, 'we turn right. Always right.'

'What's left?' Lucas asked.

'Try it one day,' Linus shrugged. 'Then you'll know why we always turn right.'

Lucas peered down the left fork; it sloped downwards at quite an angle and its floor was smooth, slippery, like stone. One false step and Lucas imagined you'd disappear.

'Right then,' he said with a little shrug, following Linus. 'So we're going to a camp in an area of England that apparently no longer exists? With no clear idea of what we're going to do when we get there?'

'Pretty much,' Linus nodded.

'I see,' Lucas said. 'Just checking. You lead the way.'

'So how are we getting to the coast? It's miles away,' Lucas asked Linus as they clambered down a sharp rock face to the ground below. They were on the other side of the hill from where Lucas had entered Linus's new lair. Having crawled through a tunnel for what had felt like hours, they now, finally, were in the open air again.

Linus shot him another infuriating smile. 'This way,' he said, winking as he dropped down to the ground below. Lucas followed suit; Linus had already started walking anticlockwise around the hill and he had to jog to catch up. 'I wish you'd just tell me,' he said.

'But where would the fun be in that?' Linus asked, his face crinkling before he turned ahead and started to walk again.

With a sigh, Lucas followed. He found himself staring at Linus's back as they walked, marvelling at the muscle, at the deep tan that seemed to cover him in spite of living in a cave for several months. He padded like an animal hunting, his eyes and ears on full alert. Lucas recognised in Linus what he had learnt himself, a state of constant awareness, constant readiness for fight or flight. Lucas suspected that Linus could predict what was going to happen way before those who carried out the actions did. Maybe he'd even known that Lucas would be coming; maybe that's why he had shown no surprise.

Finally, Linus stopped. He was in the mouth of another cave. Lucas looked at him curiously. 'We're still no closer to the coast,' he said.

'No,' Linus agreed. 'But this is certainly going to help us get there.'

He entered the cave and took out a torch, shining it into the back. Lucas saw something, a reflection of some sort, but it was only as they drew closer that he realised what it was. Something he'd never seen before. Something he'd only heard about, imagined, seen drawings of.

'It's a car,' he said, mouth open as he walked around it, touching it, getting a huge adrenalin rush as he felt its shiny surface and took in its gleaming body. This was nothing like the trucks used outside the City by Wall patrol, or the ageing vehicles resting at Base Camp. It was shiny, new-looking, a vehicle designed for pleasure, not practicality. 'It's a real car.'

'Not just any old car either,' Linus grinned, evidently enjoying Lucas's reaction. 'This is the cream of the crop. Worth a pretty penny in its day. Worth more to me now, though.'

He pressed his hand to one of the doors and the locks clicked off. 'Get in,' he said, pointing to the passenger seat.

'But how will you . . . do you have petrol?'

'Full tank of gas,' Linus said. 'And I've got myself a whole lot more right here. Only use it for emergencies, of course. But I think what we have here would be termed an emergency, wouldn't you say?'

Lucas nodded; he was too awed to speak. Instead he opened the passenger door and got inside, sighing involuntarily with pleasure as he eased into the soft, cream leather.

'How did you . . . I mean, how long have you . . . How is this possible?' he breathed.

'I found it,' Linus said, as he started up the engine. 'Beautiful, isn't she? She'd been abandoned. I found her with the keys still in the ignition as if she'd been left there just for me. Now, it's been a while since I've driven, I'm afraid, and I don't want to scrape the old girl. So if you'll just let me concentrate . . .'

Lucas nodded and slowly the car crept backwards towards the cave opening, then reversed around the corner. Linus moved a lever, shot Lucas another smile, and put his foot down. 'Enjoy the ride,' he said as they sped off, the car appearing to glide over the rocks that were strewn all around. 'Welcome to travelling Mercedes-style.'

17

'You killed my son! You killed my baby boy! You want to kill me too? Do it! Do it now and kill my baby too. You are an evil boy. You will burn in hell for what you've done. You will . . .'

Devil turned, walked, jogged, ran. He knew it was a mistake to come back to the estate. He'd been away all morning, waited for everything to be dealt with, cleared away, had thought by four o'clock he'd be safe to come back. But she was waiting for him. Waiting right in the spot her stupid son had jumped off the balcony.

'I told him he was evil,' the boy's mother screamed after him. 'I told him it was all his fault. That's why he killed himself. But it wasn't his fault. It was your fault. God will find you and he will punish you, and—'

Devil was out of breath but he kept running like his life depended on it. She was crazy. He had to get away. Far away. He hated this shit hole. Hated his dad for leaving, for making them move here. He shouldn't even be here. None of this should have happened.

He passed some of his crew but he didn't stop. He couldn't be dealing with them right now either. He couldn't be dealing with none of it.

He ran down the steps, across the playground, and through the tunnel. He exhaled heavily as he came out of it, just like he always did, but usually it was because he'd held his breath for all the time it took him to run through it, protecting himself from the stench, whereas this time he hadn't had that luxury. Man, he was out of breath. He needed to get fitter. Needed to do a lot of things. He breathed in several times, put his hands on his knees, then stood up and started to walk around the corner, onto the main road, across onto a long lane that led into town. His usual walk. And then he stopped. Because in front of him was a car. A car he didn't know. A car that did not belong, that stood out like a beacon.

It was a nice car. Very nice.

And it was empty.

Which meant its owner was either very stupid, or so powerful he didn't have to worry about where he parked it.

He looked around then approached cautiously, checking out the plates. Only two years old. Looked after. Silver, alloy wheels, tinted windows. He held his hand out tentatively, touched the bonnet; no alarm. He stroked it appreciatively for a second or two, then walked round to the driver's seat. Whoever had left this car was now in the estate. They had money. They had class. But what else? This was a gangster's car.

An empty gangster's car.

Carefully, Devil took out his pocket knife. He could get into any car; it was the first thing he learnt. No one was around; no one would see him. He could almost smell the leather, the wealth. Like his dad's car. Large, soft leather seats, the gentle clunk of the heavy doors. He wanted this car. He wanted it so bad he could scream. This was the car he deserved. This car would tell the world who they were dealing with.

But he put his knife back in his pocket. You didn't mess with a car like this without there being consequences, complications. And Devil didn't need that kind of attention right now.

Instead, he just stood next to it, imagining the sound of the doors clunking, the feeling of the soft leather, the smell, the purr of the engine. One day, he thought to himself. One day . . .

And that's when he felt the metal against the back of his neck. 'Like my car? You should get in.'

He didn't dare turn around. He didn't have to. A large man with a thickset head appeared next to him and opened the car door.

'Fancy a ride?' said the man holding the gun.

Devil didn't say anything. You didn't mess with guns. Maybe this was it for him. Maybe the Green Lanes Massive had friends he hadn't banked on. He closed his eyes, said a quick prayer, then got in.

There were four men in total. Two on either side of him, big blokes, not to be messed with, one driving, and the one with the gun was in the front next to the driver. He was the one that Devil had his eyes trained on, watching him, studying him, taking in every detail. He'd thought he was quite old, at first. He was bald, for starters, looked like he was losing his hair, But now, looking at him, he could see that he wasn't. Close up, it was clear that he wasn't that much older than Devil, in fact. Other than that his face didn't give that much away.

Devil watched him anyway, watched his hands, watched his chin, in case he gave something away, something that Devil could use. 'People always give themselves up,' his dad used to say. 'You learn to read people, you'll have them at your feet.'

He wasn't scared, not yet. No one was saying anything, and Devil was happy to wait. They were driving, the quiet hum of the car making him feel sleepy as they sped along the roads, the car barely registering the various pot holes it encountered.

His father's car had been a Lexus. The one he'd had in Hertfordshire anyway. It was only after he'd gone, only when the police came round asking questions, that he'd discovered that Hertfordshire was only one of his father's lives, that Pastor Jones was just one of his aliases, that the Church of Good Faith was only one of his little empires. Did he drive a Lexus in his other hometowns, Devil had found himself wondering. Hoping, actually. Hoping that he knew something real about the man who was his father, about the man who had run away, who had turned out to be not at all the person that Devil thought he'd known. He liked to drive a Lexus. That was something. Without that, he had nothing.

The first time his dad had beaten him had been because of the Lexus. Devil had been four, had been so excited because he'd been allowed to go to church in it, sitting in the back seat like a grown up, like his father. And he hadn't wanted to ruin it, hadn't wanted to risk being ejected, so when he'd got the urge to pee, he hadn't said anything, had held it in, had waited. But he hadn't banked on his father getting a phone call, getting angry, shouting down the phone for what felt like hours until Devil couldn't hold it in any more, until he'd pissed himself right there on the leather seat.

And years later, when his dad had finally agreed to let him in the car again, it had been in the Lexus that his father had delivered his private sermons, the lessons that Devil remembered to this day, that gave him his identity, that gave him purpose. 'Son, there are two kinds of people in this world – the haves, and the have-nots. The leaders and the followers. The brave and the weak. The winners and the losers. The people in my church, they're the losers. They need me.

They need to be told how to tie their shoes, when to eat, when to shit and when to pray. That's what I give them, son. That's why they give me their money. I give them direction. I give them what they need. And that's why I have this car. I deserve it. Not God. Me. God doesn't do anything for anyone, that's the truth. And you can sit in here with me, you can enjoy the ride, but it's not your car, it's mine. If you want a car like this for yourself, then you need to be one of the haves, one of the winners. Do you understand?'

Devil had been ten the first time he'd heard that little speech, his father's deep Nigerian accent beating into his soul. And he'd heard him. He'd heard him loud and clear.

'So then,' his father had said, smiling. 'That's our little secret, eh boy? I have a lot to teach you, son. And you have a lot to learn. You listen to me and I will teach you. But you breathe a word of what I say to anyone else, and you will know pain like no other. Do I make myself clear?'

Devil had nodded, just as he nodded every time his father said exactly the same thing. But true to his word, he didn't tell anyone, and eventually his father stopped the threats; stuck instead to the lessons. But he always returned to the car. 'Cars maketh the man' was one of his favourite catchphrases.

It was the day after his father had delivered the lesson for the forty-second time that the police had come and taken the car, taken the house. They'd wanted to take his father too, but he'd already gone in the night, to one of his other homes, one of his other lives.

And a few days later, when Devil and his family were 'relocated' to the estate, he had realised that his father had been right about everything. He was always ahead of everyone else. That's what you had to be in life: ahead of everyone else, in the driving seat, not held back by anything or anyone. They never found his dad or the money; it had gone with him to wherever he'd escaped to. Turned out the house was rented; turned out the car was on HP. Turned out even his mother's marriage certificate wasn't real.

Devil sat forward. All that was in the past now. All that was irrelevant. I-re-le-vant. This week's word. Meant that it didn't mean nothing. It reassured him. Nothing meant nothing. Leona used to mean something, but she wasn't there no more with her little voice chatting away in the background, those dolls she used to carry around everywhere she went. She was gone.

And Devil told himself it was a good thing. She'd been his weak spot. He'd have done anything to protect Leona, kill anyone who came close to her. And look where that had got them. You couldn't kill an accident. You could only blame the person who left the window open. You could only walk away and promise yourself that you'd never care about anyone again ever in your whole life because it hurt too bad, because it made you feel like your insides were going to explode.

He took a deep breath. 'So where are we going?' he asked.

The man turned round to look at him. He smiled. 'Let's not spoil the mystery shall we, Devil?'

Devil's eyes narrowed. 'And how do you know my name?'

'Oh I know a lot of things about you, Devil,' the man said, turning back to face the front as the men either side of him forced him back against the seat. 'But let's not worry about that now, shall we? I like to listen to music when I drive, if it's all the same with you. And we're nearly there. You'll get the answers you want soon enough. My name is Thomas, by the way. It's good to meet you finally.'

Devil opened his mouth to speak but changed his mind. There was no point. He knew that. So instead, he said nothing as Thomas pressed a button and the car was filled with loud music. Whatever this guy wanted, he'd turn it to his advantage. That's what it was to be strong. That's what it was to become a winner.

18

Raffy stormed towards the centre of the Settlement, not sure where he was going, but seething with anger, resentment and frustration. Because she just didn't get it. It was fine for her; coming here, embracing everything. Everyone loved Evie. Everyone had always loved Evie and everyone always would. People were drawn to her, people wanted to be around her. People like Neil. Like Lucas. Like everyone.

And they all wanted to take her away from him. From Raffy. Raffy, who no one liked, who no one loved. His own mother had barely looked him in the eye for most of his life and his brother had kept a watchful eye in case he stepped out of line. In the City, people had always regarded him with suspicion and whispered when he walked past. And he didn't care, had never cared. But that was only because he'd had Evie.

He knew he was being irrational. He knew he shouldn't have been spying on her. But she was too trusting; she didn't see people for who they really were. She needed Raffy to protect her. It hadn't been that long ago they'd been running for their lives; he couldn't just switch that off, not like Evie could.

He pushed past a table. He was in the centre of the Settlement now, where little tables and chairs had been set out for people to talk, play card games or enjoy a drink of beer made by some of the farmers. Most of the farmers came here two or three evenings a week, to blow off steam, to relax, to talk. And although Raffy had been invited many times, he had never been; having spent the day away from Evie he had always wanted to rush back to her, to be with her, to have her all to himself. And anyway, he wasn't interested in beer; he had tried it once and it tasted vile. Now, looking around, he decided that perhaps a beer wouldn't be such a bad idea; perhaps a beer was just what he needed.

As he was about to sit down, Simon, a farmer who had taken Raffy under his wing and become something of a mentor to him, came over. 'Raffy! You've come at last!' He grinned. 'I knew you'd be tempted eventually. Come on, join us.'

Raffy looked at the group – there were ten or so of them, all men he worked with, all men he liked.

He nodded and walked over with Simon, and immediately a tankard was placed in front of him.

He took a sip, but Simon shook his head. 'If you drink, you drink like a man,' he said with a wink. Raffy lifted the tankard again and downed it, nearly choking on the musty liquid as it went down his throat, reminding him of the swamps by the City gate that had flooded his mouth and nose when he and Evie had escaped.

'That's more like it,' Simon said cheerily, pouring him another. 'So where's that lovely girl of yours? Left her at home have you?'

Raffy stared at him angrily, then forced himself to nod. Simon didn't mean anything by it, he knew that. He was a kindly man, thickset, large-boned; a man whose strength had astounded Raffy when he'd seen him on the field, a man whose face was always crumpled into a grin, the lines around his eyes etched from smiling. His wife, Marion, was half his size but equally cheerful; they had five children who could often be seen running around the Settlement causing mayhem, their father smiling benignly and only getting angry if their behaviour veered towards being rude or thoughtless.

'She's reading,' he said, not meeting Simon's eyes. It wasn't a lie – at least it might not be – but it wasn't the truth either.

'Reading,' Simon nodded thoughtfully. Then he

shrugged. 'Never had much time for books myself. But it's a noble way to spend an evening. Unlike us, eh, gentlemen?'

The men laughed and drank more beer; Raffy could feel his head becoming woozy as the alcohol took its effect, felt himself smiling and laughing even though nothing particularly funny was being said. Perhaps he should have done this before, he found himself thinking. Perhaps he should have come out with these men instead of staying at home watching Evie, or pacing around waiting for her to return.

But the moment he entertained that thought, he felt the familiar clench in his stomach as he pictured her, alone and vulnerable. He imagined Neil or some other man dropping in to say hello, imagined them looking at her, thinking that they were worthy of her, thinking that the smile she gave them meant something, meant anything . . .

He closed his eyes, and all he could see was the look of anger on Evie's face when she'd discovered him spying on her. He'd never seen her look at him like that, so furious, so disappointed.

He stood up. 'I have to go,' he said, pushing the table and causing several drinks to spill.

Simon looked at him strangely. 'Easy, Raffy. What's the rush?'

'I have to go,' Raffy insisted. 'I have to get back to Evie.'

'I'm sure she's okay,' Simon said, his voice gentle but firm. 'I'm sure she won't mind if you have a drink or two.'

'She won't mind,' Raffy said. 'But I do. I need to get back to her. I need to . . .' He pushed his chair back, staggering away from the table. He could hear Simon calling after him but he didn't turn back. He had to get to Evie. He had to apologise. Had to make her see why he'd been watching her, make her understand that he was only doing it for her. Because he loved her. Because he needed her. Because she needed him.

And then he stopped. Right in front of him was the man who had caused all this, the man whose fault it was that Evie was angry.

'Neil.' He propped himself up on the table that the teacher was sitting at. 'Neil. Enjoying a beer, are we?'

Neil was sitting with a small group of men and women with earnest faces. They all stopped talking and looked up at Raffy. Neil smiled. 'Raffy,' he said warmly. 'How nice to see you. Are you well?'

Raffy's eyes narrowed. 'Well? No, not really. But don't you worry about me. You don't usually worry about me, do you Neil?'

Neil frowned. 'I'm sorry, Raffy, is something the matter?'

Raffy gripped the table. Then he leant down so that his face was just inches from Neil's. 'You leave Evie alone, do you hear me?' he snarled. 'You stay away from her. Or you'll regret it.'

Neil didn't flinch. 'If by "stay away", you mean "cease teaching", I'm afraid I can't do that, Raffy. So long as Evie wants to learn and gets something out of our discussions then I am at her disposal. Just as I am at anyone else's disposal. Yours, if you'd be interested. I could—'

But before he could finish, Raffy had grabbed him by the scruff of the neck and forced him to the floor, knocking his chair over in the process. Then he was on top of Neil, hitting him, shaking him, shouting at him, until several other men grabbed him, pulled him off, held him back.

Raffy didn't know how long he was restrained, shouting at Neil, his legs kicking out furiously. But he did notice things going quiet all of a sudden; did notice the atmosphere change as someone walked towards him.

'Let him go,' he heard Benjamin say, his voice quiet but firm. 'Raffy, come with me, please. I think we need to have a little chat, don't you?'

19

The ride was bumpy; not because of the car, Linus was keen to point out, but because of the roads. Or rather, the lack of roads. 'This beast was not made to drive off-road,' he told Lucas, stroking the steering wheel appreciatively. 'Rocks she can handle, but not craters and cracks like this. She's meant for a more civilised place.'

Lucas looked at him quizzically. 'So the old world was civilised?' he asked.

Linus shrugged. 'Some of it was very uncivilised,' he said. 'But it had its moments. And it had roads. Lovely, long, smooth roads.'

Lucas digested this as they flew over boulders and rocks, then turned to look out of the window. The landscape was desolate, just as he'd been told it would be; there were no green fields or pastures to be seen, no evidence of farming or production or houses. It was as though the City had nothing to do with its surrounding landscape; as though it existed in its own micro-environment, the large high wall keeping not only people out, but also the rest of the world too.

As Lucas watched the world speed by he realised how little he knew of the land outside the City walls, of the people who lived there. He had spent his formative years believing everything he'd been told about the Evils who roamed outside the City walls, about the death and destruction that they would invoke given half a chance. He had believed that humans were capable of such extreme evil that only by removing their amygdalas could they be safe, from each other, from themselves.

And then his father had told him the truth, had explained, patiently but hurriedly, that things were not as he'd thought, that the Brother had lied to his people, that Lucas had to be brave, had to make him a promise, had to be stronger than he ever thought possible.

Lucas had done as he'd asked; he had learnt how to navigate the System, had learnt how to ensure that the Brother noticed him, trusted him; he had given his father up as a traitor, and he had allowed his brother to grow up hating him. And all the time, he'd taken comfort from the fact that he knew, that he understood what was really going on.

But here, now, driving through landscape he'd never set eyes on before, Lucas realised he knew nothing.

'People live here?' he asked eventually.

Linus shook his head. 'Not here. No water here. City's seen to that. But there are places that are more habitable. The settlement where your brother is, for instance.'

Lucas held his breath.

'They're in the North,' Linus continued conversationally. 'About three hundred miles away.'

'Right,' Lucas said, trying to keep his voice level. 'I see.'

'Nice girl, that Evie,' Linus observed.

Lucas looked at him sharply, but Linus was staring straight ahead at the road, his expression giving nothing away. 'You want to hear some music?' Linus asked.

Lucas didn't say anything; Linus reached into a pocket on the side of the car door and brought out a thin metal disk which he inserted into a slot near the steering wheel. Moments later the car was full of loud, jangling music that caught Lucas by surprise; he lurched backwards, causing Linus to laugh out loud.

'Now this,' he said, a grin on his face, 'is the way to travel. This is what I like to remember about the bad old days.'

He tapped his fingers on the steering wheel as he

drove; Lucas sat back, letting the strange sounds wash over him. A beat, a jangling tune that somehow made him want to smile, made him want to jump up and dance.

'Yeah, the bad old days, they had their moments,' Linus said. Then he took his eyes off the road and turned to look at Lucas. 'You know, truth was, they weren't the bad old days at all. Not really. The Horrors weren't good, but before that? It was better than now, that's for sure.'

Lucas opened his mouth to respond, then changed his mind. The music was too loud, the car too jumpy; he couldn't think properly, and anyway, there was no point asking Linus to elaborate. Linus would drip information to him as he saw fit, in his usual frustrating way. To ask questions would just be to engage in his irritating game. Far better just to nod.

And so they drove, darkness descending as they sped through the landscape until Lucas felt his eyelids grow heavy, until they wouldn't stay open any more, until sleep enveloped him.

And then, with a start, he woke up and groaned. 'Stop the car. I'm going to be sick,' he said, leaning forward and clutching at the door handle.

Linus laughed. 'Got yourself some motion sickness there,' he said. 'It'll pass. Go back to sleep.'

Lucas closed his eyes then opened them again quickly when he realised it made things ten times worse. 'It isn't passing. Please stop,' he begged, clutching his stomach.

'Soon,' Linus said reassuringly. 'In about five minutes.'

'You'd better not be lying,' Lucas asked miserably. 'Because if you don't stop very soon I'm going to throw up all over your precious car . . .'

'See those lights?' Linus cut in, as though Lucas wasn't even talking. Lucas looked into the darkness, straining his eyes. He hadn't noticed any lights; had seen only black around the car as it trundled over the bumps and stones. He'd been wondering how Linus could have any idea where he was going, whether in fact Linus was taking him on a magical mystery tour that would lead only to yet another of his enigmatic smiles. But now, as he peered out of the window, he realised that Linus was right, that there were lights in the distance. Dim, tiny, but there.

'What is it? Another camp? Another city?'

Linus pulled a face; Lucas groaned inwardly and not just because of his lurching stomach. Trying to get information out of Linus was like conversing with a two-year-old. He sometimes wondered why his father had put so much faith in someone who was so incapable of normal conversation, who seemed to take great delight in making others feel foolish, out of step. He knew the only solution was to ignore Linus, to ask nothing of him, but he couldn't do that, partly because he wanted to know more, and party because talking was the only way of taking his mind off this terrible motion sickness.

'Well?' he asked, miserably, feeling like death, feeling even more humiliated by the fact that he felt so terrible. Lucas didn't do weakness; he did strength, he did silence, he protected, he fought. But now he had been floored by a vehicle and there was nothing he could do about it. 'Tell me. Is it the place that's disappeared from the map? Is this the Informers' camp?'

Linus's eyes were glistening in the moonlight. 'Part camp, part city,' he mused. 'Most interesting.'

They were close, Lucas realised with a jolt of relief. They'd be stopping soon. 'Do you have any weapons in this car?' he asked.

Linus grinned. 'Oh, we don't need weapons,' he said, his eyes twinkling. 'Not right now anyway.'

'You're sure about that?' Lucas asked uncertainly.

'We need information. You don't get that with weapons,' Linus said.

Lucas opened his mouth to ask a question, then decided against it and instead leant back in the seat and waited for the car to stop. It slowed right down and Linus started to drive towards what looked like a mountain of rock. As they approached, Lucas realised that there was an opening: Linus had chosen another cave for his car. They purred in, then he turned off the engine and they found themselves in total darkness. Seconds later, Linus brought out a torch and got out.

Lucas followed. The ground was rocky. Tentatively, he followed Linus out to the mouth of the cave, gratefully breathing in fresh air.

'Let's find out what they're up to, shall we?' Linus said, and upped his pace. Lucas nodded and followed him.

They walked for about half an hour in total silence. And then, without warning, Linus stopped, causing Lucas to almost bump into him.

'What?' he whispered.

'There,' Linus said, pointing to a pile of rocks. 'We can watch them from here.'

Silently he moved towards the rocks then began to climb up. 'You coming?'

Lucas hesitated. The lights were brighter. He reckoned the camp, or whatever it was, was about half a mile away. Even from here he could tell it was huge, far bigger than anything Lucas had imagined. It was made up of a cluster of large low buildings in the centre, surrounded by hundreds of smaller ones surrounding them.

'Pre-fab,' Linus said knowledgeably. 'Impermanent structures, but they'll have taken a while to build. These people are serious.'

'Serious about what?' Lucas asked.

'That's the question,' Linus shrugged. 'And what I think we have established is that we're not going to get anywhere watching them from these hills. We need to get inside.'

'With no weapons? You got any ideas?' Lucas asked.

'I've got one,' Linus said, a little glint in his eye. 'But you might not like it.'

'Try me,' Lucas said drily.

'Well,' Linus said thoughtfully. 'If we're found in there, we die. But if they bring one of us in . . .'

'As a prisoner?' Lucas frowned.

'Not quite. Prisoners tend to get locked up, beaten, tortured. I don't know what they're like here but we know they're not afraid of killing people. No, I have another idea.'

'So, what is it?' Lucas said impatiently.

Linus looked thoughtful. 'It's risky but I think it might work,' he said. 'Go look over there. Over the edge of the hill. Tell me what you see.'

Lucas opened his mouth to tell Linus he could go and look for himself, then decided against it and started to climb.

'I can't see anything,' he said.

'Further up,' Linus called up to him, pointing towards the top of the rock. Lucas pulled himself up; it was only as he reached the very top that he realised, too late, that Linus was right behind him; too late for him to realise what was happening, too late to stop himself being thrown head first over the small cliff to the ground below.

20

'You like this music, Devil?' Thomas turned around, a half-smile on his face. He was not a handsome man, but there was steel in his eyes that told Devil he had authority. His eyes were close set, his hair cut short, but his wrist sported an expensive Swiss watch and his suit looked hand made.

Devil shrugged. 'I guess,' he said noncommittally. It wasn't his sort of music. Jangling guitars. The sort of thing played by white boys with long fringes. The sort of thing he might have listened to years ago. 'It's a new band. I think they're going to go a long way,' the man said, his fingers drumming on his thigh, his head nodding in rhythm. Then he grinned. 'Actually, I know they're going to go a long way, because I'm going to see that they do. You know the phrase "familiarity breeds contempt"?

It's bullshit. The more we hear something, the more we like it. I hated this music the first time I heard it but now I love it.'

Devil shrugged, a non-verbal 'whatever'. He pulled his hood over his head. He didn't really know what Thomas was talking about and so he did what he always did when he wasn't sure about something and ignored him. 'Ignorance is failure,' his father used to say. 'Ignorance is weakness. And if you're weak, the strong will walk all over you. You have to be one step ahead. You have to see what's coming. You have to be educated, informed, so no one takes you for a ride, you understand, son?'

'You smoke that shit?' Thomas was looking at his cigarettes.

Devil's eyes narrowed defensively. 'They're no shit,' he retorted. 'Silk Cut. Genuine article.' They were the cigarettes his father had smoked. 'Middle-class cigarettes', his father had called them.

'They're all shit,' Thomas said. 'They pollute your insides. Kill you if they can. Nothing good about being an addict, Devil. Nothing at all.'

Devil looked at him insolently.

Thomas smiled. 'You're angry with me because you think I'm belittling you. Right?'

Devil didn't answer.

'Maybe I am,' Thomas shrugged. 'But if you have a habit like that you're asking for it. You're giving power to the cigarette manufacturers, letting them own you. People used to belittle me, but not any more. Now they wouldn't dare. I own my own destiny. I make my own destiny.'

Devil stared ahead, sullenly. He was angry, but he couldn't do anything about it. He'd take it out on someone later.

'How come you knew my name?' he asked.

Thomas smiled. 'Actually I know more than your name, Devil. I know you. Know all about you.'

'Yeah?' Devil shifted uncomfortably in his seat.

'Yeah,' Thomas said thoughtfully. 'Shame about that kid, huh? Must make you feel like shit. I mean, it was your fault he killed himself, right? You're going to have to live with that for the rest of your life.'

Devil just managed to stop himself launching himself at Thomas but just in time he remembered that he couldn't win, not with these two big guys either side of him. 'It wasn't nothing to do with me,' he said instead, his eyes dark with anger, with defiance.

Thomas laughed. 'We both know that's not true,

Devil. You know, if you play with people's lives you've got to be able to take the consequences. Live with them. Embrace them. Can't be lying to yourself. Surely your father taught you that?'

Devil's head turned sharply. Thomas laughed.

'Oh, I know about your father. Know all about him. That's why you're here.'

Devil closed his eyes for a few seconds then he opened them. 'We don't have any of his money,' he said then. 'Whatever you think I've got, I ain't. He took it all with him. I ain't got nothing.'

'I know that,' Thomas said reassuringly. Then the car indicated and pulled into a large warehouse. Devil looked around nervously. There were no other people. It looked like no one else ever came here.

'Don't be scared,' Thomas said, smiling again. 'We're just here to talk. Nothing else.'

Devil looked away. How did this guy read him so easily? It unsettled him. More than that, it pissed him off.

The man on Devil's left got out of the car, so did Thomas. Then they changed places. Devil felt his throat go dry.

'Mmmm,' Thomas said, leaning back against the seat. 'That's the mark of a great car. As comfortable in the back as it is in the front. Shows your passengers respect. Respect is important, Devil. Don't you think?'

Devil shrugged. He wished this guy would get to the point. Tell him what he wanted. Then at least he'd know what he was dealing with.

'Trouble is,' Thomas continued, 'people don't show each other respect very much, do they? People don't know what respect is. They've lost their way, Devil. They focus all their attention on things that don't matter, and none of their attention on things that do. Like respect. Like manners. They're too busy taking drugs, accumulating things. They've forgotten what life is about, Devil. Don't you agree?'

'I guess,' Devil said, noncommittally.

'You guess, huh?' Thomas replied thoughtfully. 'You think your mother has her priorities right? You think she had her priorities right when your little sister fell out of that window?'

Devil stiffened.

'Thing is, Devil, it wasn't her fault. She wasn't to blame. It's society's fault. It should have helped her instead of leaving her to fend for herself, broke, broken. She's not the first person to turn to alcohol, to drugs, to gambling, to whatever there is available. But she is part of the problem, Devil. People need leadership and no one's leading them.'

Devil didn't say anything. He hated his mother, hated her weakness, the way she crumpled when his father left, the way she cried all the time, saying that she used to be a someone, that he'd taken that away from her, when he hadn't taken anything because she wasn't no one when he married her. Or didn't marry her. Whatever. Point was, Leona was her responsibility. Not him, he could look after himself. But Leona was little. She needed her mum. And her mum let her down. Her mum was a fucking laughing stock. A mess.

But she was still his mum. It was one thing hating her; it was another thing hearing this guy Thomas slag her off.

'Whatever,' he said.

'Whatever? You can do better than that,' Thomas said. He moved closer, put his hand on Devil's arm. 'You know what I'm talking about because you sell those lowlifes drugs,' he whispered. 'You see it all around you. The scum. The sheep. You know that they're worthless. You know that. The other gangs. Your own gang. They're not winners, are they, Devil? They're losers. All of them.'

Devil didn't move an inch. 'You knew my dad?' he asked.

'Know your dad,' Thomas said. 'I know him well. And he wants to help you. Wants me to help you. See, we've got a plan, Devil. A plan to change things. To change them for good. What I want to know is whether you want to help us. Whether you want to change things. Clear the slates. Get rid of the dross. Start again.'

Devil looked at him strangely. 'I dunno what you're talking about,' he said.

Thomas smiled. 'Yes you do. You know the Bible, Devil. I bet you know it off by heart.' Devil raised an eyebrow and Thomas laughed. 'Tell me about Genesis chapter 6.'

Devil said nothing.

Thomas's eyes hardened. 'Tell me,' he said.

Devil looked at him warily. 'Noah's ark?' he asked.

'Noah's ark,' Thomas smiled again. 'A new beginning. Tell me. Tell me the story.'

Devil shifted uncertainly in his seat. 'You want me to tell you the story of Noah's ark?' he asked.

'Yes, Devil. I'm waiting. And I don't like to wait.'

Devil shook his head. He wasn't a performing monkey.

The big guy on his right moved closer. 'Tell him

the story,' he said, his voice low and threatening. Devil met his eyes; turned back to Thomas. Shit. He was going to have to do it. Shit.

Reluctantly he began to recite, his voice low, almost a whisper. Like he used to recite the Bible for his father. Wanting to please him. Wanting to see a proud smile on his face, not wanting to anger him. 'And it came to pass, when men began to multiply on the face of the earth, and daughters were born unto them,' he muttered under his breath.

'Louder,' Thomas instructed him, closing his eyes.

Devil sighed inwardly. 'That the sons of God saw the daughters of men that they were fair; and they took them wives of all which they chose.'

'And?' Thomas asked. 'Then what?'

'And the Lord said, My spirit shall not always strive with man, for that he also is flesh: yet his days shall be an hundred and twenty years.'

Devil stopped, and Thomas's eyes opened again. 'More,' he said. 'Keep going.'

Devil's eyes narrowed. 'There were giants in the earth in those days; and also after that, when the sons of God came in unto the daughters of men, and they bare children to them, the same became mighty men which were of old, men of renown. And God saw that the wickedness of man was great in the earth, and that every imagination of the thoughts of his heart was only evil continually. And it repented the LORD that he had made man on the earth, and it grieved him at his heart.'

'Grieved him at his heart,' Thomas nodded appreciatively. 'That's about right. Now come on. You're just getting to the best bit.'

Devil rolled his eyes. 'And the Lord said, I will destroy man whom I have created from the face of the earth; both man, and beast, and the creeping thing, and the fowls of the air; for it repenteth me that I have made them. But Noah found grace in the eyes of the Lord.'

Thomas's eyes opened and he smiled, broadly. 'There we go,' he said. 'He destroyed all the wicked men and he saved Noah. Because Noah walked with him, because Noah wasn't like the rest of them. See, Devil? Do you see now?'

Devil shook his head. 'See what?' he asked.

Thomas laughed. 'Never mind,' he said. 'It's time we got back.'

He opened the door. 'See what?' Devil asked again.

Thomas stopped, turned, his face still creased into a grin. 'You'll find out soon enough. You going to help me, Devil? You going to help your dad make things better?'

'Why should I?' The words came out before Devil could check himself, but Thomas didn't look angry.

'Because,' he said, 'you know you want to.'

'I don't know nothing like that,' Devil retorted, emboldened by the fact that no one had laid a finger on him. Maybe these big guys weren't so tough after all. Maybe this Thomas was all talk and nothing else.

'Oh yes you do,' Thomas said. His voice was soft suddenly, thoughtful. 'You think that running some shitty little gang in a shitty little estate is a worthwhile thing to be doing? You think that you're a someone because you can intimidate ten-year-old boys into running errands for you? You're a no one, Devil. You carry on like this and you'll be in prison within the year. A failure. A loser. You work for me, and you'll be a someone. You'll be doing something important. Something your father believes in. Something he's been working on for a very long time. So you tell me, Devil. Do you want to help me, or not?'

'You work for my father?' Devil asked, his eyes widening slightly.

'I don't work for anyone, Devil,' Thomas said. 'Just answer the question.' There was steel in his voice, an implied threat. Devil stared at him. He was angry. He'd been insulted. But even though he'd never admit it, he also knew Thomas was right. The gang was shit. Everything was shit. Ever since the boy had killed himself, Devil hadn't been able to shake a feeling of emptiness, of pointlessness, of anger, at the boy, at himself for letting it happen, for not being two steps ahead. He'd told himself he didn't care; had told himself it was a neat ending to a problem, that he couldn't have orchestrated things better if he'd tried. But he hadn't really believed it. And now . . . Now Thomas was making sense. It wasn't his fault; none of it was his fault. It was society's fault. It was all the losers, getting in the way.

Now he had an opportunity. His dad wanted his help. His dad was going to save him.

'I don't work for anyone neither,' Devil said, then. 'But I'll work with you. If that's what you're asking.'

Thomas grinned, the smile taking over his face, spreading right across from ear to ear. 'I knew you would,' he said, evidently pleased with himself.

'Welcome to the team, Devil.' He handed him a pin, a tie pin, with the letter 'I' on it.

'What's this?' he asked.

'Put it on,' Thomas said. 'It means you're part of something. Something special. Something big. See, I have great hopes for you, Devil. I think you're going to be something special. I think you've got your father's talents. And people need that right now.'

'So what do you want me to do?' Devil asked uncertainly, pinning it to his T-shirt.

'Nothing,' Thomas said, getting out of the car and moving back to the front. 'For now. But I'll be in touch. I'll let you know.'

21

Raffy's head was hurting. He was lying on some kind of daybed with sheer curtains all around him. He knew that Benjamin was in the room, but his figure was hazy through the voile. He cleared his throat. Moments later, the curtains drew back and Benjamin's face appeared.

'Feeling better?' he asked.

Raffy nodded sheepishly. 'I'm sorry,' he said.

He'd been on the bed for an hour or so. Initially he hadn't wanted to lie down; he'd been too desperate to apologise, to explain himself to Benjamin, to make Benjamin see. But Benjamin had refused to listen. Instead he had insisted that Raffy lie down, gather his thoughts, reflect, and, he added with a little smile, let the alcohol work its way through his system.

So Raffy had done what he was told, had sulked, brooded, huffed, puffed and fuelled his righteous indignation with images of Neil and Evie, of Lucas kissing Evie, of Evie's thunderous face staring at him angrily.

And then, slowly, those images had rescinded. Bit by bit his breathing had slowed down; bit by bit his anger had abated, and as it did so his embarrassment increased.

'Sorry?' Benjamin asked. 'For what, Raffy?'

'For behaving like an idiot,' Raffy said, feeling himself redden. Benjamin was sitting at the foot of the bed, his kindly eyes looking at him seriously. 'For punching Neil. For . . .'

He trailed off. There was too much he was sorry for. Too much to put into words.

'Neil is a fine teacher,' Benjamin said then, his voice quiet, gentle. 'I don't believe that his teachings have ever, in the past, led to such an outburst.'

'No,' Raffy said. 'No, I can't imagine they would.'

'And yet you were so incensed by what he said? By what he did?' Benjamin asked curiously.

Raffy shook his head. Then he sat forward. 'It's not Neil,' he said with a sigh. 'It's me. I . . . I get scared whenever anyone gets close to Evie. I can't help it. I see red.'

'You are afraid you'll lose her? That she'll see through you?'

Raffy's eyes widened. Benjamin laughed. 'We all worry about that to a degree,' he said. 'I used to worry about people seeing through me all the time.'

'Really?' Raffy asked disbelievingly. 'You?'

Benjamin nodded. 'Everyone is fallible. We all have faults.'

Raffy digested this. Then he took a deep breath. 'The thing is,' he said. 'The thing is I can't lose her. If I lost her, I'd be nothing. I'd want to die. And when I see her laughing, smiling, with someone else, it makes me . . .'

He couldn't finish the sentence.

'Want to kill them?' Benjamin asked gently.

Raffy met his eye and nodded guiltily.

'And do you think this behaviour makes her love you more?' Benjamin asked.

Raffy frowned. 'No, I mean . . .' He cleared his throat. 'She doesn't like it. I know she doesn't. But she doesn't see . . . She doesn't realise. She—'

'Doesn't see the world as you do? Full of threats? Full of challengers?'

Raffy nodded gratefully. Benjamin got it. He understood.

Benjamin smiled sadly. 'Raffy,' he said. 'Do you know why the Brother was able to keep you so restricted in the City? Do you know why he was able to do as he pleased, to take away your basic freedoms, to rule the City according to his own rules, unquestioned, unchallenged?'

Raffy nodded. 'Because of the System.'

'No,' Benjamin said gently. 'The System was part of it, but the real reason was fear. People feared the alternative. The Horrors were driven by fear, too. Fear of others. Fear and hatred and mistrust. We are all susceptible to it. We need it: without fear we would walk into dangerous situations. Without fear, the human race would not survive. But unfettered, unchallenged, fear can be a very destructive force. And that is the kind of fear tormenting you, Raffy. Neil is no threat to you. No one here is a threat to you except yourself. Act towards Evie the way the Brother acted in the City and don't you think that she will be forced to flee? Wouldn't you do the same thing?'

Raffy stared at him. Evie had said almost the same thing. He got an uncomfortable feeling in his stomach.

'I've been really stupid,' he said quietly.

Benjamin smiled. 'You've been passionate, and you've been misguided. Not stupid.'

Raffy considered this.

'I just . . . I don't want to lose her, Benjamin. Now that we're free, there's nothing holding her to me any more.'

'Yes there is,' Benjamin said, gently. 'If you can get rid of the doubts and fear, you'll see that there's everything holding her to you. Neil is not a threat to you. But you are. Your jealousy is.'

Raffy breathed out. He knew it was true. 'I'm going to really try,' he said. 'Thank you Benjamin.'

'Don't thank me,' Benjamin said with a warm smile. 'We all make mistakes. Trust me.'

Raffy pulled himself up. 'I'd better go and apologise to Neil.'

'Probably a good idea,' Benjamin winked. 'Go easy, Raffy. Everything will be okay.'

22

The estate was quiet. A few of Devil's crew were hanging out, sitting on the high wall that overlooked the walkways, smoking, drinking, using the wall on the other side for target practice with their empty cans. Business was slow, but not through lack of demand. It was like he couldn't be bothered any more. Like none of it mattered so much. And his apathy was infectious; without him setting the pace, making demands, his crew had slipped into a lethargic state that no one, including Devil, could be bothered to rouse themselves out of. Business was booming without even trying hard; the money was rolling in and there hadn't been any trouble. The Green Lanes Massive weren't interfering in their business any more; no one was. Devil didn't think about it too much, but if and when he did, the thought sometimes occurred to him that maybe it was a bit strange, maybe. But then again, maybe they had better things to do.

Truth was, it didn't matter. Because Devil definitely had better things to do. He had his eyes on a bigger game, he was moving into a different world. A world he liked. A world of smart cars and people who had real power, real respect, not just stupid gangs with their constant fighting. Like children. That's what he'd realised. All of this. It was no different from kids fighting in the playground, only now it was with knives and guns.

That's what Thomas had taught him over the past few weeks. Shown him. Thomas knew everything. It was like he'd swallowed Wikipedia or something. He knew everything about Devil, about Dalston, about his life before, about the estate, about music, about politics, about anything. Every time Devil mentioned something, Thomas would raise an eyebrow and shoot out a whole load of information. Then he'd give him one of his little triumphant smiles.

But that wasn't what he'd taught Devil. What he'd taught Devil was to think bigger than his home turf, to see his old ambitions for what they really were: pathetic.

'Who cares about Dalston?' he'd said one time, that little smile on his face. 'You think anyone outside of Dalston gives a monkey's about it? You think you're going to get respect because your gang's the biggest in Dalston? Only from people in Dalston. And who gives a toss about them?'

And Devil had wanted to punch him then, like he always punched people who disagreed with him, disrespected him. But he couldn't, not with Thomas's protection all around him, so instead he'd stayed silent and sulked, but the more he thought about it, the more he realised Thomas was right. Dalston was a nowhere place. And then Thomas took him in the car to the middle of London, to places he'd never dreamt about going. Clubs with big queues outside and they'd just walked in. Bars that stayed open all night, full of beautiful women who swarmed around them like bees. He could tell Thomas enjoyed it, enjoyed the money, the power, the attention. And Devil enjoyed it too. He drank champagne, ate food that tasted so good he salivated whenever he remembered it, had women fawning over him, laughing at his jokes, making him feel like a king.

Devil didn't know if he was part of Thomas's crew or what; every so often Thomas would send him a text, then turn up in that car with just a few hours' notice, and Devil would drop everything and get in. His crew kept bugging him, asking who the man in the car was, but Devil wasn't saying nothing. This was about him, not them. He was a winner, a leader; they were just his congregation. They got told what he wanted to tell them, that's all.

And soon he wouldn't tell them nothing at all. Soon he'd be gone. He didn't know when, but Thomas gave him hints. There was a big job, something Devil had in his destiny. He was going to be a leader. He was going to have followers, just like his dad did; he was going to tell them what to do, how to live their lives. And he'd be leaving Dalston. After that, maybe he'd have a car of his own.

He heard an engine and looked up, smiling a big toothy grin. He didn't even say goodbye to his gang these days; a nod was enough. They knew he was going on important business; they knew to keep the show on the road until he got back.

But the smile soon evaporated from his face. It wasn't the Mercedes. It was blue and white. The doors opened and two coppers, a man and a woman, got out and walked towards him. The same two coppers as before. His crew melted away, incriminating evidence disappearing with them.

'Yeah?' Devil looked at them insolently. He'd known it was too good to be true, knew they were here simply because he'd congratulated himself on the fact that they'd been leaving him alone. Stupid.

'We've been talking to people.' It was the man speaking, the one with ginger hair, in his usual threatening tone. 'It's only a matter of time before we charge you with the murder. You know that. Reckon we can add manslaughter, too. Boy you forced to do your dirty work for you. How does it feel to be a killer, Devil? Feel good? Feel proud of yourself?'

Devil rolled his eyes, affected a bored expression. 'Whatever,' he said.

'Thing is, we've got the knife, Devil. We've got the knife and we've got the mother's testimony, telling us you put her son up to it.'

'I don't know nothing about a knife,' Devil said, his eyes narrowing. 'I never put no one up to nothing.'

The female copper smiled. 'I bet you don't. But we're going to connect this knife to you, and when we do you're going down for a very long time.'

Devil stayed silent. The knife was clean; he'd seen to that. They didn't have nothing on him. Otherwise they'd be charging him instead of hanging about.

'And in the meantime' she continued, 'we're watching you. We're watching your every move. You so much as cough and we'll be onto you. You think about that,' she said, then they turned and walked back to the car. As it drove off, his crew emerged again out of the shadows.

Devil looked at them irritably. 'What?' he asked them. 'What?'

Then he stood up and put his hands in his pocket. He was sick of this place. He was sick of all of it.

He strode off angrily, down the walkway, past the losers, out onto the road. He wanted out. He wanted something better. He kicked some loose stones on the road; they hit something. A car. Not a police car this time. It was a Mercedes, driving towards him.

The door opened for him; he slid in, sat back, put on his seatbelt.

'You want to be careful, kicking stones like that.' Thomas held out his hand; he was in the back.

Devil shrugged. 'I'm sick of this place,' he said

gruffly. 'Am I joining your crew or what? What do you want with me anyway? You turn up, then you disappear and you don't tell me nothing.'

Thomas looked at him for a long moment, then the car started to move. They drove in silence for a few minutes until eventually Thomas spoke again. 'Don't worry about the police, Devil. You're safe. They won't be able to pin anything on you. And in the meantime I've got a job for you.'

'A job?' Devil's eyes widened in surprise. 'Sure, man. Tell me what and when. I can get anything you want done for you.'

'Not get it done,' Thomas said quietly. 'I don't want you getting one of your boys to do this. I want you to do it. Understand? This will be your way of proving yourself to me. Showing me you've got what it takes. You do it well and that knife will disappear. The knife, the testimony, the whole lot. You do it well and you'll never come back to this estate again. Okay?'

He was staring at him intently; Devil nodded quickly. 'Sure,' he said, his voice a little less cocky. 'Sure, whatever.'

'Good.' Thomas said, his thin lips inching upwards at the corners. 'That's very good, Devil.'

23

Raffy took a swig of water and sat back in the lush grass to enjoy a moment of sunshine, a moment of peace before the bell went, before it was time to go back to work. Work. He'd never known work like it; back-breaking, sweat-inducing work that left him gasping, that made his bones ache, that left him so exhausted he often could barely utter a word when he got home, falling onto the bed in a stupor of tiredness.

But he loved the order, the rules, the discipline and the camaraderie. For the ten hours a day that he was at work, Raffy felt like the world made sense, that he had some control over it, that everything would be okay. Work was simple, and here, at least, his work was achieving something, feeding people, nourishing them. He was a farmer; he could hold his head high around the Settlement. For once in his life he wasn't a figure of hate, of mistrust.

At least, he hadn't been.

He sighed heavily and propped himself up on his elbows. He'd apologised to Neil, had raced round to him as soon as he'd left Benjamin, had begged his forgiveness, had even said he'd take some classes, then he'd returned home, shamefaced, to apologise to Evie, to promise that nothing like that would ever happen again.

Neil had listened, had asked Raffy some questions, had watched him closely. And then he had embraced him, told him that he was part of the Settlement now, that he was his brother, that there was no need to apologise. Raffy had been humbled by Neil's outstretched hand of friendship, his immediate forgiveness, his repeated offer of lessons and whatever book Raffy wanted to read.

It had been Evie who had not met his eye, who had not been able to say anything in response to his desperate pleas for forgiveness; Evie who had simply regarded him stonily then gone to work, her back not quite as straight as it usually was, her expression reproachful even when he met her for lunch later that day. He had let her down. He had let them down.

So he'd decided to do what Benjamin had suggested

and throw himself into work, focus his mind on upholding the Settlement's values, on being part of it, a worthwhile part, a meaningful one. He had worked harder than he'd ever thought possible, arriving early, refusing breaks, carrying the load of two men, not one. And actually he felt much better. Exhausted, broken, aching muscles that he hadn't known existed, but better. And things with Evie had got better, too; gradually she was thawing, meeting his eye, sometimes even smiling at his jokes.

Things were going to be okay, he thought to himself. He was going to prove himself to her, prove himself worthy of her. And when he and Evie were married, they would be more than okay – his life would be complete. It was all he had ever dreamt of, more than he had ever expected. And when they were bonded together for ever, then he was sure that he would relax, would stop being so fearful, so paranoid that someone was going to take her away from him. He knew that Benjamin was right about trusting, about letting Evie be free. And he was trying. Trying so hard. But it wasn't in his nature to relax completely. Experience had taught him that the hawks were always circling. They had always circled over Raffy; he would always expect them.

He let his head fall backwards so that he was lying flat, looking up at the sky. Such an open sky out here, he found himself thinking, so much bigger than the City's sky, so much expanse of air, of light, of oxygen.

Here in the Settlement he could breathe.

Here he could finally just be.

He heard the bell, pulled himself up to a seated position, then put his hand down to the ground to heave himself up. And then he stopped, because there was someone standing close to him, someone he hadn't seen before, someone he didn't recognise. He stared at him, his pulse racing. There was no one else near; the men usually ate their lunch next to the building site that sat near the farmland, a site which promised new houses, new classrooms. Now that the bell had rung the builders would be clambering back onto roofs and towards cement mixers while the farmers would be winding their way back to the fields. Only Raffy chose to come out here to eat, a five-minute walk from the site, where he could lie on the grass and enjoy the smell of freedom.

'Nice-looking buildings going up. You must be excited,' the man said.

Raffy didn't say anything; he stared at the man suspiciously. He didn't recognise him and there was something about him that he didn't trust.

The man smiled. 'Sorry, you don't know who I am. I'm a friend of Benjamin's. This place is very impressive.'

Raffy's eyes narrowed. No one had said anything about a visit. 'You know Benjamin?'

'Used to, a long time ago,' the man said. 'So you're Raffy, huh?'

Raffy looked at him sharply.

The man laughed. 'Cautious, aren't you? Don't worry. I am too. Makes sense to be. Particularly in your shoes.'

'In my shoes?'

'Coming from the City, having Lucas as a brother. You know.' The man shrugged. He had a pinched face. Small eyes. Weak jaw. Raffy didn't like him. He could overpower him in seconds.

But then he remembered Benjamin. Violence wasn't one of the Settlement's core values. Instead, Raffy straightened up, every sense on high alert. 'Who are you?' he said, moving towards the man menacingly. 'What do you want?'

'Me? Nothing. Just . . .' The man cocked his head onto one shoulder. 'Look, I've got friends here. I'm not officially here . . . You don't want to be telling anyone about me. But like I said, I've got friends. Friends who are . . . concerned for you. Just don't want to tell you to your face, in case you take offence. So I said I would. No skin off my nose.'

'Friends? Who are these friends?' Raffy said,

scanning the horizon, trying to work out whether the builders on the site would hear him if he shouted and knowing immediately that they wouldn't.

The man shot him an uncomfortable look. 'Can't really say,' he said. 'Look, you're busy. I can see this isn't a great time. Just . . . the message was something about a watch. A gold watch. Apparently she got it back. I don't know what that means, don't know if it means anything to you. But that's what I said I'd tell you. And now I have. So I'll be on my way, if it's all right with you. And, uh, keep up the good work. That was the other thing.'

He started to walk off; Raffy stared after him, telling himself not to listen, not to care. His mind was racing, sweat on his forehead. The watch? Was he talking about Lucas's watch? What did he mean 'she got it back'? He started to run, couldn't help himself. 'Who are you?' he demanded as he caught up with the stranger. 'Who gave you that message?'

The man shrugged. 'Can't tell you, I'm afraid. I don't have much any more but I've got my word.'

Raffy stared at him angrily. 'Where are you from? How do you have friends here if you don't live here?'

The man smiled awkwardly, looked down at his feet. 'Got to get accepted into the Settlement, haven't you? I did my time, but I wasn't deemed suitable. Too lazy,

I'm afraid. Not like you. Still, like I say, I've got some friends who sort me out with bits of food from time to time. Anyway, I'll see you around. Look after that girl of yours, won't you?'

'Raffy?' Raffy turned to see Simon walking towards him. 'Raffy, what are you doing? You're late back.'

'Sorry,' Raffy said immediately, turning back to see the man, but he'd already disappeared.

'Come on then,' Simon said, one hand shielding his eyes from the sun, the other beckoning Raffy. 'We've got work to do here.'

Raffy took one last look behind him and, heart thumping in his chest, he followed Simon back to the field.

24

Lucas woke up slowly. He felt like he was travelling up on a lift from low down beneath the earth's surface; one false move and he would go down again. He opened his eyes but he could barely see; he felt heavy, foggy. He didn't know where he was, how he had got here, but he knew it was not a good place. He felt it in his bones.

He closed his eyes; his heart was beginning to beat rapidly and he knew that he needed to conserve energy, needed to focus, needed to remember. Slowly, he breathed, letting oxygen fill his lungs. In, out. Calm. He could hear a mechanical whirring but no voices, nothing to indicate that there were any people near him. But that was not to say that there weren't. They could be watching him, silently.

Carefully he opened his eyes again. Everything was

clouded, but gradually the world began to come into focus. He was lying down on a bed, a metal bed. There was a machine to the left of him, on the floor, connected to him. To his head. When he moved, something pulled, it hurt; he stopped moving. There was a tube connected to his left hand, too. Nothing else, as far as he could see.

He breathed in and out again, did his best to suppress the anger, the fear bubbling up inside him. Anger as he remembered what had happened – Linus pushing him off the cliff – fear as he realised where he was: inside the camp, in a bed, a prisoner. He had to stay calm. He had to figure out where he was, what they wanted from him, how he was going to get out of here. And what these tubes sticking out of his head were.

He waited. Someone would come. He just had to stay awake until they did and then he might learn something. He counted to a hundred to keep his brain occupied, then started to count down again.

He only got to eighty-three.

Lucas woke up again. He felt groggy. The light had changed in the room; he guessed it was night-time. He moved his hand to his face; his stubble had grown. He had been here a couple of days at least.

His head hurt. He was thirsty; his throat was dry. He tried to call out but it took him several attempts to make a sound. And when he did, no one appeared to hear him.

It was dark in his room but he could see more clearly; his eyes were beginning to work better. A bag of fluid was dripping into his hand.

He tried calling out again, louder this time. And then a door opened and a woman walked in. 'You're awake,' she said.

She was young, pretty, with a kind face. He managed a smile.

'I'm awake,' he agreed. 'Where am I?'

She pulled at his eyelids, looked inside his mouth, felt his pulse. 'You're in a medical centre, being looked after,' she said.

'By you?'

'Among others.'

'Others?'

She smiled. 'That's right.'

Lucas felt caught off-guard, and decided to continue the act that he'd lost his memory. 'What's wrong with me?' Lucas asked. 'I can't remember anything. Can't even remember my name.'

The nurse looked at him for a second, opened her mouth as if to say something, then changed her mind. 'I have to go,' she said suddenly, rushing out of the door and letting it bang behind her.

Lucas heard a solid lock turning as soon as it was closed. Then he fell back against the pillow. He started to count again. This time he only made it up to forty-three.

'He was definitely conscious, you say?'

Lucas woke to hear a man's voice. Lucas heard him clearly; he didn't know how long he'd been there. His voice was abrupt.

'Definitely. About four hours ago. He wanted to know what he was doing here.'

'I see.' Brisk, patronising, dismissive. Lucas lay still. This man was in charge. The doctor, maybe. 'And what did you tell him?'

'Nothing, sir. Nothing at all.' She sounded worried – fearful, even. Sir, not doctor. So who was he, Lucas wondered? 'He doesn't remember anything. Doesn't remember who he is.'

'Really?' The man leant down, or someone did; the light changed behind Lucas's eyelids, the bright lights trained on his face now blocked out by the person inspecting him. 'Not that it matters. He's of no interest to us. We can get rid of him.'

'Get rid of him?' the nurse asked uncertainly.

There was a pause. 'Shut off life support, I mean. He's obviously not going to recover.'

The second man cleared his throat. 'We have the paperwork?'

'He's not one of ours, you imbecile. We don't need the paperwork,' he said impatiently.

Another pause. Then the second man spoke, his voice lower, almost a whisper. 'This is not procedure. Outside the camp's perimeter I know you get your guys to do what they want, but in here there are laws. We can't just get rid of people.'

'Oh yes we can,' the first man said then, his voice threatening. 'We can do whatever I decide we do. Do you understand?'

'Yes, sir.'

'Okay then.'

Lucas heard the first man leave his bedside and the room, even his footsteps sounding officious as he walked away. Once he had gone, the other man cleared his throat. 'Mr Weizman wants us to switch off life support. I'll need to get the relevant forms filled in, get approval from the director. Keep him doped up for now,' he told the nurse.

'But he's not even on life support,' she whispered. 'There's nothing wrong with him. Just a head injury.'

'Then make it worse,' the man said after a brief hesitation. There was silence for a few seconds. Then Lucas heard the man breathe out. 'He's really okay?'

'Completely healthy,' the nurse said.

The man sighed. 'Okay. Just dope him up for now,' he said.

'Yes, doctor.' Lucas felt something cool going into the back of his hand. He tried to stay awake, tried to think, tried to work out what he was going to do. But the fog was closing in. It was no use. He felt himself becoming very heavy.

Linus sat, silently, his binoculars trained on the flat white building with the shining lights. He was much closer now; alone, he was able to blend in far more easily. And bit by bit he was piecing it all together: the perimeter wall designed to blend in with the landscape with an electrical current to put off any inquisitive animals; a gate with a current so high it would fry an elephant. These people certainly weren't planning on having any guests. But Linus could get round that; their system security was sophisticated, but nothing he couldn't handle. Lucas was in a room three windows from the left in the white building, the one which had its blinds drawn all the time. He scanned to the right, saw the nurse walking along the corridor, visible as she passed each window, windows of empty rooms, their doors wide open, apparently useless. Why so many? Who were they for? Linus had an idea, but it was only a theory. For now.

He thought for a moment, then trained his binoculars back on the doors into the building. He'd watched the camp constantly for the past two days, monitoring everything. And now he was ready; had clocked all the entry codes, the routines, who did what and when. The building Lucas was in had a six-digit passcode. Fancy technology, but once again, nothing he couldn't handle. He could get Lucas out no problem. No problem at all.

When it was time, that was. Right now there were more interesting places to get into. The white building might have Lucas in it, but it was the grey building behind it that Linus was most interested in. The one with three layers of security. The one that only five people appeared to have access to. That was the building where information would be found. That was the building that Linus would be visiting first. If he could get inside that building he was pretty sure he'd find the answers to his questions; and he was pretty sure he'd be able to get into their network and hide a few ticking bombs he might want to use later.

He watched, waited. Then, carefully, he emerged, just as one of the five people with access to the grey building turned the corner, as he had done for the past two days, on the walk he always took after his lunch. People were such creatures of habit, Linus thought to himself as he stunned him, dragged him to the place he'd found on the first night, took off his clothes, then tied him up. 'Going to be needing these,' he said conversationally, as he put on the man's uniform. 'Hope you don't mind.' The man said nothing; he couldn't, as Linus had gagged him. Linus regarded him for a few seconds, then shrugged. He'd be fine; Linus would free him later. And if he didn't, someone would find him eventually.

He looked back at the path, checked that no one was looking, then re-emerged, and sauntered casually to the grey building.

25

Raffy felt his heart thudding in his chest. He only had five minutes, then Evie would be back. He'd looked everywhere: among her clothes, under the bed, in the back of the cupboards. And the watch wasn't there, of course it wasn't. But Raffy had to keep searching. Because the man had known, known about the watch, and how would he know about it if he wasn't telling the truth? He'd have gone to the baker, but if it wasn't true and Evie found out . . . No, better to just search, to reassure himself.

Because Evie wouldn't have got that watch back.

She wouldn't have.

Couldn't have.

Could she?

Lucas's watch. Raffy closed his eyes for a moment, tried to push back the tidal wave of hatred and anger that the very name 'Lucas' elicited in him, the bitterness and frustration that had consumed so much of his life. Lucas was far away now, but still his shadow followed Raffy, still his very existence felt like an active attack, to suppress and emasculate him, just as Lucas had always done.

At least before it had been bearable, at least before, Raffy's seething rage had been justifiable; even if the rest of the City thought Lucas was perfect, Raffy had known about the evil that lurked within, the cold heart that had betrayed their own father. Back then it had been manageable. Back then, Raffy had known who Lucas was and what he was, and that knowledge had made him feel strong, able to withstand everyone's hatred, everyone's mistrust, because he didn't want them to like him, not if they liked Lucas.

Of course there had only been one person who liked him instead of his brother. But that was all Raffy had needed. Because that person had been Evie. Evie, who had been matched to Lucas, preferred the company of Raffy, and risked everything to creep out at night to meet him.

That alone had made living worthwhile. That alone had told Raffy that the City could think what it liked; that he and Evie were in the right and nothing else mattered.

And then . . . then everything had come tumbling down around his feet. It turned out that Lucas had been hiding the truth all these years; it turned out that Lucas was a hero. Lucas hadn't betrayed their father; their father had trusted Lucas, had made him promise to protect the family. To protect him, Raffy. It was because of that promise that Lucas had suffered all these years.

And it was because of that promise that Raffy could never forgive his brother. Because now he had nothing. Now he wasn't strong; he was weak. Now he wasn't good; he was bad: the angry young man with nothing to be angry about. Except, of course, the fact that Lucas had kissed Evie on the very night that he had sent her to rescue him, to help him escape from the City. It was to Evie he'd told the truth, the whole story about what had happened. To Evie, not him, not his own brother. And everyone expected him to be happy, to be grateful, to welcome the fact that Lucas, who had overshadowed him in the City, was now going to overshadow him here, too. Even with Evie. Especially with Evie.

Well he wasn't going to. Raffy wasn't going to let him. He was going to forget about Lucas, purge him from his mind, pretend that he didn't exist. He could do that here as no one in the Settlement knew that Lucas, the new leader of the City, was in fact his brother. Here he was Raffy, judged on his own merits, free to be who he was. And when Evie had given him Lucas's watch, the watch that their father had given him, that freedom had been threatened. He had felt the panic rise up in him, suffocating him, making him gasp for breath. But he'd dealt with it, taken the watch from Evie and then, the very next day, got rid of it again.

He should have destroyed it.

He should have ignored his hunger and destroyed it.

He sat down on the bed, took a few deep breaths. The watch wasn't here. The man was wrong. Everything was okay. He had to calm down.

He heard the door handle turn and quickly scanned the room to check that he'd put everything back in its place, then he stood up to greet Evie. She looked at him warily, took off her coat and lay down on the bed.

'I'm so tired,' she sighed, 'and hungry.' She glanced over at Raffy, then frowned. 'Raffy? What's the matter?'

Raffy barely heard her talk; his head was pounding and his stomach was clenching and he felt like the ground was opening under his feet. Because his eyes were on the pocket of her dress. Where her handkerchief was. Where, peeking up through the white linen, he could see an unmistakable glint of gold.

He reached out to the wall to steady himself, then managed a smile that didn't reach his eyes, a smile that felt like someone had drawn it onto his face like on a wooden toy. His eyes were searching Evie's face for a clue, for an explanation for her betrayal, but he could see nothing.

'Raffy?' Evie said again, getting off the bed, moving towards the door. 'Is everything okay?' She was edging away from him. As though she were scared of him.

Raffy nodded. 'Of course it is,' he said, swallowing his desperation, forcing his emotions deep down inside, where they would not consume him. 'So what did you get up to today?'

26

Devil sat back against the soft leather chair and pretended he wasn't there. But he was there, had been there for hours, ever since Thomas had brought him here, driven him into the middle of London, into an area full of tall buildings and people in suits running around. He'd driven into a car park, brought Devil in through a back door into a meeting room with no windows, and that's where he'd been ever since, gazing around, looking at nothing and everything.

He knew how to do that. It's what he did on the estate most days.

Anyway, it wasn't the first time he'd been here. The first time, Thomas had brought him here, sat him on a chair, then walked out and disappeared for about an hour. That time, Devil had been freaked, had started pacing, had found himself trying the door, finding it locked, wondering if Thomas was actually some crazed psychopath who was into imprisoning people for fun. But then, just before he really started to panic, Thomas had come back, handed him a wodge of cash and asked him stuff about God, about the Bible, told him stuff about how people needed guidance, needed to be fired up, needed to feel that life was worthwhile. They'd talked for ages, at least two hours, and then they'd gone. That had been it. Which had kind of surprised Devil, but he wasn't complaining, wasn't going to ask too many questions.

It was strange, this building. Maybe it was because Devil was so high up – they had taken a lift to the fiftieth floor – but it was like the rest of the world didn't matter here, like everything was normal. Like the chaos couldn't seep in through the solid walls.

Because outside it was chaos. Outside . . . well, to be honest, it was freaking Devil out a bit.

Then, the next time, Thomas had brought a camera. Asked Devil to look into it, to imagine his father was there on the other side, to imagine that he was giving one of his father's sermons. And at first he'd felt really stupid; at first he'd kicked his feet and looked the other way and muttered stuff about not being no Pastor Jones.

But then Thomas's face had gone cold and he'd said that maybe Devil wasn't the right man for the job, and just like that Devil had started talking. Strange thing was, he remembered his father's sermons word for word, but after a few tries he started to embellish with his own stories, with his own thoughts. And man, he loved it. He felt like a someone. Felt like he had stuff to say.

And the thing was, he was beginning to realise that Thomas was right, that people needed him. Because the world was becoming more fucked up by the day. Bombs going off everywhere, people out on the streets, riot police shooting at them. In Europe people were machine-gunning each other, just walking into each other's houses and mowing whole families down. Devil had seen it on the news, on that big television Thomas had in his office. People screaming in front of the camera, begging for help. Two people were killed on camera. Seriously fucked up. And every week he gave another sermon, reworded for his father's followers. 'Because you're going to be the new Pastor Jones,' Thomas told him. 'You look just like him. You're going to guide people out of this mess.'

Of course in this building, you wouldn't know about the men, about the violence. People walked around on the thick carpets just like they always did, in smart suits, nice hair, their voices low and calm, not shrieking like the people outside the banks banging on the doors and asking for their money.

Devil looked around the room. He wasn't on his own this time; Thomas was there and someone else had joined him, a younger guy a few years older than Devil. A geek, his hair in a ponytail, white skin, glasses, thin arms and legs, couldn't land a punch if he tried. They were drinking coffee; there was a television in there now and they were watching it, flicking through the channels, talking to each other in low voices. Devil was sitting in the corner, silently, watching.

Suddenly Thomas turned to Devil. 'So,' he said. 'I've got this job for you.'

The geek turned off the television and left the room.

Devil looked at him steadily. 'Whatever you want me to do, man.'

'Good. And here's some money to tide you over.' Thomas took out an envelope and walked towards Devil, handing it to him. Devil flicked it; he knew how to count a bundle of notes by sight and weight.

His eyes widened greedily. 'A grand?'

Thomas nodded. 'Listen carefully, Devil. Here's what I want you to do . . .'

27

Linus looked around, his eyes wide. This was most unexpected. This was . . . well, he'd have said impossible if he weren't here, looking at it with his own eyes.

He stepped towards the screen.

'Do you have a question?' it asked him, its voice silky and feminine, a voice that managed to be both sexy and disarming.

Linus raised an eyebrow. 'I'm not sure you'll give me the answer,' he said, under his breath.

'Try me,' the computer suggested.

Linus shrugged. 'Okay,' he said. 'What are you?'

'I am a G4 Benning 8 model with version 8.9 software and 1 million megabytes of memory,' the computer said.

Linus frowned. 'That's impossible,' he said, his mind whirring as he tried to work out why the name Benning reminded him of something. 'I've never heard of you.

And I know computers. I know every computer that's ever been conceived of, let alone invented.'

'I would argue that on the contrary, what you are suggesting is impossible, since I exist and am talking to you,' the computer said.

'So you talk philosophy too?' Linus asked it.

'Philosophical thought, yes, but only as part of natural discourse,' the computer said. 'For more extensive philosophical discussion can I suggest you download the philosophy app from the Alpha website? I can download it now, if you'd like?'

'No,' Linus said quickly. 'No, that won't be necessary.'

'You seem tense,' the computer said then. 'Would you like me to play some music? Or would you prefer a visual display? Perhaps of fields? Or do you prefer the sea?' Several options appeared on the screen; Linus stared at them. Then he shook his head.

'No, no images,' he said firmly. 'But tell me this. Where do you come from?'

'Alpha Ltd, 11189 East Street, Sacramento, USA,' the computer said.

'And when were you built?'

'2053. January. I was shipped in February. Top secret mission.' It sounded proud of itself.

Linus shook his head. 'That's impossible,' he said again.

'Not impossible,' the computer said. 'On the contrary, I could not have been built before this date as the latest chip technology was not introduced until 2052.'

'But there is no USA,' Linus breathed. 'Not like there was.'

'No,' the computer said, 'you're . . .' It hesitated. 'Did you know that there is someone coming down the corridor towards this room on tip-toe in order to surprise you?'

Linus raised an eyebrow. 'You're quite something,' he said. 'Just one person?'

'Just the night security guard. And thank you.'

'You're welcome.' Linus ducked down, moved towards the door.

'No, you're welcome,' the computer said.

'Okay, shut up now,' Linus hissed; the screen went blank. Then he took a gun out of his pocket, checked it was loaded, and prepared himself.

The door opened. Linus grabbed the guard, held the gun to his head and urged him to be quiet. Then, opening his bag, he took out some tape. Within minutes he had the guard strapped to a chair, tape over his mouth. He put him in front of the computer.

'Now we'd like some sea,' he said.

'Of course,' the computer said, immediately bringing

up an image of a sunny beach, waves lapping on the sand.

'One last thing,' Linus said, then, checking that the guard was comfortable but secure. 'The patient in the hospital wing. Stop his medication. And give him something to wake him up.'

'That requires authorisation,' the computer said. Linus walked over to the screen, brought up 'Security' and started to input code, searching for the information he needed. Eventually he smiled, typed in a password. 'Now will you do it?' he asked. 'And will you unlock all the doors of the hospital too?'

'It's done,' the computer purred.

'Thanks,' Linus said with a grin and walked towards the door. 'Nice to meet you,' he said, as he gave it one last look before ducking out into the corridor before the guard's back-up arrived.

28

Lucas woke suddenly and looked around the room. It was sterile, white, with one small locked window overlooking a corridor. It had a cupboard, a sink, and over him was some kind of apparatus with tubes attached to the back of his hand.

And he wasn't dead.

In fact, he felt very alive. Incredibly so: more energetic than he had for weeks, months.

He jumped out of bed, pulling out the various tubes attached to him, wondering how he could have been lying there for so long. Everything was so silent that he guessed it must be night-time, even though it was impossible to tell with no windows. He edged towards the door, tried it and to his surprise, it opened easily. Outside his room was a corridor, dimly lit; again, there was silence, no sign of movement, of nurses, of guards, of Mr Weizman.

He walked back into his room to search for anything that might be useful. He found his clothes, neatly folded in a cupboard, found a bottle of water and a bag. He took the lot, put them in the bag, put his shoes on, then left the room once more. He crept down the corridor, his slow steps gradually speeding up as he saw the door in front of him, the door that he presumed led out of this place. Then he stopped, hesitated, reached out and pulled the door just an inch. More lights. A landing, a staircase down and up. A window that told him he was higher than ground level. He took the stairs down, then stepped towards another door, a door which he knew led outside because of the glass panel that revealed a path, moonlight.

He prepared himself mentally for a locked door. Told himself he would remain calm, figure something out. But when he reached out to the handle, it pulled open easily, just as the door to his room had done. Almost as if they wanted him to get out.

Lucas hesitated. Was this a trap? He considered going back to the room, but only for a split second. A trap could be no worse than the prospect of death on that bed. Why trap him when they already had him? When they were planning to kill him?

Silently, he slipped through the door, scanned the path and tents ahead of him, then, stealthily, he started to walk carefully towards the perimeter of the compound. It would be secure, of that he was certain, but there had to be a way through somehow, and whatever it was, he would find it. He had to.

He had to get to Raffy; that had become overwhelmingly clear to him. Linus might believe he was safe, but Linus had thrown Lucas off a cliff; Linus had his own agenda and always would. Lucas's agenda was to protect his brother. Just as it always had been.

He remembered the day that Raffy was born like it was yesterday; remembered the wonderment he'd felt at this small, fragile creature with its shock of black hair, black eyes and creased face, apparently boneless, curled up, utterly dependent, its only armour a cry that pierced through every other sound and created the backdrop of the house for the next year. It had been their father who had presented Raffy to Lucas; their mother had been sleeping.

'This is your brother,' he'd said gravely to his five-year-old son. 'He's going to need you to look after him.'

Lucas had taken him, gingerly, tenderly, had held his tiny body against his. In retrospect, Lucas suspected that their father had meant nothing by his words; had said them only to make Lucas feel part of Raffy's life, to include him in his care. But Lucas had taken them seriously; as he stared down at the tiny ball that was his brother, he solemnly promised to protect him always, to look after him as best as he possibly could.

For the first few years of Raffy's life, that had meant nothing more than watching out for him, teaching him the rules of the City, helping him up when he fell. But then, when Raffy was five and Lucas had just turned eleven, everything changed.

The night his father had come to Lucas, waking him from a deep sleep to tell him to follow him, silently, to his study, was a night that Lucas would never forget. The look in his father's eye – fear, determination – filled him, even now, with grief and longing for the man he loved so much; with anger and resolve to avenge his death. Because what his father had told him had changed everything, had marked the end of Lucas's childhood. He had told Lucas that he had discovered things about the City, things that were terrible, things that were secret and safely guarded, things that were dangerous to know. He told Lucas that the labels were not governed by a desire for good, but by a desire for power; that he had been communicating with an old comrade outside the City who could help them.

And from then on, Lucas had entered a different

world, a world of secrets, of shadows, a world in which he could never again reveal his true feelings except in front of his father; a world in which he worked all day then worked again at night, learning from his father, learning everything his father had to impart.

And then one day his father came to him, told him that something had happened, something that would be discovered soon, that his label would be changed to K, and he would disappear. He told his son that the whole family would face the same fate unless Lucas did exactly what he told him to do: betray him, tell the Brother that his father was a traitor before the Brother could discover what had happened. That way Lucas could lead the family, could protect them all. That way, Lucas could continue his father's work, continue to communicate with his comrade. That way, the City had a chance.

Lucas had opened his mouth to protest, to say that he would never betray his father, never let anything bad happen to him, but he had closed it again, because he knew even then that there was no use. He had already worked through the implications, the possibilities, the various outcomes in his mind, and he knew that he had no choice.

'You must never reveal the truth until the time has come,' his father had said. 'You must never tell Raffy.

He will hate you for betraying me, and you will have to live with that. Can you live with that, my son?'

And Lucas had nodded.

'Good,' his father had said then, relief washing over his face, relief tinged with pride and love, which gave Lucas the strength not to cry. 'Then let's make some coffee one last time.'

An hour later, when Lucas had alerted the City police to suspicious activity in his house, his father had been taken away and Lucas had become the protector not just of his brother but also of his father's legacy, of everything he had fought for.

He stopped, caught his breath. In front of him now was a wall; he ducked down, knowing that it would be watched. He could see a gate to his right; could he get through? Maybe if he waited for someone to come in, some vehicle . . . But he could wait all night, could wait for a week.

He picked up a rock, threw it at the gate to see what happened. There was a resounding clank, then a torch-light shining. He shrank back.

'Careful. You might have hit someone.'

Lucas's head swung up at the sound of a familiar voice. 'Linus?' Lucas stared at the figure approaching him in disbelief. 'You're here? How? Why didn't you come and get me?'

'No need,' Linus said with a shrug. 'But I wouldn't try and leave through the gate. Go through that and you're toast. Quite literally I'm afraid.'

Lucas looked at the gate warily.

'Thanks,' he said. 'I think.'

'No problem,' Linus said. 'This way.'

29

Lucas considered berating Linus for what he'd done, but found that he couldn't really be bothered. Instead, they left the compound quietly through a small pedestrian gate to which Linus appeared to have the code, then drove all night; for once, Lucas didn't feel sick; instead he could marvel at the world as they sped past and listen to Linus as he filled him in on the Settlement where Raffy and Evie were living. And strangely his stomach didn't flip-flop when he heard her name; strangely, he just found himself smiling at the thought of seeing her again.

'I feel amazing,' he said, turning to Linus, his eyes shining.

Linus grinned. 'That computer had some pretty great drugs,' he said wryly then, seeing Lucas's expression, and laughed. 'They had you doped up, so I got the computer to stop the meds and give you something to perk you up a bit. Turns out she did exactly what I asked. Won't last long, so enjoy it.'

'She?' Lucas looked at Linus curiously.

'Oh yeah,' Linus said, his voice deadpan. 'It had a lovely voice, actually. I think we could have hit it off. In different circumstances.'

The car slowed down then pulled into a set of caves. Lucas looked around. 'Where are we?' he asked.

'North,' Linus said. The North Pennines. At least that's what it used to be called. Nice place for walking. And lots of caves.'

'So I see,' Lucas said as Linus turned off the engine and they were plunged into darkness. 'You've got this all figured out, haven't you?'

Linus took out a torch, turned it on, and shot Lucas a grin. 'Something like that,' he winked. 'So the Settlement is about an hour's walk from here,' he said, opening the car door. 'You going to be okay?'

'I'm going to be just fine,' Lucas said firmly, and jumped out of the car, then followed Linus out into the darkness.

Mr Weizman stared at the computer screen. His boss was on it, looking very angry, very angry indeed.

'Let me get this straight. You had him? He was in the compound and he got away?'

Mr Weizman nodded. He'd already explained many,

many times, that there had been no sign the prisoner had been from the City, that there had been no indication that he'd been with someone, that he had been found outside the perimeter wall with a gash to the head and brought in as a precautionary measure, that once his status as 'of no use' had been established, Weizman had given the order to terminate him. The escape, the partner, the man who had got in to the mainframe . . . there had been no indication. No warning.

He had personally gone over what had happened several times, and had fired two people. But that didn't help him now.

The man sitting at the computer let out a long sigh, then he shook his head wearily.

'You're making things much harder for me,' he said. 'You know, I try and trust other people to do things and they never get it right, never.' Then he sighed. 'Fortunately I am a few steps ahead of you. And them. Fortunately I know where they are going, and I am ready for them. But you are to take this as a formal warning. Do you understand?'

'Yes, sir,' Mr Weizman said.

His boss turned back as if surprised to see him still on his screen. 'Yeah, I'm done with you,' he said curtly and the screen went blank.

Slowly, Mr Weizman turned and left the room and decided that he needed a drink.

30

The Brother walked slowly up to the front of the Meeting House, the home to Gatherings, to the weekly sermons that had always kept the City's people enthralled, towing the line, and as he walked he enjoyed the looks, stares and murmurs as he passed his flock. Because they were his flock, had always been his flock. He had spent a year in the wilderness, his wings clipped, having to pretend to have seen the error of his ways, having to pretend to be grateful to Lucas.

Grateful? He despised Lucas. Loathed him more than he had loathed anyone in his life. Lucas was a traitor, a manipulative, secretive traitor who had become . . . The Brother shook his head in disgust. He couldn't even describe what Lucas had become. Lucas, who had appeared to be so strong, so uncompromising, had been a pathetic, snivelling ideologist all this time. Just like his father.

Still, he was gone now. And if he ever tried to return, he would regret it. Not for long, though, he wouldn't survive in the City for more than a day. Not by the time the Brother had finished with him.

He stopped briefly outside the Meeting House, looking up at it with pleasure, with relief at being back. Gatherings had been one of his favourite aspects of the City he had helped to mould. A weekly meeting, they had offered him a platform, a chance to remind everyone how lucky they were, how important it was to guard against the evil that flourished so readily, given half a chance. Everyone had sat according to their label, the most public forum for label watching that the City could offer. And the Brother had loved it; loved the contempt on the look of the faces of the A's as they regarded the sorry clump of D's, loved the way the B's held their heads high while casting envious glances in the direction of the A's, and then there were the C's, clinging on to respectability, so fearful of becoming a D that they could barely look at them lest they be tarnished immediately. Divide and conquer – wasn't that the phrase? And it was so true. So wonderfully, beautifully true and simple.

Having their place in life set out for them, that's

what people wanted, not Lucas with his pathetic attempts to let them choose for themselves. Fortunately Lucas hadn't had the stomach to lead the City; fortunately he had failed so miserably that the Brother had been more than able to pick up the pieces as soon as he'd gone.

The truth was that leadership wasn't easy, the Brother knew that all too well. It took sacrifice, time, effort. It meant constantly being on your guard, constantly looking for danger, constantly working out new ways to manipulate, cajole, fire up and quietly threaten. People were like sheep, the Brother had learnt that many years ago. They liked to be led. But if you didn't lead vigorously, if you didn't keep absolute control, another sheep might break out from the group and, mindlessly, others would start to follow.

Of course not everyone could see that. Lucas thought that if he offered people freedom they would respect him for it, would welcome it. But people didn't want freedom; they wanted rules, regulations, structure. Why else had man clung on to religion for so many years? Why else had dictators flourished throughout history? People didn't want freedom; they didn't know what to do with it. They wanted only the appearance of freedom; they wanted a belief structure that told them how to behave, that punished the bad, and made everyone else feel safe, and in return they would ignore any holes in the theories, any contradictions, any unsavoury facts that it didn't suit them to dwell on. That's how mankind had always lived. How it always would.

He walked into the Meeting House, through the centre, up to the raised platform and held up his hands. Everyone fell silent.

'My friends, brothers and sisters,' began the Brother. 'It is so good to see you all here, as it always is. Let us give thanks.'

There was a ripple of something, and it grew louder. Then louder still. And then the Brother smiled, because it was a cheer; the people were cheering him, all five thousand of them, their hands up in the air.

'Brother!'

'Welcome back, Brother!'

'Let us give thanks!'

'We are safe again!'

The Brother allowed it to continue for a few minutes, basking in the adoration, then he held up his hands again.

'Friends,' he said, seriously now. 'Friends, I am touched by your welcome, moved by your passion. But today is not a day for celebration. Today is a day for commemorating our dead, our fallen. As you know, your former leader, Lucas, left us recently, ran from the City that had looked after him all his life, taking with him one of our young. Clara, the last of the Disappeared. We don't know where he took her; I think perhaps we do not wish to know. Because when he left, brothers and sisters, we discovered the truth – the bodies piled up outside the City walls, the rest of the Disappeared. It was Lucas, brothers and sisters. Lucas who was responsible for the deaths of our young. Lucas fell prey to evil, brothers and sisters, and we did not succeed in helping him, in fighting it. We are to blame as much as he. But now we must join together; now, we must be as one, united in our desire to keep evil outside these City walls. But first, let us give thanks for all that we do have; for this City, for each other, for the food that we grow, the work that keeps our minds active and our bodies strong.'

'We all give thanks,' everyone said fervently.

The Brother's eyes fell on Clara's parents, their eyes still bloodshot, their hands entwined, clinging on to each other for support. He smiled to himself.

'Let us give thanks to this great City.'

'We all give thanks.' More loudly this time.

'And finally . . .' the Brother paused, looked to the back of the room where one man sat, camouflaged by former D's who still knew their place, who, to their credit, did not dare to sit with former A's or B's as they had done when Lucas had gathered the people together. The man nodded and the Brother allowed himself a little smile. 'And finally, let us give thanks to the System, which was shut down by the forces of evil, but which we will bring back, as soon as we can, to protect us, to look over us. So that we will lose no more of our beloved children. So that we may be protected from the evil that roams outside, that threatens to grow in this City if we are not vigilant.'

'We all give thanks.'

The Brother smiled. Everything would be okay. Everything was just as it should be once again.

31

Raffy knew the man was there the minute he sat down to eat his lunch. There was no sign of him, but Raffy had an ability to pick up on the little things, a change in birdsong, an unidentified rustle in the branches of a tree, things that others wouldn't notice, things that told him to be on high alert.

He sat, took out his food and started to eat, but really he was waiting. And sure enough, a few minutes later, the man appeared. Raffy gazed at him thoughtfully. 'You were right,' he said, his voice expressionless.

'Yes,' the man said. He sat down a few feet away from Raffy. 'I'm sorry about that. I just thought you should know.'

'You're not sorry,' Raffy said, his dark brown eyes staring at him insolently. 'You told me for a reason, and I suspect that now you're here to tell me that reason. You want something from me. What is it?'

The man smiled. 'Not much gets past you, does it?' he said.

'On the contrary,' Raffy said, staring at him, his big brown eyes half hidden behind his unruly hair. 'Quite a lot does, evidently. You had to tell me about the watch. Seems I'm the last to know about a lot of things. So tell me. Why are you really here?'

'A lot of things? You're referring to your brother? To all the lies he spun you over the years?'

Raffy didn't say anything; he took another bite of his sandwich, then wished he hadn't when he realised his mouth had dried up. He realised that he had no interest in eating now and spat the food out.

'That bad?' the man said. 'So I'm guessing you won't be too pleased to hear that he's coming this way?'

Raffy looked up abruptly. 'What?'

The man shrugged. 'He's coming here to take you away. You and your girlfriend.'

Raffy's eyes narrowed. 'We're not going anywhere,' he said, his voice low, threatening. 'Lucas can do what he wants, but I'm ready for him.'

The man pulled a face. 'I'm sure you are, Raffy. But can you really speak for Evie? Now that you know about the watch?'

Raffy didn't say anything; he wasn't going to let this man see that inside he was boiling with rage.

'She chose me, not Lucas. She'll always choose me,' he said. Then he stood up. 'Is that it? Because I'm going to get back to work.'

The man nodded. 'You haven't eaten much,' he observed.

Raffy stared at him with thunderous eyes. 'I'm not very hungry,' he replied.

The man smiled. 'Okay,' he said. 'Look, you're right. I'm sure you're right. If Lucas does come here, Evie will tell him to go; she'll do whatever you say. But, and it's a big but, if she doesn't, if things don't go entirely according to plan, I have a little proposition for you.'

'What kind of proposition?' Raffy asked, turning around, his eyes flashing. 'Who are you anyway? You never tried to join the Settlement. I asked around.'

The man laughed. 'All right, you've got me.' He looked at Raffy cautiously. Then he sat back. 'Truth is, we've got something in common. You're not wild on Lucas; I'm not happy with your brother either. Not happy about a few things that he's done. I figured we might be able to help each other. I mean, I can't imagine you're too keen on him coming here, trying to take you away from the first place you've been happy in your whole life. Trying to take Evie away from you. See, I don't think Lucas is the kind of person you can trust, is he? I mean, he's demonstrated that in the past, hasn't he? So how about you sit down again and let me tell you my idea. Just in case Evie doesn't see things like you do. Let me tell you, and then you can decide what you want to do. Does that sound okay?'

He looked up at Raffy hopefully; Raffy took a deep breath. He didn't like this man. Didn't trust him one bit. But he'd been right about the watch. If he was right about Lucas . . . if Lucas was really coming . . .

He let the breath out, sat down, looked at the man. 'Fine,' he said. 'Tell me your idea. But I'm not making any promises.'

'I wouldn't expect you to,' the man smiled, reaching his hand out. 'My name's Thomas, by the way. It's very nice to meet you.'

'This is where they are?' Lucas looked at the large fence ahead, so different from the City wall. It appeared to simply mark a boundary rather than keep people out or in. 'This is where they live now?'

Linus nodded. 'Wait here,' he said. They were a few hundred metres from the perimeter of the Settlement; Lucas watched curiously as Linus ran to the fence, waited, appeared to throw something over it, then ran back again. Lucas found Linus more irritating than he could put into words, but at times like this he could only marvel at a man twice his age who seemed as fit and lithe as a teenager, who seemed to know everything, who never ceased to surprise. Lucas, who had spent his life obeying orders, could not fathom Linus, but as he watched him running back, he shook his head in admiration. Although, of course, he had no idea what Linus was up to. As always, Linus hadn't told him anything.

'So?' he asked, not really expecting an answer, or at least not one that meant anything.

'So?' Linus repeated, distractedly.

'So what was that all about?' Lucas asked, trying not to get annoyed, trying to remember all that admiration.

'Just a little note to Benjamin,' Linus shrugged. 'Something we developed a few years back.'

'We? You know Benjamin? You never said you knew him,' Lucas said.

'I don't,' Linus said. 'But a long time ago, when we were building the City, I thought it might be prescient to meet the leaders of the various civilisations around the UK. Work through a code, a messaging system, that sort of thing.'

'And?' Lucas asked, realising that without prompting Linus was going to tell him nothing.

'And I left him a message. So he'd be ready for us. So he'd be able to prepare,' Linus said, his face crumpled in bemusement as though he couldn't understand why Lucas didn't know everything already . . . or perhaps why he wanted to know in the first place.

'Fine,' Lucas relented. 'So what now?'

'Now?' Linus asked, looking around, holding up his hand to shield his eyes from the sun. 'Now we find a place to watch until we're ready to go in.' And with that, he started to walk; Lucas watched him for a few seconds then, with a sigh, started to follow.

32

'Benjamin? Benjamin?'

Benjamin stirred, and for a moment, he was somewhere else, somewhere very different. For a moment, the sound of Stern's voice transported him back, back many years to a prison cell, a cell the two men had shared for twenty-three hours a day sometimes, eyeing each other cautiously, exchanging a few words, sizing each other up, working out who would defeat who, if it came to it, as inevitably it would, one day.

They had shared that cell for three years, seventeen years less than the sentence Benjamin had been given. And it was from that cell, or from the open area outside it, that they watched the Horrors unfold around them. When he'd been incarcerated, the violence had been limited to the bombing of mosques and churches, attacks on Gay Pride marches, street riots and a general feeling that the chaos was taking over, that it couldn't be reined in, that the police and army were only ever playing catch-up.

But that had only been the beginning. Those, Benjamin realised later, had been the good old days.

He still remembered the moment he realised that the Horrors were never going to end well, that the destruction wasn't going to stop until it stopped itself, until there was nothing left to destroy. It had been an ordinary day at the prison: kitchen work in the morning, then lunch, then free time in the afternoon. He'd enrolled on the education programme; had already passed five GCSEs and was now working towards his A levels. It had been way better than school; smaller classes and the people there really wanted to learn, even if every so often they got frustrated, even if that frustration got vented violently, even though guards would be called and prisoners dragged away for drawing a knife on the teacher when he or she put some red lines through their work. He felt like he was finally making something of himself; finally seeing who he was, what he might be.

At that time, the army was already on the streets of the UK, of much of Europe. Because of riots, mainly. And the riots were because of food shortages, which were exacerbated by the riots because half the roads were blocked off, because every vehicle that crossed the border had to be searched several times. And anyway, who wanted to drive anything into this godforsaken country? Even the relief workers were leaving food on the border and turning round immediately to go back home. Anyone with any money had already left, leaving a skeleton of doctors, managers; those who doggedly refused to leave, those that couldn't. It was left to them: the terrorists killing each other, and the rioting, hungry masses who had started to burn entire cities to the ground. And the worse things got, the fewer deliveries there were, the less food there was to go round. It had become a vicious circle; Benjamin could see that from his position of relative safety, watching the news, shooting a look at his fellow prisoners if they got in the way or made too much noise. At one point the government had considered releasing all prisoners to save on the cost of keeping them alive, but they'd decided against it; had figured that adding thousands of hardened criminals to the toxic mix on the streets would not be a sensible plan. And so, the prisons, along with hospitals and nursing homes, were one of the few bastions of civilisation, prioritised for food, so safe that many prison officers were now sleeping in the corridors, bringing their families in to keep them away from harm, away from the rioters outside.

Benjamin had been in the prison a few years and had been in enough fights to prove himself. He was part of the establishment. People didn't mess with him. And anyway, most of the prisoners wanted to listen; needed to watch the devastation. Because it was their world being destroyed, even if they weren't exactly in it right now. Their families being killed, by terrorists, by rioters, by the police or army trying to keep order. Week after week the bad news came and cupboards or walls got new holes in them from angry fists.

Things were bad; Benjamin knew that much. But it was that day that he realised how bad; that day that he started to question the point of all his hard work, of having passed all those exams. Because he understood suddenly that this was not a small, localised fire that could be put out. It was a forest fire that would rage until there was nothing left to burn. And he knew that they were all going to die, all who were in the path of the fire, it was just a matter of time. He understood that there could be no other ending, just a variation of degree: whether everyone died or slightly less than everyone, whether they suffered a great deal of pain or a little less than that.

It had just been an interview. The usual post-traumatic-event interview with the Prime Minister in

which he condemned the latest atrocity, said that the
people of the world would no longer stand for these
things, that ordinary people would fight these terrorists, these vandals, these murderers, that he was on
the side of the ordinary people, that he would put
more police on the streets, more tanks. And the inter-
viewer had barely listened to a word he said, had cut
in and said that they had another point of view. And
they'd cut to a man, Pastor Hunt, and he'd started to
talk, and as he talked, Benjamin realised he'd heard
it all before, that he knew the sermon word for word.
And when he looked closer, he saw the 'I' badge on
his lapel; when the camera panned back to the inter-
viewer, he saw that she had one too. And that's when
he'd known that there was no hope. That there was
no going back.

As Benjamin quietly watched the interview, he had
felt something change within him, and right there he
had an epiphany. He was sick of it. This stuff – this
anger, this violence – all of it was a disease, a disease
that had got past the stage when it could be cured.
Benjamin vowed that if he didn't die, when it was
over, when the fire had run its course, ravaged the
world, he would make something better in its wake.
He would build, somehow, somewhere, a better place,
a place where violence no longer held sway, where

people could express themselves without fear of attack, where they were listened to, encouraged, enabled. A place where he would lead, not from the front, not telling the people what to do, but instead from in among them.

He never thought it would happen, because he was sure he wasn't going to live that long, not now, not when he could see the destruction hovering on the horizon. But that day, straight after the news, he went back to his cell, squared up to Stern, looked him right in the eye, and said something that he remembered to this day. 'Hit me. If you want. Get it over with. Because it's your last chance. If you want to have one over me, you're going to have to kill me. And if you don't, then you're going to do as I say. And what I say is, there ain't gonna be no more fights, no more violence. I'm sick of what's going on. I'm ashamed. So we can wait here until everything's gone, we can scrap like animals. Or we can be stronger than that. I want to be stronger. I want to start something good here. I want to build something new. Something better. So hit me. Now. Or help me build it. Your choice.'

Then he'd waited for the punch to land. Only it never did. Instead, Stern had held out his hand, clasped Benjamin's. He had just got word, he told him, that his son was dead. The only thing that made his life worth living. His son, who was only three. He had been outside a restaurant that was blown up; got caught by the glass. He had been taken to the overcrowded hospital too late; left too long by the few harassed, overworked doctors who were still there. And now he was gone.

Benjamin remembered all this as though it were yesterday, and yet it also seemed a lifetime ago, not even his own lifetime, someone else's, someone he used to know. He opened the window, stepped out into the sunshine and took a deep breath. It was good to be alive, he found himself thinking. Good to be part of this place of growth, of acceptance, of new beginnings. Everyone needed a fresh start, sometimes. Everyone deserved a second chance.

He walked towards the centre of the Settlement, past the artisans making furniture for the ever-expanding population, past the bakers, past the grassy knoll where small children were being entertained, and then he stopped. Because coming out of the sewing rooms, draped in a long white dress that was about three sizes too big, was one of the Settlement's newest recruits. He smiled as he watched the women cooing over her, as Sandra pinned the dress here and there to try and make it fit Evie's tiny frame.

And then she looked up, saw him, and he was forced

to break his reverie and walk towards her. 'Evie,' he said. 'You are going to make a beautiful bride. And a beautiful citizen.'

She smiled, but Benjamin noticed that it didn't quite reach her eyes.

'Thank you,' she said. Then she turned to Sandra. 'I should take this off,' she said.

'Not yet,' Sandra scolded. 'I need to pin it. You keep getting thinner, Evie. And you haven't twirled enough. We want to see you twirl, don't we girls?'

The women laughed and egged Evie on; Evie duly turned twice, but Benjamin could see that her heart wasn't in it.

'I tell you what,' he said. 'You pin, Sandra, and then Evie and I are going to take a walk to lunch. How does that sound?'

Sandra nodded quickly and hurriedly pinned the dress before whipping Evie back into the sewing rooms; seconds later she reappeared in her usual clothes, looking up at him earnestly. That was how it was for Benjamin; he made a suggestion and before he had considered whether it was a good one, it had been carried out, quickly, efficiently. It was the sort of thing that could go to a person's head; could be quite intoxicating, Benjamin knew that all too well. But he also knew that any power he had was only as strong as the commitment he had to his people; knew that they were not sheep following him, but that rather, that it was he who served them, he who owed everything to them.

Evie looked up at him, anxiety written all over her face. He smiled. 'So,' he said, 'shall we walk? It is a beautiful day today, don't you think?'

'Beautiful,' Evie agreed.

'And soon you are to be a citizen of this place. Does that make you happy, Evie?'

She nodded fervently. 'Very,' she said, her eyes looking strained.

'But you are fearful, nevertheless. Is your fear related to this place, to committing to it, or is it more a question of love, of personal commitment?'

When he saw Evie's eyes cloud over, he knew immediately that he had got to the nub of the problem.

'I am not fearful of anything,' Evie said quickly. 'I am so happy here, Benjamin. I am truly lucky and I know that. We both do. I know that Raffy's really sorry for what he did. And actually it was probably my fault really. So please don't hold it against him. Neil said it was okay. He understood. Please don't think Raffy's . . . Because he doesn't mean to be like he is. He tries . . .' She trailed off; Benjamin could see the conflict in her face, the desire to protect Raffy competing with her own frustrations with him.

Benjamin nodded slowly. Then he stopped walking. Immediately Evie stopped, too.

'Love,' he said, 'is a difficult thing. We can love in different ways. Love our country. Love our parents. Fall in love. And out of it.' He took a deep breath. 'But love should never make us fearful, should never weigh us down. We are not responsible for each other, do you understand that?'

Evie bit her lip. 'I . . . I think so,' she said. 'And I do love Raffy. I really do.'

Benjamin smiled. 'Good. And don't worry about those wedding nerves. I believe everyone has those. Ah, here's Raffy. So, are you nervous about the big day too?'

Evie swung round; she hadn't seen Raffy approach.

'Nervous? Not at all,' Raffy said immediately, a slight edge to his voice. 'I wish it was today. And so does Evie. Don't you, Evie?'

He looked at her intently; she nodded. 'Of course I do,' she said. 'Of course.'

'Good,' Benjamin smiled, then, taking one last look at Evie, he left them to go and eat, walking back to his rooms where lunch would be waiting for him on his desk as it always was. But as he walked back towards his rooms, he saw something that he hadn't seen for many years, something he never expected to see again, and he realised that lunch would have to wait. It could have been there by accident, could well have blown in the wind from some faraway place. But Benjamin knew that it hadn't. It was old, dirty, had several holes in it. But the scrap of material that was lying in his path was without doubt a red silk hand-kerchief. And that could only mean one thing.

'What was he saying to you?'

Raffy rounded on her the moment Benjamin was out of earshot. His hand was around her wrist, tightly holding her.

Evie looked up at him warily. She'd never known him like this – after the Neil incident, he'd seemed truly sorry, had really seemed to want to change. For a few days he had been like a different person – a little too focused on work, perhaps, but easy with her, supportive, cheerful, no angry glances when she talked to other people, no reproachful looks when she came back from an evening class. And then, suddenly, he had reverted again, only this time it was worse, this time he blew up at the slightest thing, flew off the handle and nothing would calm him down again. 'He was talking to me about the wedding,' she said. 'He was saying what a beautiful day it was and how love was a powerful thing.'

Raffy nodded, bit his lip. 'And did you agree? Did you tell him that you agree?'

'I think so. I mean, I don't know, really. Raffy, you're hurting me.'

He didn't let go but instead tightened his grip. 'It is me that you love, isn't it?' he asked then. 'I mean, we're happy, right? The two of us? It's always been the two of us, hasn't it? And we're happy. We're getting married. It's what we've always wanted, isn't it. Isn't it?' He was staring at her intently; his soulful eyes boring into hers. She could see the pain in them, see the fear, but she didn't know what to say, didn't know why he was doing this.

'Evie, you okay, love?' It was Sandra, walking towards them. Raffy loosened his grip; Evie feigned a smile.

'Fine,' she said.

'Just trying to find out what the dress is like,' Raffy said lightly.

'Ah well, don't tell him!' Sandra joked. 'But she's going to be stunning. Truly stunning!' She smiled at them both before walking past.

Evie looked back at Raffy; his eyes were fiery now, full of rage.

'Raffy,' she said. 'I don't know what's wrong with you. Of course we're getting married. Of course we're happy . . .'

She felt tears pricking at her eyes, tried to force them back, but Raffy had already seen them, was already wiping them gently away with his thumbs.

'I know, I'm sorry,' he said suddenly, his face changing, the anger gone, replaced by regret, by remorse. 'I just love you so much,' he said then, leaning down to kiss her, holding her face in his hands, stroking her cheeks with his thumbs. 'All my life people have tried to take you away from me. And I'm not going to let them. I'm not going to let any of them. I'd kill someone before I let them take you away from me. Whoever it was. You know that, don't you?' He was looking at her so intently, so passionately, and Evie could see the gypsy boy she'd loved for most of her life, but she could also see the boy who wanted to keep her for himself, who didn't trust her, who would never let her be free.

'I know,' Evie said, and as she spoke, she felt a hole form in her stomach, but she refused to acknowledge it. Because she knew he was telling the truth. And she knew that there was nothing she could do about it.

33

Lucas caught sight of Evie and felt himself gasp involuntarily.

'What? What did you see?' Linus asked. They were sitting in a leafy tree, a few hundred metres outside the Settlement. They were taking it in turns to watch the gate, waiting for the Informers; had been there for hours. But Lucas had allowed the binoculars to gaze over the Settlement itself, and that's when he'd seen her.

'Nothing,' he said quickly. 'Just . . . a bird, flying towards me.'

Linus raised an eyebrow and took the binoculars from him, training them on the Settlement. Then he raised his eyebrows even more; he had apparently seen the same thing Lucas had. 'A bird, you say?' he said. 'That's a pretty big bird.'

Lucas breathed out, leant back against the tree on whose branches he was perched. Evie. She was there, so close he could almost call out, get her to see him, to come to him. She'd looked happy. Of course she was. She was with Raffy. He closed his eyes, then opened them immediately; he was so tired that if he closed his eyes he would fall asleep. Instead, he lifted his hand to his forehead and squinted, staring at the Settlement as though it might offer him some kind of answer. But he wasn't even sure what the question was.

He shouldn't be here, he realised with a thud. It had been a mistake. This was all a big mistake.

He looked over at Linus. It was early evening; the light was just beginning to fade. 'You said they were safe here.'

'Yes, I did,' Linus said.

'Maybe we should leave them here. Go after the Informers instead. They're happy here. That has to count for something.'

Linus looked thoughtful, then he put down the binoculars.

'It does. But I think the goalposts have changed a bit.'

'They have?' Lucas raised his eyebrows. 'How?'

'How?' Linus exhaled slowly. 'How,' he said again, as though to himself. 'Well, for starters, the Informers aren't entirely what I expected. I mean, they are, in many ways they are, but in many ways . . .'

He trailed off; Lucas looked at him impatiently. 'They are but they aren't? Linus, please, this is people's lives we're talking about. Stop talking shit. If you have something to say, say it.'

Linus's eyes widened in surprise. 'Got that off your chest?' he asked, a note of sarcasm in his voice, then he let his head fall back. 'Truth is, Lucas, I don't know.'

'Don't know what?'

'I don't know,' Linus shook his head. 'The technology they have. The sophistication. This isn't some group of survivors who snagged some good stuff before the Horrors destroyed everything. This goes way beyond that. The information they have. It's . . .' He pulled a face. 'It puts a different slant on things,' he said, after a brief hesitation. 'It makes me review my former belief that Raffy is safe where he is. That any of this is as straightforward as I'd believed. They have bombs, Lucas. They have weapons that weren't even invented during the Horrors. What is a group of survivors doing with bombs? Just who are they planning to attack?'

Lucas digested this. 'We need to get Raffy and Evie,' he said.

'Not yet,' Linus said cautiously.

Lucas stood up and started to pace. 'You want to

tell me why? I can get over that wall and get the two of them in five minutes. What are we waiting for?'

'We're waiting for the Informers. Because they're following us. Have been since we left their camp.'

Lucas stared at Linus angrily. 'Are you serious? We led them here? To the very people we're trying to protect?'

Linus shook his head. 'They've always known where Raffy is,' he said quietly. 'They know everything. That's what I'm trying to tell you. That computer system . . . I've never seen anything like it in my life.'

'So then why are they following us? They want Raffy; Clara told me.'

Linus shrugged again. 'I don't have all the answers,' he said gruffly. 'But I do have questions. Like why didn't Clara die? Why are the Informers on our tail? What is it that they really want? This whole thing is more complex than we can see right now. It's like a game. Only I don't know yet what we're playing for. Or who we're playing with.' He raised the binoculars again. 'Okay, I think it's time to go. Look.'

He handed them to Lucas, who shifted his gaze to the barriers that divided the Settlement from the barren landscape around it. The thin fence Linus had thrown something over; a fence that looked almost apologetic, timid, and yet Lucas found it much more confident than the City walls that were so high, so well guarded. But guarded from who? From what? Not the Informers, certainly. He heard a sound, a car engine in the distance. And then he saw it: not a car, but a small van, driving quickly towards the Settlement, dust flying as it sped along. 'They're here,' Linus whispered then, his voice barely audible. 'They're here.'

Benjamin sat very still. Around him hung a veil of silence, the only sound the hum of activity just audible through his open window. His rooms were sparse; his robes simple. But he was not without his one luxury, the only one that mattered to him. Peace. Peace and quiet. A few minutes each day without noise, without interruption, this was what he insisted upon. Time to gather his thoughts, to plan, to consider; time to let his brain wander; time to let his shoulders relax. He had had enough noise in his life. Certain noises he never wanted to hear again.

He took a deep breath and enjoyed the feeling of exhaling, slowly, thoughtfully. A wonderful thing, the human body, he mused. So complex and yet, ultimately, so simple. Air to breathe, food to nourish it, clothes and shelter to protect it, a friendly face, a hug . . . Humans strived for so much, but needed so little, really. He looked around his room, as he liked to do each day at this time, its stillness and sparseness pleasing him immensely.

Again, Benjamin breathed in and out, slowly, meaningfully, then he stood up and walked towards the window, a full-length one that looked out over a courtyard; on the other side was farmland, continually worked and tended. Food. Nourishment. He had chosen this view specifically; he wanted to see life, not death. Wanted to see hope, not devastation.

There was a knock at the door; he turned. 'Come in.'

It was Stern. 'Benjamin, we have some visitors. The Informers.'

'The Informers?' Benjamin frowned. He had been expecting visitors, but not these. But then again, he had learnt in his life that few things could be predicted. 'Where are they?'

'They are outside. They wish to speak with you.'

'Then give me a minute,' he said, 'and we'll see what they have come for.'

He waited for Stern to leave, then closed his eyes and took a deep, cleansing breath to prepare himself. The signal had rattled him earlier; it had been so long since he'd seen it he'd almost forgotten the pact he had made years before, having been visited by a strange man called Linus, one of the City's founders, who seemed almost like a prophet from Biblical times: wise beyond his years, his teaching made up of stories that Benjamin hardly knew how to interpret. But he had been a good man; Benjamin could see it in him, knew he could be trusted. And before he left, they agreed on a signal. A signal that would alert them to danger, that could not be ignored. But there it was, and now these men . . . Were the two connected? How could they possibly not be?

Steeling himself, he opened the door and went outside. The men and their vehicle were only just inside the perimeter wall, Benjamin noticed, as he walked towards them. They were not here for hospitality. They did not intend to stay longer than was absolutely necessary. Which was probably good news; it would be another transaction, an increase in demand, that's all. He often wondered if Linus had anything to do with these demands; often hoped, somewhere deep inside, that he didn't.

There were three of them, one dressed smartly, the other two in khakis. The smartly dressed one he recognised. They had met several times in the past, most notably six months after he had established the Settlement when the man had come to see him, all silky smiles and offers of protection that essentially led to demands for food. Tithes to the City; a monthly request for food to ship down to the City's people.

And Benjamin, to his eternal shame, had agreed. He had been tired of fighting. He had not wanted to see more death.

He scrutinised the other two men. Were they armed? The Informers did not carry weapons, that's what they always said; they didn't need them.

He nodded at the smartly dressed man who had chosen never to divulge his name. 'My name is Benjamin. Welcome, brothers,' he said, stretching out his hand. The two men in khakis said nothing.

'Good to see you again, Benjamin,' the suited man said with a smile. 'We've come to ask you a favour.'

Benjamin didn't return the smile. Visits from these men always meant trouble, meant that the City was either upping its demands for the Settlement's taxes or communicating some grievance. But Benjamin knew he could meet them. They would work harder, produce more, do whatever it took. Just like every other little civilisation in this godforsaken land, Benjamin knew that the Informers were too powerful to refuse; knew that paying what they asked would give them the independence and peace they so desired. He hadn't even told his people that a quarter of the Settlement's produce went to the City every month; it was easy enough to send the shipments when the Informers came, and so much better to have a people happy with their lot than one that resented a City far away. Resentment led to war, and war was something Benjamin never wanted to see again.

'A favour?' He could hear Stern behind him, clearing his throat, knew that it was his way of making a stand, of signalling his unhappiness. But Stern was not the Settlement's leader; he did not have to make the hard choices. Before Benjamin had ever had a visit from the Informers, he had heard about townships being burnt to the ground, all their people shot down. Townships that had not been so amenable to the Informer's proposition, that is, who felt that the City had enough already, that it did not need more. Benjamin had known early on that the Informers meant business. 'I didn't think we were due a visit so soon. I'm afraid you find us unprepared.'

'I am not here to collect,' the man said, a reassuring smile on his face. 'At least, not the usual produce. I wonder, Benjamin, might we talk inside?'

Benjamin nodded slowly, mentally preparing himself. The Informers never usually stepped inside any of the Settlement's buildings; they preferred their visits to be short, to the point and rarely left the side of their vehicle. On collection night (and it was always at night), they would simply check that everything was in order, then drive around the back to the collection point where goods would be loaded onto their lorry.

But though he could feel his heart thudding in his chest, he kept his expression emotionless. 'Of course,' he said, showing him the way and motioning for Stern to stay outside with the two men in khakis. They walked into his rooms, and Benjamin closed the door. 'Please,' he said. 'Sit. Make yourself comfortable.'

The man didn't sit down. He looked around the room, then looked Benjamin in the eye. 'Benjamin, we believe that two young people have recently joined your community. Young people who escaped from the City and who we are keen to have back. They are missed. That is who we have come for. I would appreciate it if you would bring them to me quietly so that we can take them home. Right away.'

'I see,' Benjamin said thoughtfully as his heart filled with dread. Until now he had hoped that perhaps there would be a way to appease these men. Now he knew there would not be. Goods he would trade; people he would not. 'Two young people, you say.'

The man nodded. 'The only two people to have joined your community in the past two years. You know who I'm talking about. Raffy and Evie. We need them, and we need them now.'

Benjamin looked at him carefully. 'All the people in our community are citizens. Handing them over . . . it's not that easy,' he said.

The man's face hardened. 'Benjamin, don't be stupid about this,' he growled. 'They haven't been here long; they don't deserve your protection. Just give them to us and we'll leave with no fuss. Whereas if you don't . . .'

'If I don't?' Benjamin asked lightly.

The man smiled. 'You know what will happen,' he said. 'And it would be a shame. It's a nice set-up you've got here. Very nice indeed.'

Benjamin digested this, made a decision. He shrugged. 'You're right,' he said. 'They are recent additions to our community. I'm sure we can let them go. Let me just find out where they are. I'll need to come up with a story for everyone. I don't want people being afraid.'

He shot the man a pointed look but he didn't seem to notice. Slowly, Benjamin walked to the door and called Stern over, whispering in his ear. Stern looked taken aback, but nodded immediately. Then, just as slowly, Benjamin walked over to his shelves and pulled out a box file and walked back towards his desk. 'Not in there,' he murmured to himself, placing the box file on the desk and opening it. 'Ah, here we are,' he said.

The man saw the glint of metal too late; Benjamin had already fired a shot. As he did so, two more rang out from outside the door. Immediately the door opened and he and Stern exchanged glances, glances that communicated everything they needed to, glances that they had learnt years ago when they had been inmates together in prison, back in the old world, the world they rarely talked about now.

'We'll need to do something with the bodies,' Benjamin said grimly.

Stern nodded.

'And would you mind walking to the gate. With this?' Benjamin handed him the dirty cloth he had picked up earlier that day. The cloth with the red mark. A mark that said *Do whatever it takes*. Benjamin had done what had been asked of him; so had Stern. And now he needed to know why. 'I think we have some other visitors. I'd like to see them right away.'

Stern frowned uncertainly and took the cloth. As he turned to walk away, Benjamin reached out and touched his shoulder. 'Thank you,' he said. 'For believing in me.'

Stern looked at him strangely. 'Everyone believes in you,' he said. 'But only you believe in me. There's no need to ever say thank you.' And with that, he disappeared, leaving Benjamin staring down at the Informer and the pool of blood seeping out all around his floor.

34

Evie woke with a start to see a face bearing down on hers. Benjamin. She stared at him uncertainly, her heart thudding in her chest as she pulled the sheets around her.

'Evie,' he said gently. 'I'm sorry to disturb you so late but you have to get up.'

'Get up?'

'That's right,' a voice said, a voice so familiar that she thought she must be dreaming because it couldn't be him, couldn't be Linus, it made no sense. She sat up, stared at Linus and Benjamin standing over her. And then another face appeared behind them that made her eyes widen and her face flush and her heart thud loudly in her chest, and she knew without question that this had to be a dream. Had to be.

'Lucas?' It was Lucas. It actually was him. She stared at him, unable to move, unable to think, her heart thudding, her hands suddenly clammy and wet. Was this a test? A warning? A—

'Lucas?' Evie turned at the sound of Raffy's voice. He had woken and was sitting bolt upright, staring at Lucas feverishly. 'What are you doing here? What are you all doing here?' His voice was gruff, angry and he moved in front of Evie as though he could block her from view.

'I'm sorry Raffy but we have to leave this place,' Lucas said, his voice low. 'You're both in danger.'

'Leave? No,' Raffy said, turning away. 'We're not going anywhere.'

'Raffy,' Benjamin said seriously. 'I'm afraid you must. Men have come looking for you. We have dealt with them, but there will be more. And worse. It is imperative that you leave now.'

There was a soft knock at the door; Evie saw Stern's face appear as it opened. He looked taken aback to see the room so full of people but quickly sought out Benjamin and moved towards him silently.

'I have tidied up,' he said, looking at his leader meaningfully.

Benjamin nodded grimly. 'We don't have long,' he said.

'An hour at most.' He looked at Linus. 'And you say the City is not behind this? And yet they were the City's men. The Informers.'

Linus pulled a face. 'The Informers might appear to do the City's work, collecting food for them. But in truth it's the other way around. The Informers are not from the City. These two men might be doing the City's work, but they're doing it for their own ends. Either way, they're more dangerous than you can imagine.'

Benjamin appeared to digest this, then gripped Stern by the arm. 'Stern, I need you to take leadership of our people for a time. The Settlement is under great threat; I need you to evacuate, take everyone into the hills, just as we've practised. There are food stores that will last several months, if that's what it takes.'

Stern nodded silently.

'Follow the drill, ensure that it's followed to the letter. I'll make sure that Raffy and Evie leave safely, then I will join you.'

'Of course, Benjamin,' Stern said, his face filled with confusion.

'Remind everyone to be strong, remind them that we're in this together.' He released Stern, shot him one last look. 'Now go,' he ordered, then turned back to Raffy. 'You must leave. Now. Your lives are in danger.'

Evie caught Lucas's eye and flushed, looking away quickly, studying the floor, the bed linen, anything.

'Maybe if you could . . . leave us for a few minutes,' she suggested, 'we could get ready?'

She smiled at Benjamin awkwardly; immediately he nodded.

'Of course. I'm sorry. We'll be outside.'

'You can stay outside,' Raffy said. 'We're not going anywhere. Neither of us.'

Linus looked at him archly. 'You've got five minutes,' he said. 'Then we're taking you, dressed or not.'

He walked out, followed by Benjamin and Lucas. Evie picked up a bag, started to throw things into it. Raffy sat up. 'We're not going, Evie. Put that down. It's a trick.'

Evie turned to him in disbelief. 'A trick? Raffy, are you mad? Benjamin said himself we have to go.'

'Because Lucas convinced him to. This is all about Lucas,' Raffy said, shaking his head, his eyes narrow. 'He just can't bear me to be happy. You don't know him. Not really. I'm not going anywhere with him. And neither are you.'

Evie shook her head in bewilderment. 'You have to get over this anger at Lucas,' she said. 'This is not about the two of you. It's not all about you and Lucas.'

Raffy glowered at her. 'I see he's got you where he

wants you,' he said darkly. 'But then he always did, didn't he?'

Evie shook her head despairingly. Then zipped up her bag. 'You know what?' she said, tugging at some robes. 'I'm going. If after everything we've gone through you're going to act like such an idiot then that's fine, but I'm not hanging around. You stay here. You do what you want.'

She started to walk towards the door, but Raffy jumped up, grabbed the bag from her and threw it on the floor. 'No!' He rounded on her, grabbing her wrists. 'If you love me, you won't go. You'll stay with me.'

'Ready?' The door opened and Linus's face appeared. He frowned when he saw Raffy restraining Evie. 'Come on, we don't have long.'

'We're not coming,' Raffy said, his voice low and tense. 'If Benjamin doesn't want us here, we'll go somewhere else. But on our own terms. Without any help.'

'No, Raffy,' Evie said. 'Let go of me.' She stared at Raffy's hands. Then he released her wrists and his hands fell limply back to his sides. 'Now, pack,' she ordered.

She'd never heard herself sound more angry, more in control. And to her amazement, Raffy didn't argue; didn't threaten her, didn't lose control. He just stared at her, his eyes flashing, then shook his head and picked up a bag.

35

Devil looked around. Put the briefcase in the walkway, that's what Thomas had said. The walkway in his own estate. Hide it where no one will see. Then walk away, far away. But Devil didn't want to walk away; he knew what was in the case. He'd looked.

He put the case down, started to pace around. His forehead was covered in sweat. Thomas knew what he was doing. He had to. He was clever. He knew stuff. Knew stuff about Devil. He had chosen Devil, and Devil didn't want to let him down.

He was supposed to leave, get the hell out of there. That's what Thomas had said.

But he couldn't. Not yet. Not till he was sure.

Sure about what? What else was he going to do with the case? He opened it again, tentatively, his fingers slipping on the clasps. He swallowed, a huge lump appearing in his throat, his stomach lurching. Thirty minutes. That's what the timer said. Thirty minutes and thirty-five seconds. Thirty-four seconds. Thirty-three . . .

This was what Thomas wanted him to do. What his father wanted him to do. Thomas talked about his father a lot. Told him that he hadn't forgotten Devil, not at all. He'd had to leave, but he'd asked Thomas to look out for him. Told Thomas that Devil was a winner, that his father wanted him to take over his flock, that he wanted him to be a leader just like him. Soon, Thomas told him on a regular basis, Dalston would seem like a bad dream.

Bad dream or a fucking bombsite?

Devil wiped his forehead. His heart was going so fast he thought it might explode. Twenty-eight minutes and twelve seconds. Eleven . . .

He had to get out of here. This wasn't on him. He was just doing a job. Just proving himself. Proving he had what it took.

What it took to do what? Kill people?

He stared at the case. Stared back at the sprawling estate. He hated it. Loathed it. But he didn't want everyone to die. The people who lived here were all right. They were just getting by.

'Do this job and a new life awaits you, Devil.'

He looked around, agitatedly. Then, suddenly, he stood up. Picked up the case. Started to run. He'd never run so fast. To the wasteland behind the estate. He shouted as he ran, scattering the few people hanging out towards the back of the estate. 'Get away from here,' he yelled. 'It's dangerous. Get the fuck away! This thing is going to blow!' And they ran, they ran quickly, away from Devil, away from the case in his hand. And then he found what he was looking for, the hole dug for the foundations of the youth club. Two metres or so. Maybe three. He threw the case in, braced himself for the explosion but none came.

Then he turned and started to run again; he was getting out of there, as far away from the estate as possible.

As he ran, the phone in his pocket started to ring and he saw Thomas's name.

'Yeah?' He was panting.

'You've done it?' Thomas asked.

Devil hesitated. 'Yeah.'

'Good,' Thomas said. 'Where are you?'

'Just leaving now.'

'I'd run if I were you.'

'I'm running,' Devil said. 'I'm running.'

And as he ran he saw that the few people he'd shouted at before were getting people out of the estate; they weren't just running themselves, they were rounding people up, moving people out, banging on doors. And he didn't know why but he started to cry, because people weren't sheep. They weren't weak. They were good. They were so much better than him. And he turned again and ran back, and banged on doors himself, and pulled people out, and told them stories about gangs coming to burn the estate down, to make them see they weren't safe inside, and there was no time, but still he ran, and shouted till he was hoarse, and they were all out, all as far as he could see. He started to run himself, following the crowd of people who had no idea where they were going or why. And then his phone rang again.

'Are you far away now?'

'Not really,' Devil said.

'Start running then,' Thomas said. 'You're going to be famous, Devil. I'm going to be posting your sermons in just a few minutes. You're going to be *infamous*. People will follow you.'

'What do you mean?' Devil asked, his eyes fixed on the estate, on the land behind it, waiting.

'Genesis,' Thomas said. 'You told me yourself.

'And the Lord said, I will destroy man whom I have created from the face of the earth; both man, and beast, and the creeping thing, and the fowls of the air; for it repenteth me that I have made them. But Noah found grace in the eyes of the Lord.' That's you, Devil. You're Noah. And God himself. Punishing the wicked, offering salvation to the others, if they follow you, if they do what you ask them to do.'

Devil shook his head. 'It's not going to work, Thomas. There ain't no one dying here today.'

'What do you mean?' Immediately, Thomas's voice went cold, angry.

But Devil didn't notice. Because he'd just seen something. The kid. The little girl. The one whose bike he nicked. On the walkway, looking down, her face scared, uncertain. And there were only seconds left to go, but Devil bounded back towards the estate, up the stairs. He picked her up and put her on his shoulder, and then he was running, but he knew he wasn't going to make it, and as he reached the bottom of the steps there was a crash, a bang, like a million fireworks going off at once, only louder. 'It's started,' he heard Thomas through the phone. 'The flood waters are coming in.'

And Devil could smell smoke, could hear people running, screaming, but he was paralysed, couldn't move a muscle because of the smoke in his nose. He hadn't smelt smoke like that since . . . not for a long time. And then he could move, but all he did was fall to the ground as the memories flooded in. The smoke. He remembered it. Remembered it filling his mouth, his nose. He remembered being scared, worrying about the cigarette he'd been smoking, the cigarette which had caused the smoke, because if his mum found out she'd beat him, beat him senseless. And then he remembered running out of the flat, to safety, away from the smoke, away from the fire.

And he remembered not even thinking of Leona.

He could feel the warmth, could smell the death in the air, clawing its way into his lungs. People were shouting but Devil wasn't listening to them. Because he was somewhere else, somewhere filled with smoke, smoke and heat. He remembered it. He was back in the flat, back in the flat the day Leona died.

Devil realised he was holding something. The girl. She was in his arms, his phone pressed against her shoulder. Leona?

Not Leona. How could it be Leona?

Leona hadn't fallen out of that window. His mum probably hadn't even left it open.

Leona had opened it.

Leona had jumped.

She'd jumped because he'd started a fire and then left her to burn.

A flash of red filled Devil's mind and he slowly pulled himself up. The girl was coughing; she was alive. She looked up at him, her arms around his neck. And he held her. He held her and he wept.

'Tell me what's happening, Devil,' he heard Thomas's voice shouting out of the phone. 'You tell me right now . . .'

He looked over at the phone and kicked it away. He held the girl for a few more seconds, feeling her warmth against him, her life. Then, as the sirens drew closer, he put her down, stroked her head, said goodbye and started to run.

36

Evie trudged silently in the darkness, her eyes fixed ahead. Next to her was Raffy, his hands shoved in his pockets, his eyes thunderous. She watched him for a few minutes, remembering how his anger at the world used to intrigue her, how his refusal to fit in made him so irresistible. Back in the City, it had been her and Raffy against the world; their secret meetings had been the only thing she ever looked forward to. He was the only person who seemed to question things like she did; who found the rules of the City constraining, like wearing chains.

But now, now things were different. Except Raffy had continued to be angry, resentful, jealous. Like nothing had changed. Like it wasn't the City that had made him like that after all.

And whereas his anger used to make him seem

exciting and dangerous, now it irritated Evie more than she could put into words.

Raffy was walking next to her, slowing his pace when she slowed hers, speeding up when she did. And as she walked, she realised that she was trying to shrug him off, that she'd been trying for a while now, that he'd never let her, that the more she tried to edge away, the more he would come after her.

And all this time she had let him have his way, had reasoned with him, tiptoed around him, let him make his demands, let him get angry for no reason. Because she knew he needed her. Because she thought she owed him. Because she wanted to be happy in the Settlement, because she didn't want to cause any trouble.

They were leaving the Settlement and something terrible was happening. And all Raffy cared about was keeping pace with her, making sure that he was right beside her, making sure that she wasn't out of his sight, even though he'd been quite willing to keep her in the Settlement in spite of Linus telling him their lives were in danger.

Because it wasn't her that he was thinking of.

It was himself.

Always himself.

Evie felt her heart thudding in her chest in indignation, frustration at herself for not seeing it before.

Even Raffy's anger with Lucas was self-sustaining, self-imposed. It wasn't about the kiss; he'd despised Lucas long before that. Even when he discovered how much Lucas had suffered to protect him. He should be grateful. He should let Lucas speak, let him explain, give him the benefit of the doubt for once.

He should grow up.

Evie thrust her left hand into her pocket and allowed it to wrap around the cool, metallic object that she'd hidden there, that she'd hidden for nearly a year, secreted about her person, buried at the bottom of drawers, continually moved to make sure it was never found. It had been the first thing Evie had put into her bag, the only item she'd known she couldn't leave the Settlement without. Before leaving the room she shared with Raffy, she'd transferred it to her coat pocket, just in case she lost the bag, just in case Raffy opened it.

It was Lucas's watch, the watch she'd worked so hard to get back after Raffy traded it; the watch she had hidden for so long with no real idea of what she was going to do with it.

Now, holding it in her hand, she felt herself getting stronger, felt her old energies returning. She wouldn't put up with it any more. She wouldn't allow Raffy to get his way.

She allowed her gaze to rest on Lucas, who was

walking a few feet in front of her. He was about the same height as Raffy, maybe an inch or so taller, but even compared to Raffy's new muscular frame, Lucas was still broader. He walked tall, too, his eyes looking straight ahead but his entire body on alert; Evie could see it, even though she wasn't quite sure how, or even what it was she was seeing. She just knew that he was watching, listening, just like he used to in the City.

She wondered what he'd been doing since they last saw each other. She wondered if he had anyone to talk to or whether he'd retreated back into his shell. In the City he'd always been so impenetrable, as though he had no heart, no soul. She had hated him; had seen him as the epitome of everything she despised about the City. And then . . . then she'd seen the real Lucas. When he'd confided in her, told her the truth so that she would convince Raffy to leave the City and escape certain death, she'd seen how hard it was for him; not the telling, but the stopping up of his emotions. It was like the pipe was full to bursting of water and he'd had to turn on the tap just enough to let out a trickle before closing it again.

Lucas stopped, turned and spoke to Linus, to Benjamin. She looked around and saw that there was a large rocky hill in front of them; she'd been so preoc-cupied with her thoughts that she hadn't even noticed her surroundings.

'Okay,' Lucas said. 'We stop here. Linus is going into the cave ahead to get his car.'

Linus disappeared into the darkness; Raffy shuffled towards Evie. 'Linus has a car?' His eyebrow arched upwards as he regarded Lucas, his tone of voice was one of insolent disbelief.

Lucas turned to him, his eyes steely. 'Yes, Raffy, he has a car. Any other questions?'

Raffy shrugged as though to demonstrate his lack of interest. 'Come on, Evie,' he said. 'Let's wait over here.'

He moved towards a rock and sat down; Evie looked at him but didn't move. Raffy glared at her, but still she stayed where she was. Finally she turned to Lucas. 'When did he get a car?'

Lucas caught her eye and she felt herself getting hot. 'I don't know,' he said, looking away quickly. 'I think he might have always had it. Trying to get an answer out of him is impossible.'

He looked down at the ground.

'Trying to get anything out of him is like that,' Evie laughed awkwardly. Her voice was shaking slightly, her whole body coursing with adrenalin, but Lucas had already turned, and was inspecting a stone on the floor; their conversation was over.

She felt a lump appear in her throat and found herself

walking over to Raffy. He moved so that she could sit facing him, but she faced the other way instead; away from Raffy, away from Lucas. Then she folded her arms and looked up at the sky.

She didn't know how long they remained like that, the three of them together but entirely separate, lost in their own thoughts. But eventually she looked back down again, and when she did she saw that two lights had appeared on the horizon, far away at first but nearer and nearer until the glare made Evie reach her hands up over her eyes. The car stopped and Linus jumped out. 'What do you think?' he beamed.

Evie, relieved to have him break the intolerable silence, jumped down off the rock. 'Looks great,' she said, trying to muster some genuine enthusiasm.

'Then get in. You'll love the inside.'

Evie nodded and walked towards the car.

'Get in the back,' Linus said. 'Lucas gets car sick; he needs the front seat. Don't you, Lucas?'

Lucas walked up behind her and opened the door for her. She felt his hand brush against hers for a second and her heart missed a beat. 'Not car sick,' he said. 'I just . . . don't like cars very much.'

She caught his eye and that's when she saw something she never expected to see on Lucas, on the man who was so contained she'd often wondered if he had any emotions at all. What she saw was a boyish expression of embarrassment, sheepishness. Because he didn't want her to see his weakness. Because he didn't get that his weakness made him suddenly so human, so vulnerable, it made Evie catch her breath.

37

'Okay, slow down. You're going to have to speak more clearly,' the policeman said as he rummaged around for a pencil. 'You're saying the explosion an hour ago was you? That you let off a bomb?'

Devil nodded. He was sweating; he'd run all the way here, had waited impatiently in line and was now finally at the front desk of the police station, a grey squat building in the middle of the high street. 'Yeah. This bloke got me to do it. His name's Thomas. I need to talk to someone. Someone in charge. This is big, man. Really big. He's crazy.'

The policeman nodded carefully. 'Just one minute.'

He left the desk, leaving Devil to catch his breath. He'd never willingly been in a police station before; had only been here a few times, late at night, dragged here by coppers to account for his whereabouts during some crime or other. Usually he'd been as uncooperative as possible, his expression sullen, his eyes full of hate.

But not now. His breath was still laboured; he gripped the counter in front of him to steady himself.

A policeman appeared next to him. He was wearing a suit; he was senior, Devil could tell from the tone of his voice. Relief flooded through him. They knew about the explosion. They were taking him seriously. 'Would you like to come with me?' he asked.

Devil nodded, followed him around the back, into an interview room.

The man sat down; motioned for Devil to do the same. Devil sat down on the metal chair, took a deep breath, looked up at the policeman, waiting for the question, for the 'So . . .' that would get him started.

But no 'So' was forthcoming. Instead the policeman just stared at him. Devil stared back, his instinctive response, eyes fixed, mouth set, his entire face a challenge. Then he checked himself and looked away; he wasn't squaring up for a fight – he was here to tell them about

Thomas. He had to make them see they could trust him, that he was telling the truth.

He looked around the room. There were usually two coppers in interviews. Maybe that was only when you were under arrest, he found himself thinking. Maybe one senior cop counted as two regular ones.

'You going to tape this?' he asked, looking around for a tape recorder but not seeing one.

'That won't be necessary,' the policeman said, a half-smile on his face.

Devil considered this. 'I think you should,' he ventured. 'Get every word. Because what I'm going to tell you . . . The guy behind this is a nutter. He's dangerous. You've got to stop him, man. But he's got friends. Works for a big company. In town.'

He drummed his fingers on the table. The policeman opposite him had a nondescript face, with dark hair growing out of his nose. Long ears. 'So you going to ask me questions, or what?' Devil asked impatiently.

The policeman shook his head. 'Like I said, that won't be necessary.'

'So . . . what then?' Devil asked suspiciously. He looked over at the door. Was it locked, he wondered. His heart started to beat more rapidly. 'Didn't you hear why I came here? What I've got to tell you?'

'Yes, you did,' the policeman said. 'But the thing is, Mr . . .' He looked down at his notes. 'Mr Jones, is there hasn't been a bomb.'

Devil shook his head. 'Hasn't been a bomb? Nah, man. Of course there's been a bomb. There are people dead, man. People injured.'

'There was an explosion,' the policeman said. 'But it was caused by a gas leak. Forensics have been there with the fire brigade.'

Devil shook his head. 'Are you kidding me?' he asked incredulously. 'It was a bomb. I had it. In a case. It went off. It was a bomb.'

The policeman smiled tightly. 'So, if there's nothing else?'

He stood up, and as he did so, Devil saw something, a little pin on his shirt. With an 'I' on it.

He felt the blood drain from his face.

'There's nothing else,' he said, his voice shaking slightly.

'Good. And we won't worry about paperwork, shall we?' the policeman said. 'Don't want you charged for wasting police time. The explosion probably just confused you. Made you think things were happening that weren't happening. Do I make myself clear? If I were you, I'd lay low. I wouldn't go bothering people, stirring things up. Do you understand? We wouldn't want anything happening to you, after all.' He leant closer. 'You screwed up, you little prick,' he hissed. 'Months of work ruined because of you. So I'd run away now before Thomas gets really angry. Before he decides to come after you. Okay?'

He was looking right into Devil's eyes. Devil knew a threat when he heard one. He'd given enough of them in his time.

He nodded. 'Yeah, man. Whatever. I don't want no hassle,' he muttered.

'No, you don't,' the policeman said and opened the door, showing Devil into the corridor, through another door, out into the front of the station. Feeling dazed, Devil walked out into the road. It was the same road as before but somehow it felt different now, like a switch had been flicked that changed the atmosphere, changed everything. He started to walk, but he felt like he was being followed; he turned, there was no one there, just an old woman grunting as she heaved her shopping down the road, another younger woman having a screaming row with a toddler. Were they working for Thomas too? Did they have one of those pins on? No, of course they didn't. Don't be stupid. Just keep walking.

He put his head down, walked faster, back towards the estate. No bomb. A gas explosion. How many people did Thomas have working for him anyway? Why hadn't they just killed him instead of all this?

Because Thomas wanted to show Devil who was boss, he realised with a thud. Because Devil had turned the tables, turned himself in. Because Thomas didn't like to lose, because he wanted Devil to be scared, every day, wondering what was coming, when it would come.

The estate was barely recognisable. Half the building was missing; the whole area was covered in police tape, loads of signs up saying 'Danger'. Ambulances were treating people; outside the tape women were screaming, children standing around wide-eyed. Two buses pulled up. Coaches. A man got out, started shouting. Residents were being taken away somewhere else, he said. No one could stay here. Devil walked towards the tape, towards the estate. Several security men stood in his way, preventing access. 'Sorry, mate, too dangerous,' one said to Devil.

'I live here, man,' he said, trying to get past.

The man pulled him back. 'Fill in a form,' he said. 'Everyone's moving to temporary accommodation. You can collect your stuff later. What's left of it. There's going to be compensation, though. You know it was a gas leak? Hold on to that form. You might make some money.'

Devil took the form. 'A gas leak?' He looked down at the form, but couldn't focus enough to read it properly. A gas leak. People were really buying this shit.

'That's right. Apparently they knew about the dodgy pipes a year ago, council should have fixed it and didn't. There's a bus leaving in half an hour, over there. You wait for it. And remember to fill in the form.'

Devil walked in a daze towards the large group of people waiting for the bus. His mum was standing next to a man Devil recognised, a man she was friendly with. She was looking drained, confused. The girl was there with her mum, Nelson too. He shuffled over to Devil. 'Fuck, man,' he said.

'Yeah,' Devil said, his mind racing. 'Yeah.'

Then he put his hand in his pocket, took out the money that Thomas had given him. A grand to blow up his estate, to kill all these people. He walked over to his mum. 'Here,' he said, pressing the money into her hands. 'Look after yourself.'

His mother stared at him uncertainly, then nodded.

'You look after her for me,' he said to the man.

Devil walked back to Nelson. 'You keep an eye on them,' he said. 'Make sure no one takes her money. You get me?'

Nelson looked at him in surprise, then shrugged. 'Yeah, man. Whatever.' Then he frowned. 'Where you going then? Why don't you make sure no one takes it?'

Devil didn't say anything. He didn't know. Not yet. He watched as the bus doors opened and people started to get on. Most of them were covered in dust. And that's when Devil saw him, the man driving the bus, as he got down to help an old man on; that's when Devil saw the ring on his finger, the ring with an 'I' on it.

'You get the bus, man,' he said to Nelson. 'I'll catch you later, okay?'

'Later? But—' Nelson started to say, but Devil was already walking away, already running. And as he ran, he took the pin off his hoodie, the one that he'd worn all this time, and he threw it onto the ground, treading it in with his shoe.

He wasn't one of Thomas's gang. Not any more. He paused a moment, stared at the pin with loathing, with shame, with fear. Then he started running again.

And as he ran, he realised that he would always be running. Running, or doing whatever Thomas asked of him. Because men like Thomas didn't give up. Men like Thomas didn't let people like Devil slip through their fingers. He could look over his shoulder all his life but it wouldn't be enough; there would always be someone, something he missed.

He was never going to be free because he knew too much.

And right then, Devil knew what he had do to. The only thing he could do. The only thing he wanted to do. Because he didn't want to run from Thomas, but he didn't want to run from himself any more either.

And so he ran back into town, back into the police station, pushed past the queue, stood at the desk and banged his hand down.

'I want to turn myself in,' he shouted.

The man at the desk pressed a button; immediately the policeman, the one with the 'I' badge came out of a door, walked towards him.

'You again,' he said, his face cold. 'I told you not to waste police time. There was no bomb. There was no . . .'

'Not that,' Devil said quickly. 'I want to speak to the ginger policeman.'

'Pete?' the man at the desk said. 'You want DC Wainright?'

'That won't be necessary,' the policeman said. 'You can talk to me.'

'I want Pete,' Devil said desperately. 'Please,' he begged the guy at the desk. He shrugged, picked up the phone. The door opened and the ginger-haired policeman appeared. He looked at Devil uncertainly.

'He's wasting police time,' the senior policeman with the hair growing out of his nose said. 'I'm handling it.'

'Right you are,' PC Wainright shrugged and turned to go.

'Wait,' Devil cried out. 'Wait.' He looked PC Wainright up and down; there was no pin, no ring.

'What is it?' the PC said.

'I want to turn myself in,' Devil said.

'For something that didn't happen,' the thin-lipped policeman said.

'For the Green Lanes Massive murder,' Devil said, banging his hand down on the desk. 'For drug dealing. Running a gang. You know all about it. You were there. You spoke to people. You know it happened. I want to confess. I want to confess . . .'

38

They had been walking for forty minutes and had already made good progress; by daybreak they would be safe, hidden. It had been Linus who had taught Benjamin about the safety of caves, about nature's gift to those seeking to survive. It had come up the first time they'd met: Linus had quizzed him on the Settlement, on how it was run, on how it provided for its people. So many questions that Benjamin had grown suspicious, had threatened to have Linus removed if he didn't come clean about his reasons for being there. But Linus hadn't seemed fazed, not in the slightest; he had just continued to talk, to notice, to ask, to make suggestions. He told Benjamin that his Settlement was vulnerable, that he was vulnerable as leader. 'Always have a fallback position,' he'd told him. 'Always have somewhere to run to. Trust me, you'll thank me one day.'

'You think we'll be all right?' he said.

Stern looked at him strangely; Benjamin didn't often ask for reassurance. Perhaps twice in twenty years. Then he nodded. 'We're all alive. We've got food and water. The caves are ready and waiting,' he said. 'Of course we'll be all right.'

Benjamin nodded uncomfortably. They were all alive. But for how long? Where was he leading everyone, anyway? Who was he to decide he was their leader, the person who made all the decisions? Sometimes he heard people talking about him as though he was some kind of deity, some kind of saviour sent from heaven. But he knew what he really was. He knew he was nothing like a God.

Then again, it wasn't like God had ever done much for people. The Old Testament God had been more interested in brutality, killing and maiming like a warlord. Then he sent his son to preach on his behalf and allowed him to be tortured and murdered. Perhaps his son had displeased him, Benjamin found himself thinking. Perhaps he had been unhappy with his son's interpretation of his message. Because Jesus talked not of punishment, but of forgiveness, of patience, of living a simple, good life, of being tolerant of others, when it was abundantly clear that his father was not tolerant at all. His father did not forgive; he was a man of rage, hell-bent on absolute power, demanding total loyalty and submission from his followers. Sure, the Bible made out that God sacrificed his son to save the world, but that never really rung true for Benjamin. Jesus just didn't seem to be talking from the same script as his old man. Maybe he got carried away. Maybe his dad hadn't banked on him having a mind of his own. Benjamin allowed himself a little smile, imagining Jesus as the son of a dictator, trying to modernise the regime, trying to make it appear more people-friendly, more acceptable when his father hadn't been interested in changing the status quo. Perhaps it was for this, not to save anyone, that Jesus paid the ultimate price.

'It may not be a bad thing, angering the City,' Stern said suddenly. 'Maybe now we can tell our people the truth. Now that we've stood up to them.'

Benjamin turned, startled. He had thought that Stern wanted what he wanted; that appeasing the Informers was better than more bloodshed. 'You've wanted me to stand up to them before? Even though it puts our lives in danger?'

Stern didn't stop walking. 'A life lived on its own terms is generally better, even if it's shorter than one lived in subjugation.'

'But no one knew that we lived in subjugation,' Benjamin said.

'I did,' Stern said simply.

Benjamin nodded and felt his shoulders grow heavier. He had wanted his township to be a proud place, one of quiet dignity. The Informers had taken that from him. And he had taken it from Stern.

He walked, and took a deep breath, deciding that Stern was right, that this was a new beginning, a chance to start again. They didn't need much to live well. Air to breathe, food to nourish them, clothes and shelter to protect them, a friendly face, a hug . . .

'I'm sorry,' he said. 'But Stern, you must know. These men are not from the City. They act on its behalf, they collect food for it, but they are not the same. They have their own agenda. And crossing them is dangerous. You must be prepared.'

'I'm always prepared,' Stern said with a shrug.

Everyone was carrying a bag, but just one, and not a large one. People could travel lightly when they needed to, and yet so often they tried to do the opposite. Benjamin still remembered the days of plenty, of greed, of material things piling up in every room, every cupboard, infecting their owners, polluting the land. So many things, and yet everyone was always in a hurry to buy more. Like an addiction, he thought to himself. As though things could fill the void, as though they somehow provided the answer.

It seemed a lifetime ago. A time when everyone considered themselves invincible, just as he had done. No one could know what was to come; no one could predict the Horrors.

Except for one person.

He stopped walking, as the familiar nausea washed over him, the nausea that always accompanied that thought, that knowledge. Then he frowned, turned to Stern. 'Can you hear something?'

Stern shook his head. 'Hear what?' he asked.

Benjamin put his hand on Stern's arm, concentrated. Was he imagining it? Of course he was.

But then the whistle got louder. Stern heard it too, and others. Seconds later they all heard the explosion; as his people screamed and ran, Benjamin said a quick prayer to a God that he knew didn't exist, then ran after them to get them to the caves as quickly as he could.

'What is this place?' Raffy asked cautiously, his eyes darting around, resting on Evie every so often, then over at Lucas, before darting back around the room.

'This,' Linus said, walking towards the biggest computer, 'is my little hideout. My research centre. Please, have a seat.'

Raffy ignored him. 'But what are you doing here?

What's with all the computers? I thought we were going to Base Camp.'

'You assumed we were going to Base Camp,' Linus shrugged. 'I doubt thought had much to do with it. You made an assumption based on previous experience.'

Raffy's eyes blackened.

Lucas stepped forward. He wasn't in the mood for this. Wasn't in the mood for Linus's little jokes and evasion tactics. 'Linus, stop patronising Raffy and tell him what we're doing here,' he said. 'Or let me tell him.

Linus raised an eyebrow, and even Raffy looked taken aback. 'You don't think we should make tea first?' Linus asked quizzically. 'Come on, Lucas. Let's be civilised, shall we?'

Lucas opened his mouth to argue, then closed it again. He hadn't meant to snap like that. He didn't want to be here. Didn't want to be in this cave with them, the two of them. He'd thought he would be okay, but he wasn't. He wasn't at all. His brother evidently hated him; Evie was being polite but it was clear that she was unhappy. And why wouldn't she be? There was nothing to be happy about. His father had died for nothing; the City may not be in the grip of the System any more, but now it was under threat from the Informers, the murderers who were now looking for Raffy. It wasn't a better place. It would never be a better place, and it made him feel ashamed.

He caught Linus's eye, saw his face crease into a half-smile, saw the kindness in and amongst the lines etched into his cheeks, around his eyes. And for a moment he saw not Linus the infuriating renegade, but instead Linus the man who built the System, who believed in it, who was forced to escape from the City when he discovered that it was being corrupted, that everything he had worked for was being usurped. And as they looked at each other, there was a brief moment of recognition. Because Linus had been hopeful too, once.

'Tea, then,' he said quietly. 'But after that we tell Raffy and Evie everything.'

Linus nodded, held Lucas's gaze for a second or two more, then went in search of an old teapot. A few minutes later he started to make a fire.

Raffy stared at him. 'You've got enough electricity to power all these computers but now you need a fire to make a pot of tea? What about the kettle over there?'

Linus frowned. 'I thought Lucas was going to make the tea,' he said with a little shrug, his eyes twinkling with their usual mirth. 'I'm just building a fire for us to sit around. Raffy, help me, will you? There's some wood over there.'

Raffy hesitantly shuffled in the direction Linus was pointing; Lucas smiled to himself and went about making the tea. Evie, meanwhile, joined Lucas in Linus's makeshift kitchen and collected together some cups, the two of them seeming to dance around each other, not meeting each other's eyes, not bumping into each other, touching each other . . . She was avoiding him, he could see that. And he totally understood why. So he did the same, doing everything he could not to even make eye contact. He owed it to her. Owed it to Raffy.

A few minutes later, Lucas brought the teapot over to where Raffy was adding logs to a fledgling fire. Somehow, in being busy, the atmosphere had defrosted slightly; Evie and Linus were talking and even Raffy didn't look quite so thunderous. Maybe Linus had been right to insist on tea, Lucas realised. Maybe Linus was right about more than Lucas gave him credit for.

'Right,' he said, pouring the tea into the cups and handing them around. 'Let's talk, shall we?'

'Okay,' Linus said, gravely. He sat down and took a gulp of tea. 'The thing about the Informers,' he said, looking at Raffy carefully, 'is that they've been in the City from the start. I'm beginning to think they were even involved in its genesis.'

'So they're City citizens?' Evie asked, curiously, leaning forwards as though primed for action.

Linus shook his head. 'Not citizens, Evie. No, I don't know where they're citizens of. All I know is that after the Horrors, they watched and waited. And when they heard about the City, heard about the plans, they came to Fisher, came to our Great Leader . . .' he raised an eyebrow to emphasise the irony, 'and offered funding for his new City, offered help and support. Fisher didn't tell me. He just took what he could get and brought the Brother in on it later, got him to help them run their little scam. And in return for the help, the Informers have, as far as I can tell, had the run of the place. They've been watching it all this time. Why, I'm not sure. What I do know, though, is that all this time they've been building their own civilisation with technology that is way ahead of anything I have, that's been developed since the Horrors in places that are meant to have been completely destroyed.'

'But why do they want Raffy? I mean, I know you said it's because they think he can turn the System back on, but why?'

'That's what we need to find out,' Linus said, breathing out heavily. 'We need to find out what they want with the City and the System. We need to work out why they're here. Because one thing is for sure, they are not a force for good. And they're also very clever. Which in my book is not a great combination.'

He rubbed his head. Evie's eyes narrowed. 'What?' she said.

Linus looked her curiously.

'What else,' she said, folding her arms. 'You're not telling us everything. I can tell.'

Linus grinned. 'You can't tell,' he said, raising an eyebrow curiously.

Evie raised an eyebrow right back at him and Lucas felt his heart lurch hopelessly.

'Fine,' Linus relented. 'It's nothing, really. Just a hunch, an idea. But looking at the chronology of this civilisation, the way it was in place before the Horrors finished . . .' he trailed off as though unwilling to finish the sentence.

'Tell us,' Evie said, frowning. 'Tell us your hunch.'

Linus sighed. 'It just seems too . . . fortuitous. Too clean. It's almost like they knew. Knew what was going to happen.'

'But that's impossible,' Lucas said, frowning.

'Maybe,' Linus pulled a face. 'But looked at from a different angle, what seems impossible one day might look possible the next,' he said. 'In fact, most things that people think they know are actually not the truth at all. People used to think the world was flat. People used to think that the sun revolved around the earth.

349

People think a whole lot of things that turn out to be wrong. People think what is easiest to believe. I haven't got the right angle to look at this yet. Maybe, if I keep looking at it hard enough . . .'

'So you might be wrong?' Evie asked, then, her intelligent eyes penetrating Linus's fearlessly. 'I mean, you just said most of what we think is wrong, so you could be wrong now, couldn't you?'

Linus didn't seem to take offence. He smiled. 'Could be,' he conceded. 'But either way, there's a civilisation out there that has kept itself a secret for a very long time, that has been able to hide itself from me.'

'And they're going to want to hide if they don't want to be destroyed by me,' a booming voice said from the ledge behind them, and a tall, majestic-looking man with dark skin and short, slightly greying hair appeared. 'They have destroyed the Settlement. Everything we built. Everything . . .'

'Benjamin!' Raffy jumped up, ran towards him and helped him down. 'What happened? Why are you here? You shouldn't be here.' He looked genuinely upset, Lucas noticed, genuinely worried.

'What happened,' Benjamin said, putting his arm around Raffy and walking slowly, grimly towards the group, 'is that we are at war again.'

He walked over to Linus and held out his hand; Evie

could see tears pricking at his eyes. 'I'm at your service,' he said. 'If you want me.'

'Of course I do,' Linus said, moving so that Benjamin could sit down. 'Otherwise I'd never have told you how to find this place. But tell me. What happened?'

'What happened was what you told me would happen. But the attack was from the air. A bomb. The whole Settlement was destroyed.'

Lucas saw Raffy's face drain of blood. 'It's been destroyed?' he said, looking ill.

'Only the buildings,' Benjamin said, gravely. 'Our people are safe in the caves,' Benjamin nodded, shooting Linus a look of gratitude. He looked older, Evie noticed. As if he'd aged a decade in just a day. His eyes were flashing with anger, but his body looked defeated, beaten. 'They'll be fine for a few weeks. But I am not fine. I am angry.'

'You came on foot?' Lucas asked. 'How did you get here so quickly?'

Benjamin shook his head. 'Linus suggested many years ago that I keep a vehicle in the cave, just in case. I never thought I would need it.'

'Well I'm glad you came,' Linus said, moving towards him and putting a hand on his arm. 'Not about why you came, but it's good to have you here.'

'I am here to get justice. I am here because I need this to stop.' Benjamin's eyes were flashing, his jaw set firm. 'It was a good place, the Settlement. We troubled no one. We gave the City what it asked for.'

Linus raised his eyebrows. 'These people don't care about that,' he said with a shrug. 'You know that as well as I do. They don't care about the City, for that matter. Acting for the City was just a means to an end for them.'

'So what do they care about?' Evie asked, her voice wavering.

Linus breathed out. 'There's a question,' he said. He leant forward. 'Maybe they cared about something else, a long time ago. Maybe they thought there was some justification for what they were doing. The trouble is, Evie, that anyone who thinks they have an answer, a solution, anyone who thinks that they're right, will inevitably become a tyrant. As soon as you proclaim one right answer, all other answers must be wrong. Dictators, religions . . . they think they want to save us, but all they really want to do is tramp over everyone and attack anyone who challenges them. It's all just megalomania with a story attached to justify it.'

'So they're megalomaniacs?' Evie frowned.

Linus smiled. 'Something like that. Ends justifying means. Violence brushed under the carpet, dissenters silenced. Believe me, it's nothing new. But we have something they need, or at least the key to it. We need to play this very carefully. That's the only way we're going to win this little battle.'

'You mean the System?' Lucas asked.

'The System,' Linus nodded, breathing out slowly. 'What I really want to know, though, is why.'

He left the question hanging for a few seconds, then clapped his hands together. 'Now, however, it's time to get some rest.'

'Rest?' Evie asked indignantly, then stifled a yawn.

'Sleep,' Linus said firmly. 'Come on, I'll show you where I keep the blankets.'

39

Thomas Benning watched the news and smiled as desperate reporters stood in front of cameras, trying to interpret the latest attacks that had devastated the City of London and Birmingham on the same day: the first, an attack on wealth and capitalism; the second, the work of religious extremists.

Or so they thought, Thomas thought to himself with a smile.

He wandered into Adrian's office. 'Two more weeks, then we go big,' he said.

'Big? You mean . . .'

'I mean war. I mean armies, destruction on a global scale. It has to feel like the world is coming to an end.'

Adrian appeared to consider this. 'But . . . the bombs here. They're already pretty big.'

'Yes, yes,' Thomas said impatiently. 'But they're just *here*. Now it's time for phase two. We block off information from the rest of the world. Total blackout.' Adrian's face screwed up as he opened his mouth to ask a question. 'A blackout that no one is aware of because we simultaneously fill the void with the content we want them to see,' Thomas continued, before Adrian could interrupt. He found explaining all the time so tiresome. 'And do the same going out from the UK.'

'So no one knows what we've done?'

'Would you know that I'd taken over the airwaves if your television channel continued as normal?' Thomas asked.

Adrian shook his head.

'Would you know your friend in Europe was dead if you continued to receive emails from her, phone calls and web updates?'

Adrian shook his head again. 'But when people come here, when they fly out, they'll see the reality,' he said.

'Which is why the curfew and the closure of airports comes first,' Thomas said, rolling his eyes. 'You don't think I've thought of everything? You don't think I've got every single detail worked out?'

He laughed. 'Just do as I tell you, Adrian. Do what I ask and everything is going to happen just as it's supposed to.'

40

Evie followed Linus towards the cupboard where he kept the blankets and took some out. Lucas was behind her; she gave one to him. He looked awkward. 'Thanks,' he said. 'Are there enough?'

Evie glanced up at him; she could smell him, could feel the warmth of his skin. He looked so different from the man she'd known in the City, like a completely different person. But not a stranger. He looked older than he had when she'd seen him last; lines had appeared around his clear blue eyes. He looked exhausted. Like he'd almost given up on himself, she found herself thinking.

She nodded. 'There are plenty,' she said, clearing her throat. 'Take another. It'll probably be cold.'

Raffy was a few metres away; too far away to hear

them talking, but she could feel his eyes scrutinising them, could feel his anger.

'One's fine.' Lucas forced a smile. 'And I'm sorry. Sorry you had to come here. Sorry it had to come to this.' His eyes kept meeting hers then looking away again, as though he couldn't bear to actually look at her, as though he wanted to forget what had happened between them.

Evie forced a smile. 'Don't be sorry. It's not your fault. You're only trying to protect him. Protect the City.'

Lucas nodded. He was still just inches away from her; neither of them seemed able to move. 'I thought I'd never see you again,' he said suddenly, his voice was husky, low. And he was looking right at her now; Evie felt his eyes boring into her, like they might consume her if she wasn't careful.

'I thought I'd never see you, either,' she said, her voice catching. Her nails were digging into her palms, reminding her to hold it together. 'So how was the . . . I mean, in the City . . . what have you . . . ?' She had no idea what she was saying. Her brain had stopped working, had become a blank screen.

'Evie? Are you coming?' It was Raffy, walking towards them. Immediately Lucas moved away, the spell broken. Evie watched him go, then turned back to Raffy, her heart thudding in her chest.

'I'm coming,' she said.

They found places to sleep – Raffy and Evie in an area near the kitchen; Lucas in front of the fire. Linus and Benjamin had set themselves up on the other side of the cave; Lucas suspected they had intended to talk, not sleep, but already he could hear gentle snores coming from their direction.

He closed his eyes, allowed his head to loll backwards. His head hurt and he needed to sleep, needed sleep more than anything in the world, and yet he was finding it impossible because he couldn't relax, couldn't stop thinking, not for one moment. It felt like his brain had knotted together too tightly, as though someone were squeezing it together, wringing out any moisture, any air that might bring him comfort. His thoughts felt compressed; he couldn't untangle them, couldn't think straight. He felt heavy with tiredness but was too alert to sleep, his mind too active, his body too primed for action.

He'd thought it would be easier, thought that he was stronger, wiser. But he wasn't at all. Watching Evie with his brother was like physical pain itself, like a red-hot poker being jabbed into his eyes. If he'd hoped that he'd be able to remain impassive, that hope had been dashed the moment he'd set eyes on Evie, seen those eyes of hers, those eyes that were so alive, so questioning, so knowing. And every time he looked at her, he knew that he would never find peace, never find happiness. Not when she was with someone else, not when she was with his brother.

He took a deep breath. He had to sleep.

He remembered the hospital, and decided once again to count, not to stay awake this time but to take his mind away from this place, away from reality. He counted, up to a thousand and then down again. And as he counted, he felt himself get heavier. And as he sunk into a deep slumber, he saw Evie's face next to him, and he imagined Evie was caressing him, that she was embracing him, whispering in his ear that everything would be okay, that he was with her now, that all the pain had gone for ever.

Evie watched Raffy silently, watched him sit on the edge of their bedding, refusing to look at her but refusing to go to sleep. And the more his angry silence went on, the less Evie felt capable of breaking it. It was as though she'd run out of things to say to Raffy, but she knew that she hadn't; in fact there was a flood of things, but she just couldn't start because if she did she might not stop, and now wasn't the time. So instead, Evie had got into their makeshift bed and told Raffy she was tired. He looked at her balefully, then slowly stood up, got undressed and crouched down on the corner of the blanket. And that's where there'd been for the past hour; Evie not sleeping, Raffy not moving. She knew that he was struggling, knew that he was angry at the loss of the Settlement, angry at the Informers, at Lucas, at Linus. And she knew that it was up to her to help him, to allow him to express himself, to get out the thoughts that would currently be jumbling his mind. That's what she always did; acted as his sounding board, his confidant, re-assuring him, explaining things to him. Now, though, she did not know the right sentence to say that would unlock his confusion and fear. All she could find were silent images of Lucas flashing through her head, making her stomach lurch and her heart quicken, making her redden every time Raffy glanced at her, flooding her with guilt, flooding her with anger because Raffy was so obstinate when it came to his brother, so impossible.

'Raffy,' she said, finally, knowing that only she could break the stalemate; that Raffy would never speak first. 'Raffy, come to bed. Stop being so angry. Lucas came because you were in trouble. And everyone is here because of it. The Settlement doesn't even exist any more. This is bigger than you and Lucas. This is more important than that.'

Raffy opened his mouth, then closed it again, stood up, his eyes anguished. 'You don't get it, do you? After all this time, you just don't get it.'

'Get what?' Evie asked uncertainly.

Raffy shook his head. 'It doesn't matter. You know what? It just doesn't matter any more. I'm going to sleep.'

He got into the bed, lay down, facing away from Evie and pulled the blanket over him. Evie pulled the blanket back.

'It obviously does matter,' she said, trying to keep her voice calm. Now was not the time, she kept reminding herself. But it was no good. 'So tell me,' she said, sounding like a schoolteacher, her voice tight and cross when it should be sympathetic and supportive. 'What exactly has Lucas done that's so terrible? Apart from pretending to be someone he wasn't all his life to protect you? Apart from risking everything several times to keep you alive? What has he done that's so terrible?' Raffy grunted; Evie moved away wearily. 'I wish you'd stop being so blinkered,' she said. 'Lucas isn't the bad guy. I don't get how you can't see that.'

'Because he is,' Raffy said suddenly, sitting up, his eyes dark and thunderous. 'You're the one who can't see it.'

'So then tell me why,' Evie said in frustration. 'Give me an actual reason why he's so bad.'

Raffy caught her eye, then shook his head. 'There's no point,' he said quietly. 'It's too late anyway. He's done what he set out to do.'

'Which is what?' Evie said, her voice at least an octave higher than usual. 'What has he done? What?'

But Raffy wouldn't answer; he was lying down again, his back to her, the pillow pulled over his head. Minutes later, Evie could hear the sound of his deep breathing that signalled he was asleep.

She stared at his still body mutinously. How could he sleep? Her whole body was zinging with outrage. How could Raffy be so unreasonable? So unmovable? So . . . stubborn?

The more she watched him, the more angry she became and she needed to calm down, needed and clear her mind so that she had some chance of getting some sleep. He needed her, she knew that; wouldn't rest until they were married or living away from all other human contact. But right now the thought of being with him, only him, for ever . . . It made her sweat, made her breathless, like she was gasping for air, like her oxygen was slowly being sucked away.

It made her feel like she used to feel about marrying Lucas, back in the City, back when she'd thought that the only person she cared about in the whole world was Raffy.

She closed her eyes. Was it her? Was she incapable of being happy, of giving love? She breathed out heavily, opened her eyes again and stood up, then carefully padded out to the kitchen. Perhaps a glass of water would help. She could sit by the fire for a few minutes, let it warm her, let it hypnotise away her dark thoughts and desires. She was angry with Raffy, but she knew it wasn't really his fault. She was angry at herself, angry at the world. But she wouldn't be for ever. Things would calm down. And then she would probably be fine again.

She could see Linus and Benjamin sleeping on the other side of the cave, so she poured herself some water then walked over to sit by the fire, to warm herself, to calm her thoughts. But as she approached she saw that Lucas was there, sleeping under a pile of blankets. And she wasn't sure why she did it, but she found herself walking over to him, sitting just a few inches from where he lay; found herself studying him, his face, the bandages wrapped around his head, his arm, his hand. He looked so peaceful, so calm. She imagined him in the Informer's camp, so afraid, but still calm and rational, just like he always was. And she realised, as she watched him, that she had never seen him anything other than in control; he was always being strong for everyone, taking the lead. She had never seen him quite so vulnerable, and she found that she couldn't look away; couldn't possibly look anywhere else.

And then, without really thinking what she was doing, she found her own hand stretching out, touching his, lightly, then less lightly, her palm over the back of his hand, resting. Her hand looked so small compared with his, so delicate even after a year at the Settlement. She left it there for a few seconds, felt the warmth of his skin against hers. Then, silently, she took her hand away. She shouldn't be there; she knew that. But whether she had intended to or not, what she'd done had worked; sitting there next to Lucas had calmed her and she felt ready for sleep. Watching his chest rise and fall had slowed her own breathing, slowed her racing mind. So quietly, carefully, she stood up. And that's when Lucas's eyes opened. Evie reddened, looked at him anxiously. 'Sorry,' she whispered. 'Go back to sleep.'

But Lucas shook his head and looked right into her eyes. 'Don't go,' he whispered. 'Stay.'

The hairs on the back of Evie's neck were upright. Covered with goosebumps, she sat down again.

'How's Raffy?' Lucas asked softly.

Evie managed a half-smile. 'Asleep,' she said. 'Angry with you. Angry about everything.'

Lucas emitted a hollow laugh. 'Asleep is good,' he said. 'And what he thinks about me is irrelevant. Once this is over, he can go back with Benjamin. You can . . .' He hesitated, cleared his throat. 'Both of you, I mean. You can get married, like you were going to.'

Evie nodded slowly, her eyes meeting his, unable to look away. And that's when she saw something in his eyes, something that gave her hope, something that made her afraid; something that could only be the start of one thing and the ending of another; something that brought to a head everything she had been feeling for so long.

'Maybe,' she said. The word came out before she'd been able to mentally process the thoughts that had been tumbling around her head; before she could caution herself, before she could consider the implications.

'Maybe?' Lucas frowned, sitting up.

'Maybe,' she whispered, biting her lip.

He reached out, his right hand cupping her jaw, his thumb caressing her cheek. 'You deserve to find peace, Evie,' he said then, his eyes looking into hers so intently she had to look away.

'No,' she shook her head. 'No, Lucas. I don't deserve anything. She reached up to the bandage on the side of his head. 'What happened?'

'Linus,' Lucas said with a shrug, 'threw me off a cliff.'

She removed the bandage, brushed her thumb against the wound, felt the rough edges. 'Does it hurt?'

'Not really.' Lucas's voice was barely audible.

Evie nodded. Her hand moved down slowly so that her palm was against the back of his neck. She wanted to show him that there could be happiness and joy as well as pain and suffering; needed him to know that at least one person saw him as he really was.

'You should go to Raffy,' Lucas said huskily. 'He'll be waiting for you.'

'No,' she said, and as she spoke she realised that she'd known for a long time. Known that Raffy was the boy she'd grown up with but not the man she loved; not any more. 'You should go to Raffy,' Lucas said again, breathlessly, as he moved his arms around the small of her back, pressed her towards him, his hunger for her evident in every touch.

She shook her head, brought her other hand up to Lucas's face, pressed them into his hair, then she moaned as his lips found hers, as she felt her whole body ignite with desire, with need, with a connection so strong it almost overwhelmed her.

'Evie,' she heard Lucas whisper. 'Evie, Evie . . .' Again and again he said her name as he pulled her to him, as his lips moved around her face, her neck, as she clung to him, pressed herself against him, knew that she would surrender to him completely, knew that things were about to change for ever.

41

Raffy sighed and opened his eyes, then frowned as his hands patted the bed, stretched out, but were met with nothing. He sat up, looked around, tried not to feel the familiar clenching fear that consumed him every time Evie was out of his sight. She'd gone to the bathroom, gone to get a drink. She'd be back in a minute. But a minute went by and still there was no Evie and with every second he felt his chest constrict with terror, terror that she'd left him, that she'd been taken from him, that he was all alone, that she was with Lucas . . .

He stood up, slowed his breath, put his hand against the wall of the cave to steady himself. He had to calm down, had to take control of himself. She wouldn't do that to him; she wouldn't, no matter what that guy Thomas said. He was wrong; he didn't know Evie.

Although he'd been right about everything else.

Raffy closed his eyes, then opened them again when images of Evie and Lucas flashed into his head, images that had tortured him ever since she'd admitted to him that they'd kissed that night, the night they'd left the City. Evie and Lucas; Lucas and Evie – the very thought brought him out in a cold sweat. Lucas, who had everything else, could not have her; would not have her, not if Raffy was still drawing breath.

He started to pace; she would be back. Thomas was wrong. He had to be. And yet Raffy could hear his words so clearly still, could hear the solution he had offered . . .

Raffy took a deep breath, counted to three, then counted to ten. He had to calm down. Lucas hadn't come to steal Evie; he had come to help them, just as he always had. Raffy knew that and yet his resentment had only grown again. Lucas the hero; Lucas the saviour. Lucas the elder brother that Raffy had hated his whole life, hated so much it had become integral to his identity, as though if he were to stop despising his brother he would cease to exist. That's what Evie didn't get, what she didn't see. Discovering the truth about Lucas had only made Raffy hate him more.

Because Lucas's courage and determination only emphasised more clearly Raffy's own failings. Because against Lucas, Raffy would always be the also-ran, the let-down. And because one day Evie would see it, and leave him for his big brother.

He shook himself. He was being paranoid. He was letting that Thomas person play with his head, and his head was messed up enough already. Evie wasn't with Lucas. She loved him. When this was all over, they'd go back to the Settlement with Benjamin, help rebuild it, get married. Everything would return to normal. Everything.

But she still wasn't back. Maybe he'd just go and check. Just in case.

He picked up his torch and made his way down through the tunnel towards the computer room. If Evie wasn't in the kitchen or the sitting room he would wake Lucas, ask him if he had seen Evie. Not that he needed help, but more because it would give him an opportunity to talk to Lucas. To be mature. Reasonable. Just like he knew Evie was desperate for him to be. He'd do it for her. He'd thank Lucas for coming. He'd ask how things had been in the City.

He walked purposefully, his ears on high alert. And then he stopped; he could hear something. Evie. Her voice was muffled, a whispered cry, but it was definitely her. He moved quickly, anger flaring up inside him. If someone was hurting her he'd kill them; more than that, he'd rip them limb from limb, cause them more pain than they'd ever known before. He raced towards the sound of her voice and then he stopped, and his mouth fell open, and his whole world came crashing down around him.

She was not in trouble.

It was something else completely.

42

Evie crept back to bed, and when she saw Raffy lying there, his head on the pillow, unknowing, unsuspecting, she started to cry. Even her tears made her hate herself more because she had no right to cry; had no right to feel anything, not when she had just betrayed the boy she had always loved, the boy who depended on her for so much.

She lay down, closed her eyes, tried to sleep. And sleep came, eventually, but with it were feverish dreams that made her toss and turn, that made her sweat, that made her scream out and sit up. And when she opened her eyes and saw that daylight was creeping in through the cave's natural skylight, she reached over to Raffy.

And that's when she realised that he had gone.

Not gone, she told herself, just not in bed. He could be anywhere. Was probably mooching around. He didn't know anything. Couldn't know anything. He would be talking to Benjamin, arguing with Linus. Of course he would.

Quickly Evie got up, dressed and rushed out, trying to look relaxed, trying not to look guilty. But when the first person she saw was Lucas, when she saw his eyes, she knew that what happened between them couldn't stay a secret, not when he was looking at her like that, his eyes naked, every thought and emotion clearly visible in them, just as they were probably visible in hers.

She forced a smile. 'Seen Raffy?' she asked, her voice light but shaking because she was trying to sound normal, but she'd forgotten what normal sounded like, because nothing was normal, nothing would ever be normal again.

Lucas shook his head and his forehead creased. 'He's not . . .' Evie knew the end of the sentence: 'with you', words that Lucas couldn't bring himself to say. Had he suffered all night knowing that she was returning to sleep in bed with Raffy, she wondered? Had his night been as fitful as hers had been?

She shook her head. 'You didn't see him out here?'

Lucas shook his head again; Evie started to move more quickly through the cave. She called out Raffy's name but was met by silence. Soon Lucas was calling out too, walking then running through the cave, checking everywhere, shooting each other concerned glances as they searched.

'What's up? Lost Raffy?' It was Linus, emerging from his sleeping bag.

'He . . . he was asleep. But now . . .' Evie said worriedly. 'I'm sure he's here somewhere.' An image filled her head, an image of Raffy waking in the night, coming to find her, seeing her with Lucas . . . But she pushed it away. No. No . . .

Linus looked at Lucas, whose face was more serious than Evie had ever seen it. 'We can't find him,' he said.

Linus's face fell, went a grey colour. 'The Informers got in here and took him? No, it's impossible. No one can get in here. Not unless you know how. Not unless . . .' He ran to wake up Benjamin. 'Benjamin, did anyone follow you? Did you check? Double-check?'

Benjamin woke with a start, then slowly stood up. 'No one followed me,' he said, quickly. 'So what's going on?'

'Raffy's gone,' Linus said grimly. 'They must have got in. But how? And how did they take Raffy without waking Evie? It doesn't make any sense.'

'I was not followed,' Benjamin said categorically.

'I know I wasn't. Could they have found us some other way?'

Linus was pacing up and down, his arms wrapped around his chest. 'No. I mean yes, obviously, because they did, but no, it's impossible. And to get in, to take Raffy without us hearing anything . . .'

'Either way, we have to find him,' Lucas said. 'I'll find him. I'll go out, they can't have got far.'

'You're not going anywhere,' Linus said, his eyes narrowing.

'Yes I am,' Lucas replied, his blue eyes full of determination. 'We can't wait for you to work out a plan. Raffy's in danger and I'm going after him. I'm going to find my brother.'

'No, Lucas,' Evie said anxiously. 'They might be waiting.' It wasn't the Informers. That wasn't why Raffy had disappeared. She knew it, knew it in her stomach. He had known something. Somehow he had found out. But she couldn't say anything, because she knew no one would blame her; she knew they would blame only Lucas.

Lucas walked over to her, reached out to touch her then seemed to change his mind. 'If the Informers took Raffy, they would have taken us all,' he said, his voice slightly strangled. 'It's not them. I'll be fine.'

And when she looked into his eyes she knew why

he was going, knew that he didn't believe that Raffy had been taken either. He knew, just as she did, that they were responsible for his disappearance, not the Informers, that he had run away of his own accord. And she knew that he would never live with himself if they didn't bring him back safely. Neither of them would.

'We'll all go,' she said, her voice husky with emotion. 'We'll spread out and search. He might have left because we – we argued last night. We'll be able to find him if we all go . . .' She looked at Linus and Benjamin imploringly but was met by stony faces.

'Why would he have gone?' Linus asked. 'The Informers are hunting for him; he knows that by leaving this cave he's vulnerable, that they'll find him. So why would he do that? Why would he leave?'

Evie stared at him defiantly. She would carry her guilt, carry her anguish, but she wouldn't let Lucas be judged, wouldn't allow him to be blamed. 'You know he didn't want to be here,' she said. 'He wanted to go back to the Settlement.'

'There is no Settlement,' Benjamin said, walking towards her. 'Not any more. And he would not leave without you. Evie, is there something you're not telling us?'

Evie looked over at Lucas, who shook his head.

'There's nothing else,' he said, firmly. 'Raffy was there when you went back to sleep, wasn't he, Evie?'

Evie nodded; she was hot now with everyone's eyes on her.

'So let me go and find him. Before the Informers do. Before they . . .'

'Kill him?' Linus said quietly. 'They won't do that, Lucas. If they do find him, they won't harm him. They need him. If they find him, they'll take him to the City.'

'So then I'll hunt for him here. And if I don't find him, we'll go to the City,' Lucas said, running towards the exit.

'First *we'll* hunt for him here,' Evie corrected him, running to join him. And then she heard more running and it was Linus and Benjamin behind her.

'We look for ten minutes. No more,' Linus said gruffly. 'Although you know even that is pointless. If the Informers have got him, he's far away; if he left of his own accord, he's had several hours on us.'

'So why are we searching?' Benjamin asked as they climbed out of the cave.

'Because otherwise Lucas and Evie stew in angry guilt and be no use to anyone,' Linus shrugged.

Evie shot him a look, then stopped. 'What's that?' she asked. It was a loud, thudding sound, coming from outside the cave, stopping Lucas in his tracks. It was causing a wind, too, a wind so strong that Lucas was having to hold the side of the walls to remain upright.

'It's a helicopter,' Linus shouted, rushing towards Lucas.

'A what?'

'A flying machine,' Benjamin said, reaching out to take her hand. 'Evie, come back. Come back with me.'

Evie saw Lucas and Linus shouting, struggling to be heard above the sound of the helicopter, and then, finally, they were running back to where she and Benjamin were, Lucas's face white with anger, Linus looking more fearful than she'd ever seen him.

'Back,' he shouted. 'Back inside. Quickly.'

They all scrambled back inside, and Linus looked around at each of them, his eyes frantic. 'They've found us,' he said to no one and everyone, rubbing his head as though it might produce the answer somehow. 'I don't know how but they've found us.'

'Linus,' Benjamin said, then. 'They know where we are, but not how to get in. You taught me about caves, about the structure of the more complex ones. It would take anyone hours to figure out how to get in here. Days, maybe. So can I suggest that we all calm down? That we take a moment and work out what we're going to do?'

Linus nodded vaguely, ran towards his computers.

'I have to delete files,' he said. 'I have to protect my work.'

'Protect your work?' Lucas stared at him in disbelief. 'What about protecting Raffy?'

'It's too late for that now,' Linus said, not looking up. 'They have Raffy. You know that, I know that. Otherwise they wouldn't be outside this cave. They must have spotted him outside, or picked him up and figured out where he came from. I cannot let them get hold of this information, and we know that they're not going to hurt Raffy until he's done what they want him to do. So let me do this and then we'll go and get him. Okay?'

Lucas didn't say anything; Evie reached out her hand but he didn't take it.

'Can I help?' Benjamin asked, crouching down beside Linus.

'You know how to erase a hard drive?' Linus asked.

Benjamin shrugged. 'I can give it a go,' he said, pulling up a chair and getting to work.

'Lucas, pack up some essentials, just in case,' Linus grunted.

Lucas looked at him mutinously, then went to find some bags; Evie followed him. And then she changed her mind and walked back towards the bed she'd shared with Raffy. Her bag was there; Raffy's was not. If he had been captured by the Informers it was because she had sent him to them.

She put her hand into her bag, brought something out, put it in her pocket and padded back to the kitchen where Lucas was methodically packing up food and water.

'Hi,' he said, not looking her in the eye. Then he stood up, reached out to hold her shoulders. 'You know that this isn't your fault, don't you?' he said. 'It's mine. I shouldn't have come – I should have let Linus go alone. But what happened, I won't tell a soul. Not ever. Raffy needs you. I realise that now – he needs you and I promised to protect him, and if that means . . .' He choked, cleared his throat. 'You can be happy,' he said. 'The two of you. Be happy. When he comes back. Because we are going to get him back. We are going to find him. We are—'

'Of course we are,' Evie nodded, and she found that she was crying, and she tried to brush them away but it was no use. And all she could feel was the watch in her pocket, the watch that she'd worked so hard to get back, the watch that had meant so much to her, meant so little to Raffy. She wrapped her hand around it, took it out, pressed it into Lucas's hands. He looked down at it, surprise on his face, then confusion.

'But it's Raffy's,' he said.

Evie shook her head. 'No,' she gulped. 'No, he didn't want it. It's yours, Lucas. You have to take it. You have to have it.'

And she didn't know if Lucas understood, if he understood at all, but he took it, and he didn't put it on, and for that Evie was grateful, even though she wasn't sure why.

Then Lucas picked up the bag and they all grouped around Linus, who was sitting at his computer typing furiously.

'Come on,' Lucas urged him. 'We need to go.'

'I don't know,' Linus said, frowning. 'That helicopter's still outside. If they've got Raffy, why aren't they using it to take him to the City?'

'Because they don't have him,' Evie said, her eyes shining with hope. 'Because they're still looking. Maybe he started to leave then heard it. Maybe he's in the cave somewhere. We have to go and find him.'

Benjamin shook his head. 'In here we're safe,' he said. 'We have to stick together.'

'And do what? Wait?' Lucas asked impatiently. 'If Evie's right, we can't leave him out there, not with the Informers searching for him.'

'Yeah, they're not actually searching for me,' a voice said suddenly.

Everyone turned to see Raffy walking towards them, a sheepish look on his face.

'Raffy!' Evie exclaimed and rushed towards him. 'Raffy, where have you been? We were so worried.'

But Raffy just looked at her strangely. And that's when Evie saw that he wasn't alone, as out from the shadows stepped a man. A man she'd never seen before. A man she knew immediately was one of them.

'You,' Benjamin said breathlessly. 'You . . .' He jumped up, lunged forward, but Linus reached out, grabbed him in time, held him back. Evie could see that Benjamin was shaking, that his face had turned a grey colour.

'Me, indeed,' the man said with a smile. 'Hello, Devil. It's been a long time but I knew I'd catch up with you eventually.'

His smile broadened as he turned to Evie. 'Thomas Benning. Nice to meet you. And you . . .' He turned to Linus, who looked at him curiously, his blue eyes creasing as he peered closer at the man's face, then gasped and shook his head. Benning. He remembered the name now, shaking his head in disbelief.

Thomas laughed. 'It's good to see you again, too, Linus. Time to fulfil your contract, wouldn't you say?'

43

'You know this man?' Evie turned to Linus then Benjamin, who said nothing, their faces contorted with disbelief, with fear. Evie had never seen either man look scared before and it brought her out in goosebumps. She swung back to stare at Thomas, and found herself looking at a slim-built man with short, silver hair and a nondescript face. Not someone she'd even be able to pick out in a crowd. Was he really one of the Informers? How could anyone be that evil? She remembered being told in the City that all people were evil, that with their amygdalas in place, all humans were capable of all manner of terrible things, that evil was there all the time waiting to flourish, waiting for the right opportunity. And she had never truly believed it, had never believed that a baby was born with evil thoughts, that a good person could turn bad at just the flick of a switch. But now, looking at Thomas, she realised that while not all humans were capable of genuine evil, some were. And he was one of them. And from the look in his eyes, he didn't even care.

Then Benjamin spoke, his voice trembling. 'You're still here,' he breathed.

'Oh yes,' Thomas smiled. 'I'm still here.'

'How do you know this man?' Linus asked, his voice so strangled it was barely recognisable.

Benjamin's eyes narrowed. 'He is an evil man, and one whom I had the misfortune to cross paths with.'

'Cross paths?' Thomas laughed. 'How would I ever have crossed paths with you? You were chosen because I believed you would be useful. You were the result of a research exercise, that's all. And you proved yourself to be useless.'

Linus shot him a look. 'When did you know him?' he asked. 'When?'

'Before the Horrors. The beginning of them,' Benjamin said, his eyes not leaving Thomas. 'He started them. That's what he wanted me to do. To lead people into war.'

'Started them?' Thomas sneered. 'I did more than that. I created them. Orchestrated them, directed every move.'

'You can't orchestrate a global war,' Linus said, angrily.

'Maybe not,' Thomas smiled, thinly. 'But then again, maybe you can. What matters is what people think is happening, remember. Not what's really happening. Perception is everything. You taught me that.'

Linus stared at him, his face creased into a frown.

'So why didn't you do something about it?' Evie rounded on Benjamin suddenly. 'If you knew what he was doing, why didn't you stop him?'

Benjamin took a deep breath. 'It's a question I ask myself every day, but I still don't have an answer. The only one I have is that I was scared. Of what he could do. He could change the facts, he could make things that had happened disappear. And he had friends everywhere, even in the police. I wasn't strong enough. I . . .' He exhaled. 'I had my own problems. My own issues to resolve.'

'That's one way of putting it,' Thomas shrugged. 'Another is that you went to prison because you were a violent thug.'

Benjamin moved towards Thomas, stopping when he was just an inch away. 'I was in prison because I turned myself in to escape from you,' he said, his voice low. 'Because you made me realise that if there were going to be sides, I didn't want to be on yours. Because

I wanted to pay for what I'd done. Because I wanted to start again.'

Thomas pulled a face. 'Whatever gets you through the day, Devil,' he winked.

'Benjamin,' he said. 'My name is Benjamin.'

He immediately stepped back; Lucas grabbed Thomas by the scruff of his neck.

'Hand my brother over,' he said, his tone dark and menacing. 'Let Raffy go or you'll regret it.'

'Will I? I doubt it,' Thomas sneered, then he shrugged. 'You can have your brother,' he said, casting his eyes in Raffy's direction, 'but only because he's served his purpose. Raffy and I had an understanding, didn't we, Raffy?' He turned back to Lucas. 'He's actually been tremendously helpful.'

Everyone turned to look at Raffy, who stared back defiantly.

'Raffy?' Evie asked. 'Raffy, what's he talking about?'

Thomas smiled. 'He's been helping me out a bit. Haven't you, Raffy? Helping me track down my old friends. And now, here we are. Frankly, I have no need for him any more. You're welcome to him, Lucas. If he wants you. Of course I very much doubt that he does, but that's none of my business.'

Evie looked over at Raffy, her heart beating loudly, her head throbbing as what Thomas had just said sank in. 'You brought him here? You told him where we were?' she asked, barely trusting herself to speak.

Raffy looked at her thunderously. 'What was I supposed to do? He told me Lucas was coming. He told me he was going to take you away from me.'

'No,' Evie gasped. 'No, you're lying. You can't have done that, Raffy. Tell me you didn't. Tell me!'

She looked beseechingly at Raffy, but he just shook his head, his eyes dark and angry. 'I thought I could trust you, Evie. I kept telling myself I was imagining it, that I had to believe you when you said you loved me. But you don't. You love him. I saw you with my own eyes, Evie. I saw you. You betrayed me. Just like Thomas said you would.'

His hands were in fists, his eyes full of pain, and for a moment Evie could see the fearful boy she used to see in the playground, the boy who intrigued her, who stared at her like he could see her thoughts, like he knew who she really was. But that Raffy would never have done this; would never have brought this odious man anywhere near her. She'd done that to Raffy. She'd changed him into what he was now.

'You saw?' she asked, her voice so quiet she hardly heard it herself.

Raffy nodded, then moved towards her. 'It's okay,' he said then. 'It's not your fault. It's Lucas's fault.' He took her hand, stroked it with his thumbs, squeezed it. 'Come with me. We're free to go, Evie. You can come with me and we'll go away, anywhere we want to.' His voice was husky, low, his eyes looking right into hers as though there was no one else in the room. 'Thomas – the Informers – they don't want me, Evie. They never wanted me. Or you. Thomas just wanted to find Linus. And now he has. So we can go. Come with me. Come with me now.'

Evie looked at him carefully, and as she looked at him, she realised what he was saying, what he'd planned with Thomas, what he thought might happen. 'Where to, Raffy?' she asked, her voice catching slightly. 'Back to the City? Back to the Settlement that he's destroyed? Just where do you propose that we go, exactly?'

'I don't care,' Raffy said, his expression intensifying. 'I don't care.'

'No,' Evie said, shaking her head slowly in disbelief. 'You don't. I can see that now. But the thing is, Raffy, I do care. I care that you brought this man here. That you sold out Lucas, Linus, Benjamin, people who were protecting you, people who had put themselves in danger to keep you safe.'

'No,' Raffy said, his hands squeezing hers tighter. 'Don't say that, Evie. Thomas told me about the watch, Evie. He knew all about it, how you got it back from the baker. And I didn't believe him. I told him he was wrong. But he wasn't. He wanted to help me. Help us.'

'Where did you meet this man, Raffy?' Linus asked then, his voice devoid of emotion. 'How long have you been planning this?'

'We met at the Settlement, didn't we, Raffy?' Thomas smiled.

'So you've known all this time?' Evie gulped, felt herself choking. 'You knew that you were going to lead him to us all this time?'

Raffy didn't blink. 'I did what I had to, Evie. You'll see that one day. You'll see why I did it. I had to get you away. I had to—'

'I will never see that,' Evie shook her head, tears pricking at her eyes. 'I will never see, I will never understand, and I will never forgive. Never, Raffy. Don't you see that? Don't you see what you've done?' She glanced over at Lucas, who was staring at Raffy wide-eyed in disbelief. He caught her glance and immediately his eyes changed; they were filled with hunger, with love, with all the things he'd hidden because of his brother, things he'd tried to resist, things that he hated himself for succumbing to. But he wouldn't hate himself any more.

Raffy stepped towards Evie. He looked like he'd been punched in the face. 'No, Evie,' he said desperately, shaking his head, moving towards her, reaching out to hold her arms, her shoulders. 'No, don't say that. Don't . . .'

'I've said it,' Evie said. 'And I meant it.' She pulled away, unable to look at him, unable to face what he had done, what Raffy had done because of her.

And suddenly Raffy wasn't next to her any more; he was running at Lucas, fire in his eyes. 'This is all your fault,' he shouted, throwing Lucas to the floor. 'You had to take the one thing I had, didn't you? I hate you. I've always hated you . . .' He hurled himself at his brother, kicking and punching him with such malice that Evie found herself screaming and rushing towards him; she and Benjamin managed to pull him off, but still Raffy wouldn't stop kicking out.

'Raffy,' Benjamin said, firmly, and grabbed his hands, pulling them behind his back and turning him so that he was unable to move. 'That's better,' he said. 'Let's just cool it, shall we?'

'Let me go,' Raffy seethed. 'Let me go. I want to go. Evie. Tell them to let me go.'

But Evie said nothing. Instead she shook her head and walked towards Lucas. 'No, Raffy,' she whispered. 'No.'

'Nice action,' Thomas said to Benjamin. 'You're looking well, my friend. Very well.'

'I am not your friend,' Benjamin said quietly. 'I have never been your friend.'

Thomas shrugged. 'So come on, Linus. Enough of this sideshow. Let's get down to business, shall we?'

Linus was pacing around rubbing his head, shaking it from side to side, muttering loudly. He looked up at Thomas, then shook his head again. 'No,' he said. 'No. It isn't possible. No. No . . .'

But Thomas just laughed. 'Linus, I told you a long time ago that anything is possible. You should have believed me then. You should be grateful. Don't you see what I've done for you? Created the perfect environment. Everything you said you needed. I even gave you a car, left the keys in the ignition for you. And how about Ilsa, my G4 Benning 8? Isn't she great? Aren't you impressed?'

His eyes looked manic, terrifying. Evie shrank backwards. Linus, meanwhile, was staring into mid-air, shaking his head. 'But . . . how? No. No, I won't . . . It can't be,' he was saying, his face ashen, his eyes darting around but not focusing on anything, as though he were somewhere else completely.

Thomas rolled his eyes impatiently. 'Linus. This is getting boring. Look, let's just get down to brass tacks, shall we? I need you to reboot your System. Get it working again. That's all. Do that, and we're good.

Do that, and we'll all walk away and enjoy the rest of the day.'

And then suddenly Linus's face changed again. Became calm. He looked Thomas in the eye. 'I . . . I can't do that,' he said, his voice low. 'I changed the code. Can't be restarted. It's dead.'

Thomas shrugged. 'I was worried you'd say that. So then we go with Plan B. Actually my favoured option, if a little risky.'

'And that is?' Linus asked.

'You come with me,' Thomas smiled. 'And build me a new one. Because either way, I'm getting my hands on the System. You owe me, Linus. And I'm here to collect.'

44

There was silence for a few minutes. Then Benjamin spoke. 'Linus isn't going anywhere,' he said, his voice menacing. He moved forwards, towards Thomas, towering over him.

'Yes, I am,' Linus said then, and Benjamin swung round, still holding Raffy.

'No,' he said.

'Yes,' Linus replied, reaching out to touch Benjamin's arm, to squeeze it. Then he met Evie's eyes and for a moment he held her gaze, then he looked away. 'I have to go,' he said. 'Don't you see? This started because of me. I have to go with Thomas.'

'Just like that?' Evie demanded, her voice sounding brittle under the strain. 'After everything he's done?' She could feel Lucas behind her and she reached her hand back; Lucas immediately caught it, held it, pressed his fingers against hers. She wanted to fall against him, be enveloped by him; she wanted to pretend nothing else mattered except the two of them pressed against each other, together. But she didn't. Everything else did matter. It mattered a great deal. She and Lucas would find their moment later. Later . . .

Linus was still pacing, his eyes distracted, darting around, apparently unable to focus on anything. 'But I can see now that Thomas and I have some unfinished business. It's been the System all this time. That's what it's been about. What it's all been about. From the beginning. I should have seen, I should have realised. I was looking at everything else, everyone else, and not where I should have been looking . . . At myself. I should have . . . And we shut it down. We . . .' He stared at Thomas. 'How did you do it? Convince the world that the UK didn't exist any more?'

Thomas smiled. 'So much radioactive waste,' he said with a little shrug. 'Such a shame, it was a great country until the Horrors.'

'And they didn't happen anywhere else? At all?' Linus asked.

'What are you talking about?' Benjamin interjected. 'What didn't happen anywhere else?'

'The Horrors,' Linus breathed.

Benjamin's face creased in confusion. 'I don't know what you mean. The Horrors were global. They were killing each other in Europe. Everywhere. They were dropping bombs. Japan wiped out half of China. I saw it with my own eyes.'

'You saw what Thomas wanted you to see. Everyone did,' Linus said, turning back to Thomas. 'So what, a complete communication blackout?'

Thomas's face lit up. 'Total,' he said. 'It was genius. And I've never been able to tell a soul. Can you imagine? All that work! And no one has any idea.'

'Wait,' Benjamin said, his voice deep and resonant. 'Wait a minute here and talk slowly. Linus, what is he talking about? What's going on here?'

Linus shook his head as if unwilling to speak. Thomas smiled. 'Linus is just beginning to understand what I masterminded. A global war that didn't exist. A country that the rest of the world believed to be destroyed by nuclear weapons. A country that itself believed contains the only survivors. It's really quite brilliant when you think about it.

'And all this. For what? To what end did you destroy so many lives, Thomas?' Linus asked.

Thomas looked baffled. 'For the System, of course,' he said. 'So you'd build the System. So it would be ready to roll out. I was on the brink, Linus, I really was. And then you pulled the plug. Most inconvenient.'

'Most,' Linus looked at him incredulously. 'So all this time you've been playing your little game and it never got out? Your secret was never discovered? That's impressive.'

'Information,' Thomas shrugged. 'It's easy, really. If you have information on people, you own them. And I own a lot of people. Including you. So maybe we should get going. Back to the real world. To do what you should have done a long time ago.'

'You're taking me off this island?'

Thomas laughed. 'Don't you get it? This island doesn't exist any more, not as far as anyone else is concerned. Just you wait, Linus. What you're going to see . . . It'll blow your mind.'

Linus took a deep breath. 'You know, Thomas, it's a lot to take in. What you've just told us.'

'I know,' Thomas said, his eyes shining beadily. 'And the tragedy is that no one will ever know. Apart from you. And obviously you won't be allowed to tell anyone. Or see anyone.'

'Obviously,' Linus said. 'But before we go, how about we catch our breath a bit? How about some tea for the road?'

Thomas raised an eyebrow. 'I don't think so, Linus. It's time to go.'

Linus shook his head. 'Thomas,' he said, 'what you've just told me . . . What I think you've told me . . . What you've asked me, it's a lot to get my head round. I think we all need a moment. And I need to say goodbye to my friends. So let's have some tea. Just one cup?'

Thomas stared at him uncertainly. 'You're kidding me, right?'

Linus shook his head. 'You've got us covered. We can't go anywhere. I've agreed to go with you. So let me have some tea first. You've waited this long. You can wait a few minutes more, can't you? We can be civilised about this. Let's be civilised, Thomas.'

Thomas scrutinised Linus's face, as though searching for a clue, searching for a sign. Then, apparently giving up, he shrugged. 'I guess,' he said. 'But you're right about not going anywhere. Just remember that there's a helicopter right outside, an army of men just waiting for my command to rush in here and . . .' He smiled. 'Well, I don't need to go into detail.'

'No, you don't,' Linus said lightly. 'Evie, you want to give me a hand?'

Evie nodded tentatively and followed Linus into the kitchen; Thomas watched them like a hawk as they boiled the kettle, collected mugs together and washed them, then put tea bags in the teapot and poured the water over it.

'Breathe,' Linus whispered to her as she stirred. 'It's all going to be okay. Don't worry.'

Evie did worry, because things weren't going to be okay – they would never be okay again. But she forced a smile, tried her best to act like everything was normal, like the world wasn't crumbling under her feet.

'Sugar?' Linus called out.

'Not for me,' Thomas said.

'So, shall we sit down?' Linus led them all to the area just behind his computer where cushions were scattered on the floor. 'It's not much,' he said. 'But let's at least try to be comfortable, shall we?'

They sat, Evie next to Lucas, who was next to Benjamin, who was next to Linus. Opposite them, a few feet from Evie and Linus, sat Thomas, Raffy still in Benjamin's grip.

'Sit,' Benjamin ordered him, his booming voice making Evie jump; Raffy sat, behind Thomas, facing away from the group, shooting looks at Evie every so often, who did her best to ignore them.

'So,' Linus said then, looking at Thomas, his blue eyes now clear, his face relaxed. 'Tell me.'

'Tell you?' Thomas asked. He looked down at his tea. 'Swap cups,' he ordered Linus.

Linus shrugged and swapped. 'I'm not trying to poison you,' he said. 'I'm not stupid.'

'And nor am I,' Thomas said with a little smile. 'So, what do you want to know?'

'Everything,' Linus said, looking at him intently. 'Everything from the moment I left Infotec until right now.'

'Infotec?' Benjamin asked.

'The company we used to work for. Well, I say work. I was there for a couple of weeks on work experience,' Linus said.

'I for Infotec?' Benjamin said then, looking at Thomas. 'Your ring. The one the policeman wore? The pin you gave me?'

Thomas looked very pleased with himself. 'They were my idea,' he nodded.

'You've been pretty busy,' Linus said. 'You've done an awful lot.'

'I have,' Thomas agreed. 'Yes, I have. But I did it for you. For us. For the System. It's what you said you needed. What you said would never happen. I did it, Linus. I did it all.' His eyes were glistening almost manically, Evie found herself thinking and she edged backwards; she felt Lucas's arm stretch around her and it comforted her.

'So tell us,' Linus said quietly. 'I bet you've been

itching to tell someone. Tell us. Tell us what you did.'

Thomas thought for a moment, then he smiled, his whole face lighting up. 'But you know, Linus. I just did what you told me to do.'

'What I told you to do?' Linus asked quietly.

'Of course!' Thomas grinned. 'You said you needed a small community who wanted a System that would control them. Cut off from the rest of the world. I thought about shipwrecking some people but it wouldn't have worked – I tried it, putting in a fake "you" to see if they'd buy it and they didn't. And anyway, I didn't just want to create the perfect environment to build your System; I also needed the rest of the world to need it too, eventually. The Horrors was just the perfect thing. Created your little group of survivors, the perfect little community for you. But it also created fear everywhere else. And when people are scared, they forget all about liberty and turn to surveillance, to armies, to anything that might protect them. The world is ready for your System now, Linus. The world is ready to be controlled beyond anything anyone thought was possible. And guess who's going to be the one controlling everything? Guess who's been controlling everything ever since you walked out of Infotec?'

He took a sip of tea, and looked around the group. 'The thing is,' he said, 'it was so easy. So incredibly, scarily easy.'

'What was easy?' Lucas asked stiffly.

'The Horrors,' Thomas replied. 'All I had to do was light a few matches, and soon the forest fire had taken hold.'

'Blowing up my estate, you mean?' Benjamin asked, his voice choking with emotion. 'Killing innocent people.'

Thomas shrugged. 'That was a low point. A wasted effort,' he said. 'But it didn't matter, not in the great scheme of things. You were just one of many, Devil. You know it's very easy to assemble an army, if you know what it is that people want, if you know who they are, what their insecurities are, their hopes and fears. People are so easy to manipulate when you know everything about them. Pathetic really.' He glanced over at Linus. 'But that's the point, isn't it? Know people and you can do what you want with them, control the world!'

Linus smiled encouragingly at him. 'So you started the Horrors,' he said. 'Then what?'

Thomas narrowed his eyes. 'I'm not telling you everything, Linus. I'm not giving away all my secrets.'

'Okay,' Linus shrugged. 'Fair enough. But how

about the City? I'm guessing you were behind that, too?'

Thomas smiled broadly this time. 'Oh, the City,' he said, his eyes gleaming. 'That was quite something. I wanted to approach you direct, of course, but I was nervous, in case you didn't see things the way I did, in case you . . . changed your mind. So I watched and waited, made sure that you were okay, looked after, made sure you had what you needed, kept an eye on you. All the time, Linus, I was looking out for you. And then, soon after the Horrors had finished, I stumbled across Fisher. I was watching you, and you met with him. I quickly found out what he'd proposed, what the two of you were planning. And I made it happen! I made the City happen, Linus!'

He had the same childlike expression, and Evie suddenly realised why. He was looking for Linus's approval. Looking for him to say 'well done'.

'But you didn't build the City,' Linus said carefully. 'We did that.'

'Oh, you did the manual work,' Thomas shrugged. 'But I did what it took behind the scenes. I spread the word, made it sound convincing, made Fisher sound like a guru instead of a nutcase. I made sure the City had water, food, everything it needed. Made sure it had generators. You ever wonder about the resources the City had?'

Linus shook his head.

'No!' Thomas said triumphantly. 'Because you were too busy building your System, just like I knew you would. I created the perfect environment, Linus. I made the impossible possible.'

'And then we turned off the System. And you started to panic. You sent your men into the City to restart it. Only they were discovered, weren't they? By those young people. So you killed them. Every single one,' Linus said, his voice suddenly very serious.

Thomas looked at him incredulously. 'Of course!' he said agitatedly. 'We had to get it working again. And we couldn't be disturbed, couldn't have people asking questions. When the System was up and running no one asked any questions; no one ever went where they weren't supposed to be. So we had to get rid of them.' He smiled to himself. 'Of course, the Brother was all for it. Thought he could use the Disappearances to stir up fear, to help overthrow Lucas. That last one, the one you escaped with?' He looked at Lucas triumphantly. 'The Brother used her disappearance as proof that you're a murderer.'

Lucas's face flushed with anger.

'Not that it matters either way,' Thomas shrugged

then. 'You led me to Linus in a roundabout way. That's all I've ever been interested in. You're remarkably elusive, Linus, when you want to be.'

'Which is always,' Linus said, a little smile playing on his lips.

Thomas turned to him, his eyes shining. 'And there we have it. I'm a genius, you have to admit.'

'A real genius,' Linus nodded slowly.

'So,' Thomas said then, clapping his hands together. 'Lovely though it's been to catch up like this, you need to come with me now.'

'And where is it that we're going?' Linus asked. 'Your camp on the coast?'

Thomas raised an eyebrow. 'Oh no, that place is being dismantled as we speak.'

'And will it show up again on the map now?'

Thomas laughed. 'I thought you'd like that. But really, you have no idea. No idea at all, Linus. You've got no idea what you're in for. What I'm going to show you. You're going to be amazed. Truly astounded.'

'I bet,' Linus said, quietly.

Benjamin turned to him. 'You're not really going, are you? We can overpower this freak. We can fight.'

'No we can't,' Linus said flatly. 'Not any more. He's destroyed the Settlement. He'll destroy the City. He'll destroy everything. He looked at Thomas. 'But

405

if I come with you, everyone else goes free. You leave them alone. Leave it all alone. Do you understand?'

Thomas looked at him for a moment, then he shrugged. 'Whatever you say.'

'And I need my computers,' Linus said, looking around. 'I'll need them all.'

Thomas smiled. 'Of course. My men will bring them all.'

Linus nodded, stood up, walked towards his computer. 'I'll just get it all ready,' he said, beginning to unplug machines, fold up laptops. As he did so, Evie noticed him take something out of the side of one of them; he glanced over at her then, and as he walked around to disconnect another machine, he dropped it just next to Lucas's hand. He immediately moved his hand to cover it, manoeuvred it into his pocket without Thomas seeing.

Thomas turned to Benjamin. 'Wish you were still working for me, Devil?' he asked, his eyes glinting.

Benjamin didn't answer; he just stared straight ahead.

'No,' Thomas said thoughtfully. 'No, well, I suppose we can't all be visionaries.' He stood up. 'Okay, I'm done,' he said, looking at Linus. 'Let's go.

Linus got to his feet. 'Okay,' he said. 'But let me say goodbye to my friends.'

Thomas pulled a face. 'You know what?' he said. 'I don't think that's actually going to be possible to leave them here after all. I've developed a real hatred of loose ends. We will all get onto the chopper and your friends will . . . Well, we'll think of something. Something painless.'

'You said I could leave with Evie,' Raffy stared at him angrily.

Thomas shrugged. 'I lied.'

Linus's eyes hardened. 'You want me, you leave everyone else. That's the deal.'

'How about you cooperate or I'll kill them all. That's a better deal, I think,' Thomas said smoothly as Benjamin's grip tightened around Raffy, this time to stop him hurling himself at Thomas.

Linus held his gaze for a few seconds. 'Seems you've got me,' he said eventually.

'Yes,' Thomas smiled. 'Yes, I have. So, shall we go?'

Linus nodded heavily and started to walk, but as he brushed past Lucas he whispered something, so quietly no one noticed except for Evie, who was right behind him.

She saw his hand reach back and she took it; as he pulled her towards him he murmured in her ear, 'At the drop, we turn left, not right.' And she didn't know exactly what he meant, but she nodded earnestly, pretending to stumble so that Benjamin would help her up and she could convey the same message to him.

They walked, Linus at the front, then Lucas, Evie, Benjamin, Thomas, and Raffy at the back. And then they were at the cave's exit. Linus turned right. Lucas turned left and immediately disappeared. Evie followed him but before she could take another step she felt a hand gripping her. 'No. No!' It was Raffy, leaping forward to grab her; she pushed at him, screamed for him to let go, but it was too late. Thomas was beside her, his face white with rage.

'Get up here,' he shouted to his men, who were now visible at the mouth of the cave. 'Get up here and get these prisoners onto the chopper.'

'No,' Evie cried out as several armed men descended and started to drag them out. 'Where's Lucas? Where is he?'

'He's safe,' Linus called out to her, the noise from the helicopter almost drowning him out, his arm reaching out to her as he was bundled towards the strange, scary flying machine, as Evie herself was pulled towards it. 'I'm sorry. I'm sorry, Evie . . .'

Epilogue

Lucas took a deep breath and surveyed the woman sitting opposite him. Amy Jenkins. She was the first person to get an interview with him after he'd returned to the City, broken, battered, but knowing that with Clara at his side, he had to appear strong, had to appear to be triumphant. Martha had wanted to keep him at Base Camp for a few days, to nurse him back to health, but he'd refused. Having run all the way there from Linus's cave, he had eaten just one meal before setting off again, with Clara, to return to the City.

It was a triumphant return; after a brief spell in prison, accused of murder and worse, Clara's testimony had led to his release, then Linus's recording of everything Thomas had said about the City, about the Brother, had led to the Brother's own incarceration; when the memory stick Linus had dropped next to him was played in the Meeting House to a stunned silence, all of Lucas's former doubters had sobbed in regret.

Of course, they only saw part of the recording, the part that Angel had edited for him; Lucas didn't want to take all hope away from the City's people, didn't want them to be filled with anger like he was.

Amy was smiling at him. His last interview with her felt like so long ago. A lifetime ago.

Now things were very different.

No more search parties were roaming the streets of the City; instead, crowds were gathered outside his offices, braying for the Brother's blood. Now he was met only by humble, apologetic faces, by men and women asking to shake his hand. Now, finally, people were beginning to embrace their freedoms, beginning to finally shake themselves free of the Brother's doctrines, of his grip on their minds and hearts.

And Lucas tried to be happy for them, tried to feel pleasure in the fact that he had finally achieved what he'd set out to do. But instead he was battling a constant fog of nihilism. Because the City had not been created from the ashes, but through design. Because it was not a beacon of survival, but the creation of a madman, a game, a project.

And because Evie was with that madman, away from Lucas, a lifetime away.

'None of us believed you,' Amy said. 'And yet now we realise just how wrong we were to doubt you.'

Lucas nodded, trying hard to focus, trying to push everything else out, for now at least.

'What you have to remember,' he said, his right hand moving inadvertently to his left wrist, 'is that the System enslaved us. Its judgements were arbitrary, controlled by the Brother to keep people fearful, to separate them, to reward his friends and punish his enemies. It was corrupt. Just as the Brother was corrupt. He is responsible for what happened, for manipulating the people of the City to believe him and not me. No one should blame themselves. We need to look forwards, not backwards. We have to start living. I want us to start living again.'

He said the words, but he wasn't sure how he kept a straight face. He knew nothing of living. Not any more. Not since Thomas had taken Evie, not since he'd turned left at the cave's exit to find himself spinning down a tunnel to the ground below, unable to turn back, unable to respond to Evie's cries. He had tried scrabbling up; had shouted, screamed, ripped his hands to shreds trying to get to her, to all of them, but it had been no use. He'd had to watch as she was taken away, taken off in the helicopter with Linus, Raffy and Benjamin. Taken to a world that was meant to have been blown up. Taken to a world that Lucas still couldn't comprehend, no matter how hard he tried.

Had Linus known that he alone would make it? He didn't know, but he had his suspicions. Suspicions that kept him awake at night, that filled his head with feverish thoughts, questions. Was that why Linus had given Lucas the memory stick, the recording of Thomas revealing everything to them: his involvement in the Disappearances, the Horrors; the Brother's treachery? Was that why Linus had made sure that Lucas was right behind him? He didn't know; all he knew was that he was empty inside, that he would remain empty until he saw her again.

'So what,' Amy said, her eyes narrowing, 'would you suggest as a suitable punishment for the Brother? People are calling for his death; after all, he enabled the brutal murder of the Disappeared.'

Lucas closed his eyes for a few seconds, then opened them again, stood up and walked to the window, large and broad. He had considered a new office, a new building, a new start. But in the end he had settled for a new window. A large window that allowed him to see the sky.

'I think we can find a suitable punishment,' he said quietly. 'I intend to gather a jury of citizens, men and women of this City, to determine whether he be imprisoned within the City or exiled from it. The people will decide. It was the people that he betrayed, after all.'

'And what else do you have in store for the City?' Amy asked then.

Lucas thought for a moment, then turned around to look at her. She had no idea that this was all a sham, just like everyone else in this country had no idea that they'd been duped, used, their lives destroyed. And all for a computer system.

'Peace,' he said eventually. Because they didn't need to know. Not yet, anyway. Not when they'd already suffered so much. 'Peace and prosperity for the City's people. Hard work. Resilience. Humour. Fun. Love. I want people to be free to enjoy the small things, the big things, free to talk, free to disagree with each other, with me; free to take pleasure in the world again. I want to lower our walls, to engage with the other communities around us. I want us to stop being afraid.'

Amy scribbled furiously, then she looked up at Lucas, cocked her head to one side. 'And you?' she asked. 'Will you find peace, do you think? After everything that's happened?'

Lucas looked at her and his eyes were drawn to his desk, behind her. Over on his computer he could see a message flashing up for him, a message that could only be from one person, a message that reminded him of the years he spent sending and receiving messages to and from Linus, not knowing who he was or where he lived, just that his father trusted him and that he must, too. Now they were using the same device to communicate again; no words yet, just a signal, to let Lucas know that they were alive, that things were okay. Five seconds later, it disappeared to be replaced by his screensaver, a picture of Clara celebrating her sixteenth birthday two weeks before, her parents' faces radiant, their loved one returned. To remind him that his fight had been worthwhile, for her family at least. To remind himself that people came back. That Evie would come back. That he would find her again, one day . . .

Lucas took a deep breath, then forced himself to smile.

'I can hope,' he said. 'I can always hope . . .'

END OF BOOK TWO

Acknowledgements

Thank you, as ever, to Kate Howard, my editor, and everyone at Hodder who has worked so hard to bring this series to life, especially Eleni Lawrence and Justine Taylor.

Thank you to Dorie Simmonds, my wonderful agent. And huge thanks to Alan Greenspan, whose thoughts and ideas prompted a major rewrite of this book, for the better, I hope . . . !

And finally thank you to all of you who find the time to get in touch and spur me on. I couldn't do it without you!

Reading Group
Guide

'If you want to write, I always say that the best thing to do is . . . write.'

Meet Gemma Malley . . .

'So, where to begin? School? Hmmm. School was okay. Great in some ways, not so great in others. I'm someone who likes to do things my own way, rather than following rules and that's not so easy in the regimen of the classroom. But I loved English – I had a wonderful teacher, Miss Pitt, who got me super excited about Chaucer. I really looked forward to those lessons.

Then university. I studied Philosophy, which I loved too – it's basically about arguing your point. Not just arguing your point; it's about challenging assumptions, asking difficult questions, having to come up with cogent reasons for things you've always just 'known' to be true. And I joined a band, too. Lots of fun. We toured Japan, toured France, had an album in the indie charts . . . I edited the university newspaper, too. If you want to write, I always say that the best thing to do is . . . write. Don't talk about it, just do it, and if you wind up writing about something that doesn't entirely fascinate you then great – writing is hard and you have to work at it. My first job in journalism was writing about pensions – if you can make them interesting, you can make pretty much anything interesting. Going for the hard option is often the best way to learn in my opinion.

So anyway, that's a bit about me. But

you're probably not really that interested in what I got up to years ago. Maybe you're more interested in why I wrote my books? If you are, read on . . .'

Which children's authors most inspire you?

My favourite children's authors are those who, in my opinion, make the most of the genre with great story-telling, extensive imagination, and who aren't afraid to tackle difficult and complicated subjects. Philip Pullman is certainly one, as are Meg Rosoff, Jennifer Donnelly and Jacqueline Wilson. I think that Oscar Wilde's fairy tales are also absolutely wonderful.

Do you have any particular habits or rituals when you write?

I don't have too many rituals when it comes to writing — I sit looking out into the garden, which is lovely and I can't even start thinking about writing until I've had a cup of hot, steaming tea. Other than that, I try to clear my mind completely, think about my characters, and then write as much as I can before my next tea break!

What career path would you have taken, if you hadn't become an author?

I'd like to say an astronaut or an adventurer, but I think I would have ended up writing in some way — perhaps as a journalist, or perhaps working in education. I might even have become a teacher — I think

'My favourite children's authors are those who aren't afraid to tackle difficult subjects.'

The Disappearances

'Sometimes a book just flows out of you; other times you have to wrench it out.'

working with young people and getting them excited in a book, a subject or the world around them is about the most rewarding thing you can do.

Does it take a long time to write a novel?

It really depends — it can take weeks, months or even years! Sometimes a book just flows out of you; other times you have to wrench it out.

What inspired you to choose the dystopian setting?

I love to think of a utopia – in this case, a world without evil – and turning it on its head, looking for the flip side. Because the truth is, I don't think that utopia exists. Humans are fallible and that's what makes life such a roller-coaster ride. I like the ups and downs; without them things would be very dull. And don't we all appreciate the summer more after a long, cold winter?

MY TOP TEN DYSTOPIAN FILMS

1 THE MATRIX
Just such a brilliant concept and makes you really think about what happiness really means.

2 NEVER LET ME GO
A brutal look at our desperation for health and longevity and what we'll do to achieve it.

3 1984
Unlike many film adaptations, this film is almost as good as the book itself. Utterly haunting.

4 LOGAN'S RUN
Life is for pleasure and everyone dies before they're 30 . . . Essential viewing for young people everywhere!

5 BLADE RUNNER
Dystopia, sci-fi, human drones . . . My idea of film heaven!

6 THE TERMINATOR
I love this film and its sequels. Just the right mix of action, emotion and philosophical/political thought.

7 METROPOLIS
A world divided into 'thinkers' and 'workers' who need each other to survive yet never meet... Made in the 1920s but just as relevant now...

8 A CLOCKWORK ORANGE
Utterly terrifying but so well made and very convincing.

9 BRAZIL
Confirms everything I've always hated about bureaucracy...

10 SLEEPER
The funniest dystopian film ever made and a warning bell against conformity and following all the rules.

'Dystopia, sci-fi, human drones . . . My idea of film heaven!'

Discover the first book in Gemma Malley's
powerful and gripping dystopian series

THE KILLABLES

Everyone accepted that people were different physically.
But inside?
Inside, they were different too.
You just had to know how to tell, what to look for.

Evil has been eradicated. The City has been established.
And citizens may only enter after having the 'evil' part of
their brain removed. They are labelled on the System
according to how 'good' they are. If they show signs of
the evil emerging, they are labelled a K . . . But no one
knows quite what that means. Only that they disappear,
never to be seen again . . .

Available now in paperback and eBook

HODDER

Take a look at what some of Gemma's readers thought about THE KILLABLES:

'*The Killables* is amazing. The story has an excellent quality which is as soon as you put it down you're itching to pick it up again just so you can know what happens next. Or your mind is reeling at all the different possibilities of what could happen. That's a thing I love to have in certain books because it completely sucks you in and is unbearable to put down.'

Charlotte Wheeler

'I found *The Killables* by Gemma Malley very enjoyable and hard to put down . . . I can't wait to read Gemma Malley's next book in the series – *The Disappearances*. If it's as good as her first then there's no doubt I will enjoy it!'

Amy Langston

'In *The Killables*, Malley creates a denunciation environment. Although this was not my typical genre of book I would read I found myself gripped after the first page.'

Bethany Ellis

'I really enjoyed this book as I enjoy dystopian novels. I thought the plot was really clever and I loved the love triangle between Raffy, Evie and Lucas.'

Darcy Frayne

'The vivid descriptions and debatable morals help this book seem like a realistic and terrifying future for the world. With developments in science and people becoming more corrupt, it doesn't seem unrealistic that a city would surface, where evil was supposedly eradicated.'

Eleanor Gadsby

'It really did captivate my imagination and send me into the universe in which this book is set.'

Grace McGarry